FIND
THE
GIRL

BOOKS BY HELEN PHIFER

FIND
THE
GIRL

HELEN PHIFER

bookouture

Published by Bookouture in 2022

An imprint of Storyfire Ltd.
Carmelite House
50 Victoria Embankment
London EC4Y 0DZ

www.bookouture.com

ISBN: 978-1-80019-605-6
eBook ISBN: 978-1-80019-604-9

For Sofie Ravetta, you're such a beautiful soul inside and out. xx

PROLOGUE

AUGUST 1997

Anna had managed to find the campsite with the help of a friendly local who had been cutting back hedging along the main road. She had cycled from the small train station at Windermere with her tent, backpack and sleeping bag secured on the saddlebags, and was exhausted. The roads had been narrow in parts and steep, but she had made it in just under four hours. Now she was hot, grimy and in need of a hot shower. Even a cold one would be fine. As she wheeled her cycle along the narrow road that led to Forest Pines Campsite, she took a moment to look around at the scenery. She'd been so focused on reaching a shower that she hadn't really taken a minute to appreciate just how beautiful it was here. The campsite was situated along the edge of Whinlatter Forest, and she was looking forward to spending some time here alone, exploring the area and getting away from her lonely life and the family she'd been working for in Manchester, who were just awful. Her friends had raved about working as au pairs, but she hated it. The kids were spoiled and mean, the wife was rude, and the husband was forever making a pass at her. She'd lasted two weeks before she'd packed a bag, helping herself to a small tent, sleeping bag and a bicycle from the garage. Then she'd taken her suitcase full of her worldly belongings and put it into a luggage locker at Manchester Piccadilly train station, hopping on a train to the Lake District with a couple of changes of clothing, and a copy of *The Art of Happiness* by the Dali Lama she'd also helped herself to from the overstuffed bookcase full of unread books. She had hoped to take in some of the stunning views and try to figure out what to do with her life: she was twenty and didn't have a clue what direction to take and figured that she should enjoy it while having no one to answer to.

She pushed the mountain bike to the campsite office to pay her money and be told where her pitch was. Inside was a burly boy in his late teens who was watching a small television. A much younger boy was sitting on the floor playing with two plastic figures, clashing them against each other.

'Hello, I'm Anna.'

He looked at her and shrugged.

'I have a pitch booked for the week.'

He jumped out of the chair and stood up. 'Oh, you're late. Very late.'

Looking down at the boy, she smiled. 'You like Power Rangers?' He smiled at her, nodding, then turned his attention back to his game.

She nodded. 'I didn't expect the ride here to be quite so up and down, very big hills.'

He grinned at her. 'You biked here from where?'

'Windermere train station.'

His eyes widened, and he nodded his head. 'Wow, that's some bike ride. I didn't think you were coming; people usually turn up in the afternoon, not this late. I let your pitch.'

She didn't understand what he meant; she had an idea but her English wasn't perfect.

'I'm sorry, I don't understand.'

'I'm really sorry, but a family turned up two hours ago and I didn't think you were coming. I gave your spot to someone else. We're full now, sorry.'

'Sorry? I rode a very long way. I smell and I'm tired. Please can you squeeze me in somewhere? I'm on my own, I don't need much room.'

Anna hated crying in front of people, but she knew that if he turned her away, she was going to. In fact she might scream because she was too tired to go anywhere else. The tears were pooling in the corners of her eyes, and she began to blink to wash them away. The boy lowered his head, grabbed a map off the counter, and nodded his head in the direction of the kid who wasn't even looking their way. He whispered, 'Follow me. I could get in trouble for this. We have rules and regulations about how many campers and vans are allowed on the site, but I know a spot I can put you. It's a bit further away from where you would have been, and I'm sorry about that, I really am, but at least you can get your tent pitched and have a hot shower, clean clothes and get some rest.'

She followed him out of the hut, and he pointed to a cycle rack. 'You can leave your bike there, save you falling over it. I'll keep an eye on it for you.' He waited while she parked it, then led the way through the paths.

The sun was setting and the sky was streaked with swathes of orange and red; the forest looked dark and gloomy in the background, and she shivered. It was beautiful, but a little foreboding. The boy carried on walking past tents with families gathered around camping stoves, laughing and chatting. Anna wanted to climb into bed more than anything. She had never been so tired in her life and wondered if she was crazy. She should have just got a train to the airport and a plane back to Lithuania. As they were literally edging onto the dark forest, the boy stopped suddenly; it was at least fifty metres from the nearest tent and there were no lights this far down. She turned to look at him.

'I may as well camp in there.' She pointed into the trees.

'I know, but there's no washrooms or hot showers over that fence. I won't charge you either because I messed up. You can stay here for free, and my dad won't even realise.'

'You don't want money?'

He shook his head, pulled a key out of his pocket and held it out for her. 'For the showers.'

She took it from him, pushing it into her pocket. 'Thank you.'

He nodded and turned to walk away.

'Hey, one last thing.'

Turning back, he smiled at her. 'What?'

'Can you help me with my tent? I don't know what to do.'

Shaking his head, he crossed towards her, and she shrugged the heavy bag from her aching shoulders. Kneeling on the floor she tugged out the compact rolled-up tent, and he laughed.

'You're not much of a camper, are you?'

'Why?'

'This is a two-man pop-up tent, they're more for kids. You'd better hope it doesn't rain much or you'll find yourself floating down the side of the hill into the trees.'

It took him less than ten minutes to erect her tent. He secured it with pegs using his boots to stomp them into the ground. When it was up, she looked at him and laughed. He laughed with her.

'Come on, I'll show you where to shower.'

She opened the tent, threw the bag inside and grabbed some clean clothes and a towel, then followed him up the hill to a large building.

'The key will open the door.'

'Thank you.'

He waved his hand at her and carried on walking.

* * *

Sometime later, after curling up into her sleeping bag and drifting off immediately, Anna opened her eyes. She couldn't see anything; the side of her head was throbbing so much she could feel the blood pounding inside her mind. She opened her mouth to call for help and almost choked on the material that was pushed inside it. She wasn't lying down in the tent. She could feel the roughness of a tree as the bark pressed against her soft skin. Her arms and legs were stretched around its trunk, and she realised that she was bound to the base of the tree. There was something warm and sticky running down the side of her face, and she knew she'd been hurt. She had to get away from here. A muffled cry was stifled by the gag, and she squeezed her eyelids shut, hoping to wake up and find she'd just had the worst nightmare of her life. But the bark of the tree was pressing into the skin on her forehead. It was sharp, painful and she'd never had a dream like this ever. A branch snapped in the distance, and she knew someone was there. She was blind, but she could sense someone watching her. She began panicking, trying to loosen the rope that was tied around her arms and legs. Her limbs were stretched so far around the trunk they felt like they were on fire. Footsteps crunched through the twigs, coming closer, and she stopped struggling. Rough hands tugged down the blindfold, and she squinted; the sky was beginning to get light. The man stepped back from her and crouched down. She looked at him in the early half-light. He was dressed in camouflage trousers and jacket, with a matching baseball cap pulled low so she couldn't see his eyes, but she could see his lips and he was smiling at her.

'Now then, what's a pretty young thing like you doing camping on your own with that poor choice of tent?'

She stared at him; he was still smiling.

'Don't you know that it's not safe to be out on your own like that? Whatever is the world coming to? You women thinking you can be out on your own, doing whatever you please without any help is what is going to be the downfall of you all. If you ask me, it's trouble, yeah that's exactly what it is, trouble. Don't you wish you had stayed at home? I bet you do now.'

He reached his hand around to the back of him and slowly brought the biggest hunting knife she'd ever seen into view. She could feel her whole body begin to tremble. He tossed it into the air and caught it again and again. Anna watched the blade as it fell, hoping he was about to slice his fingers off.

'So, what do you want to do with your life? Have you ever really thought about that, have you got any big plans? Do you want to live or die? Let's play a little game. You nod your head yes or no when I ask you a question. Do you understand?'

She nodded as hard as she could against the tree, the skin grazing on her forehead, sending needles of pain shooting through her body.

'Good, that's good. Are you on your own? Before you start, let me just tell you I'll know if you're lying, so you best be truthful with me.'

She nodded again, wondering how he could know anything about her. She had never seen him before in her life. She could see tufts of sandy-coloured hair sticking out from the sides of the cap he was wearing and was trying to memorise everything about him to tell the police.

'Are you married, engaged or have yourself a boyfriend?'

Her head shook from side to side, tiny scratches of sharp bark grazing her skin with each movement.

'Do you live alone?'

She paused for a split second, wondering if she should tell him no and let him think she shared a house with someone. A shaft of sunlight broke through the trees, glinting off the steel blade. She nodded; she couldn't lie, for some reason she believed that he already knew everything about her.

'Are you sure about that, you wouldn't be fibbing?'

She nodded frantically, despite the pains in the side of her head.

'Well, isn't that a shame. If you'd said you lived with some-one, I'd have had to untie those ropes and let you go.' A rumble so low came from his throat, and she wondered what the noise was until she saw his lips moving and realised he was chuckling to himself.

A fear sharp and cold ran down the full length of her spine so violently that she shuddered against the ropes and began to shake. He was laughing at her. He stood up, wiping the palms of his hands on his camouflage trousers. She looked him up and down. Combat trousers, desert boots. Camouflage jacket, base-ball cap, sandy hair. She focused, desperately trying to imprint his image into her mind.

'I'm just fooling with you. It doesn't matter if you live on your own or with ten people. That was mean of me and I'm sorry for that. I shouldn't be teasing you when you're probably already scared to death. That was in very poor taste.'

He stepped closer, and she began to scream into the thick band of material that was wrapped so tight around her mouth it was cutting into the side of her cheeks. Then he stepped even closer. She began to throw herself against the ropes binding her to the tree.

'Hey, calm yourself down. There's no point getting yourself all worked up like that; you're only hurting yourself. Be a good girl and take what's coming to you. It's easier for you if you don't fight; although I do like a bit of a struggle. It's more of a challenge.'

His words echoed in her mind, *a bit of a struggle*. Had he done this before? If so, how many times had he got away with it? She felt her body go limp as the hopelessness of her situation drained her strength. Her head lolled forwards, pressing against the bark, and then he was there, looming over her like an angel of death, blocking out what little light there was, making her naked skin bristle with goosebumps. A twig snapped some-where behind him, and she realised they weren't alone. He crouched down behind her. His hand grabbed a handful of her honey-coloured hair, and she felt her head being yanked upwards, his face inches from hers. He smelled bad, and she found herself staring into the blackest eyes she'd ever seen.

'Yep, you're definitely the prettiest.' He released his grip on her hair and bent close enough to whisper in her ear. 'Give me a kiss and I'll set you free.'

She did the only thing she could, waiting until his lips were so close she could feel them touching her cheek, then she snapped her head back as far as it would go and threw it side-ways into his nose and forehead as hard as she could. There was a loud crunch as his cartilage cracked, sending a hot spray of blood over her cheeks. She closed her eyes and mouth. He let out a scream so loud that it echoed around the trees, and she found herself praying to God that someone from the campsite heard it, or whoever was nearby would come and rescue her. A sudden burst of pain in her temple signalled just how hard she'd headbutted him. He fell backwards and rolled onto the ground. She didn't waste another moment, frantically twisting and turning to loosen the ropes.

'You broke my nose, you bitch.'

He was still on the ground. Anna felt the ropes give enough that she could slip her slender wrists out and began to untie her feet. Her feet were numb with pins and needles, but she pushed herself forwards, hobbling barefoot away from him. Pulling the gag from her mouth she screamed at the top of her voice, still limping forwards. She opened her mouth to scream again when she was hit from behind by what felt like a sheet of iron. She fell onto her knees, then was face down on the forest floor in the leaves, a dead weight straddling her back. The man yanked a handful of her hair, pulling her head so far back she thought it might snap, and then the world stopped as he drew the blade across her throat.

Anna lay still, bleeding out onto the forest floor. She heard the sound of a bird cry out in the distance and then there was nothing.

ONE

PRESENT

Detective Constable Morgan Brookes was parked in a plain white divisional car, no markings on it whatsoever to alert the public it was being used as an official police vehicle. She was in the small car park opposite Fell Street, where she suspected she'd seen escaped serial rapist and killer Gary Marks, who also happened to be her biological father. Not that she had any feelings for the man except perhaps contempt. He'd killed her mother in cold blood when she was a little girl, and more recently, he had been on the run from HMP Manchester for seven months, with no clue as to his whereabouts until last week, when she thought she'd spotted his familiar figure disappearing around a street corner. She still wasn't a hundred per cent sure if she had actually seen him or whether it was wishful thinking, but she wasn't taking any chances. She had been monitoring the location ever since whenever she had some downtime. If Morgan saw Gary, then, obviously, she would alert her sergeant, Ben, and inspector, Tom, but until she was sure she was doing this alone. And if she got the chance to bring him in, well, she would. There were only a few people around today, which made it easier to be a little more discreet. Logically,

Morgan didn't see how Gary Marks would have the audacity to come back to Rydal Falls, where he had terrorised the small community in 1999, and manage to live here unnoticed. People noticed, and they gossiped. The place wasn't so big that he could move around without anyone spotting him. Then again, how many people who lived here now had been here back when he was preying on women by the side of the river?

Lifting the latte she'd bought from the little coffee shop around the corner, she took a sip as her radio crackled to life, making her hand wobble and her coffee dribble down her chin.

'*Any available patrols for Forest Pines Campsite or anyone near to the area?*'

Morgan listened for a reply, but it was silent, like tumble-weeds rolling through the radio waves. It made her fingers itch to press the button and answer them. She could offer to go, but Amy, her friend and colleague, would berate her when she saw her because they were detectives and not response officers. If no one offered next time they asked, she would go. It wasn't in her nature to shirk away from any jobs that came in, no matter how big or small. She turned the rotary dial on the handset so she could hear the conversation, and the car was filled with the sound of Cain's deep voice, her favourite police officer who gave the best hugs.

'*Sorry, I was with a member of the public – is that a job, control?*'

Morgan smiled. He was always the one to answer any jobs that were passed. She would have enjoyed working on shift with Cain if she hadn't ended up thrown in at the deep end on her first day of independent patrol and working alongside Ben and the rest of the team in CID. She turned her attention back to the quiet street, studying each shop entrance and the extra doors which led to upstairs flats. Just how would Marks get a deposit together or references for a flat when he'd been in prison since 1999? It didn't make sense; he couldn't unless he was stopping with someone, but who? She wondered if he could have struck up a friendship with someone in prison, like one of those pen pals. There were lots of people who wrote to prisoners that were locked up for long stretches, but would anyone be so gullible and stupid to let Gary stay with them when he was on the run? She decided to go back to the station and check the intelligence system to see if there were any known criminals living on Fell Street, or single women who would be foolish enough to fall for his charm and feel sorry for him.

Morgan didn't even make it to the gates of the station before her phone began ringing. She stopped at the side of the road and answered it. Cain's voice echoed in her ear.

'*I guess you're at work, Morgan?*'

'I certainly am. Can I help you?'

'*I can't get hold of Ben; thought I'd try you. Are you busy?*'

'Not really, things are a bit slow at the moment. Ben's taken Amy to go and pick up some stuff from Barrow, and Des is on rest days.'

'*I could do with a second opinion.*'

'Where are you again? I never caught the name where they sent you.'

'*Forest Pines Campsite near Whinlatter Forest. Do you know it?*'

She nodded, realising he couldn't see her. 'I do, spent a couple of summer holidays camping there when I was a kid.'

'*Good, could you come here then? There's a missing camper, well her friend who was supposed to meet her for lunch today thinks she's missing. The guy from the campsite thinks she's gone for an early hike and will turn up soon.*'

'What do you think?'

His voice became a whisper in her ear.

'*I think her friend is genuinely upset and telling the truth.*

Where's she gone missing to? She was seen by the owner of the camp last night going back to her tent; her stuff is here. I mean she might have got up early and gone for a walk, maybe she forgot about lunch.'

'Nah, women never forget about a lunch date, Cain, especially not with friends. It's something that we just wouldn't do. I'm on my way. Have you asked Mads what he thinks?'

'Can't get hold of him. I thought I'd ask the expert.'

'Flattery will get you everywhere.' She ended the call with a smile on her face and a list of questions forming in her brain, hoping that by the time she'd driven fifteen minutes to Forest Pines the missing woman would have turned up and everyone would be happy.

* * *

The campsite entrance looked a lot better than the last time she'd visited as a kid. Morgan remembered her adoptive dad, Stan, swearing because he'd driven past the narrow road multiple times before they spotted it. Then, it had been overgrown and the signage partially hidden by trees. Now, the road was wider, probably to accommodate the much bigger caravans and campervans that dominated campsites now. There was a huge sign which read 'Welcome to Forest Pines'. As Morgan turned onto the lane she smiled to herself. They'd spent a great week here camping. Her parents had seemed relaxed, and Stan had even taken her swimming in a lake. They'd eaten food cooked on a tiny camping stove, and every night she'd fallen into bed exhausted after all the exercise and fresh air. She'd almost forgotten all of the good memories from her childhood because the bad ones preferred to take up space in her mind.

Finally, the road opened up onto a much larger campsite than the one she remembered, which had been more caravans and campervans than actual tents. The office building, which had been a glorified shed, was now a sleek brick and glass building.

Morgan parked next to the police van and went inside. Cain was leaning on the counter staring at a television monitor. He looked up and smiled at her.

'Thanks for coming, Morgan.'

'No problem.'

A red-haired woman with matching eyeliner flicks and tattoos stepped out of the small office, and it was like looking at her double. Cain was watching Morgan's reaction with amusement.

'Morgan, meet Sofie Ravetta, this is Sara's friend who was supposed to meet her for lunch.'

Sofie held out her hand. 'Sofie with an F, hi sweets.'

Morgan smiled and shook her hand. 'Hello, I'm Morgan.'

Cain interrupted. 'Detective Constable Morgan Brookes, she's our resident expert on missing persons' investigations.'

Morgan side-eyed him, warning him to shut up.

'Can you tell me why you think your friend is missing?'

'I've known her since college. She's one of those outdoorsy types, completely opposite to me. You know the sort, walks, climbs, does triathlons, runs marathons, goes hiking and mountain climbing. But she also enjoys catching up for coffee and lunch. In all the years I've known her she has never missed a coffee or lunch date, especially if it also involved wine or cocktails. She's not like that, she's super organised. In fact she's a personal assistant, so she has to be, she gets paid to be so well organised. We were supposed to meet at The Black Dog, but she never turned up and there were no messages or texts. I phoned her and it went straight to voicemail. It didn't even ring.'

'Is she camping here alone?'

Sofie nodded. 'Yes, she loves it. Whenever life in the city gets a bit much she comes back here and goes camping.'

'Is her car still here?'

A man in a checked shirt, faded jeans and work boots walked through the door.

'I've checked the showers, toilets, and walked the perimeter of the site. I can't see her.'

Cain nodded. 'Morgan, this is John Winder. He owns the site. Thanks, John.'

'How are you getting on with the cameras, any sign of her leaving?'

'Not up to now. I've watched from last night when she left the washrooms, and she goes out of sight but heading in the direction of her tent.'

Sofie was shaking her head. 'Well, if she didn't leave, she must still be here, somewhere.'

Morgan reached out and grasped her arm gently. 'She may have got up early and gone into the forest. Can you show me where Sara's tent is? Cain, can you get onto the forestry commission and ask them to scramble a search?' She turned back to Sofie. 'She may have fallen and hurt herself along one of the more secluded tracks, and you can guarantee her phone died when she needed it. It's always the same, they either die or you can't get a signal. There's no reason to worry yet, maybe she's a little hurt or lost. Have you got a photograph of her we can email to officers and the wardens at the forestry commission so they can look for her?'

Sofie nodded and took out her phone. She began scrolling through her photos.

'Does she like swimming? Would she hike down to Bassen-thwaite Lake and go in the water there?'

Morgan was thinking that the lake was much deeper and colder than most people realised. Someone swimming alone could quite easily get tired very quickly or overcome by the cold. Although it didn't sound like Sara was an amateur when it came to the outdoors.

'She loves it, but it's a bit of a hike down to the lake to swim then hike back up and meet me for lunch at twelve.'

Morgan looked at Cain. 'Show me Sara's tent.' She walked outside away from Sofie's earshot. 'She could have got into difficulty swimming, got lost in the forest, that's a lot of area to cover. Is her car definitely here, she didn't sneak off?'

He pointed to a small, mint green Fiat 500. 'That's her car, the engine is cold, and John said it hasn't moved since she arrived yesterday. I PNC'd it just to double check.'

'So, she's somewhere in this area, we just have to figure out where?'

'That's why I asked you to come take a look. I didn't make a fuss of it before, but her tent is ripped. I wanted you to see what you thought before I upset her friend.'

He was striding down the path towards the area where the tents were pitched, nearest to the edge of the forest, down a steep slope. The caravans and campervans were on a flatter area. They walked past couples sitting in deckchairs around camping stoves. The air was filled with the aroma of frying bacon and sausages. There were a couple of barbeques on the go, and Morgan suddenly felt hungry for a huge burger with fried onions, lettuce, tomato, cheese, relish, and a big blob of mayonnaise. She wished there was a Five Guys nearer than Manchester. Her stomach growled; she'd not eaten since her bowl of tropical fruits granola with a protein yoghurt for breakfast and it was late afternoon now. Amy had convinced her that it was a far better breakfast for her than the usual cup of coffee and bowl of dry cornflakes she ate most mornings. They didn't even have a McDonald's in Rydal Falls, the nearest one was in Kendal. Morgan looked around at all the people, who looked genuinely happy, smiles on their faces as they embraced the outdoor life, and felt a touch of envy that she didn't make the time to do these sorts of things herself. They finally reached the end of the tents. There was a smaller one set a little apart, near to the fence that bordered the forest. Morgan looked around. It was just out of line of the lights that were dotted around the paths and really quite secluded. A heavy feeling settled inside the pit of her stomach. She tried to push it away, but it wasn't going anytime soon. She whispered to Cain. 'I have a bad feeling about this.'

He turned to look at her. 'Oh shit, I knew you would say that.'

'Tell me that's not her tent?'

'That is Sara's tent.'

'Have you looked inside it yet? And don't you think it's a strange place to put a woman who is camping on her own?'

He shrugged. 'No. Sofie said she rattled the tent and unzipped it a little, saw Sara wasn't there and came straight back to the office. It's a campsite in the Lake District not some seedy hotel in the middle of a red-light district. This is probably one of the safest places you could be on your own.'

'I think I have to disagree with you there.' Morgan tugged a pair of gloves from her pocket and snapped them on. She bent down and unzipped the tent, the chill wind making the door flutter. Morgan's breath caught in the back of her throat as she looked inside. A silken eye mask lay on top of the empty sleeping bag, blood red dots ruining the cream fabric. She glanced at Cain and pointed to it, whispering, 'Look at that.'

He peered over her shoulder. It didn't smell of anything bad, and next to the sleeping bag was a backpack, book and notepad. There was a torch and a cool box. She lifted the lid to see unopened cans of mojito, porn star martinis and three huge bars of Galaxy chocolate. Sara was a girl after her own heart; Morgan loved chocolate too. The back of the tent was ripped wide open and flapping in the gentle breeze. She stood up and walked around to take a look. This side of the tent faced the forest. No other tents overlooked it. Her instinct was telling her not to go inside the tent. She looked at the rip that ran the full length from top to bottom and felt a shiver running the full length of her spine when she noticed the grass was flattened and there were two tracks which led towards the wooden fencing.

'Cain, did you notice those? They look like drag marks in the grass or crawl marks; either way it's not good.'

He came closer and whispered, 'Jesus, I didn't look inside the tent, I called you.'

Morgan held her hand out for his radio. She'd left hers in the car. Unclipping it he passed it to her, and she spoke quietly, not wanting the family who had just arrived back at the tent nearest to Sara's to hear what she was about to say.

'Control, I need a PolSA lead, CSI, dog handler and DS Matthews to attend Forest Pines for the missing camper. I also need every available patrol and PCSO you can gather. Can you also contact the rangers at the forestry commission and ask for someone to be a liaison between us and them? We have a missing woman with what looks like a cut to the rear of her tent and what could be drag marks in the grass.'

'*Hang on, Morgan, PolSA, dog, CSI, available patrols and a who?*'

'Someone from the forestry commission, preferably someone who knows the trails and has transport. We might even need Mountain Rescue, to help search the forest, but I'll see what the ranger has to say. I think they have their own system for searching for missing walkers.'

Morgan's phone began to ring, and she answered it, passing the radio back to Cain. 'Ben, where are you?'

'*I'm turning the car around and on the way to you. We just got back to the station; what's going on?*'

She filled him in, and he never said a word until she stopped talking.

'*Do you think this is a crime scene?*'

'Yes, I do, one hundred per cent. It looks as if there's a

bloodstained eye mask inside the tent, and there are clear marks in the grass leading to a fence which borders the forest. Someone took her in there or she crawled, either way we need to find her soon. Should Cain and I go in?'

'*Not until the dog handler has been and had a look. Is there a dog on for South? Please tell me there is?*'

'Yes, she booked on an hour ago and is on her way. Cassie should be here soon.'

'*Good, let her take the lead then you two can follow if needs be. You're going to have to secure the area. Put a cordon on. How far is the tent from the main path?*'

'Quite some distance. It's surrounded by families having a great time.'

'*Sorry, you're going to have to ask them to either stay inside their tents or go up to the clubhouse out of the way. Is there a clubhouse? Amy's driving so we'll be there soon. She's worse than you for speeding.*'

'Charming, thanks, boss.'

He hung up, and Morgan turned to look at Cain. 'What do you think, should we go into the forest?'

'Is that what Ben told you to do?' He arched an eyebrow at her.

'The opposite, but we can't stand around here. What if Sara needs our help?'

'Morgan, have you seen how big Whinlatter Forest is? It's almost four and a half miles give or take. There are loads of different trails and paths running through it.' He was pointing at the thick band of trees that edged along the wooden fence for miles.

'I wasn't suggesting walking it all. I thought we could have a look around the immediate area in front of us. If Sara is in difficulty, we might be able to help her. What do you think?'

'I'm all for saving life and limb, but we don't know how long she's been in there, or, more to the point, who could have taken her. If we trample the scent, the dog might not pick it up and then we might have prolonged finding her.'

Morgan knew that made sense, but she wanted more than anything to clamber over the wooden struts of the fencing and begin calling out to Sara. Sirens echoed around the fells, and she hoped it was Cassie and her search dogs coming to the rescue because it was killing her standing here and not being able to dive over the fence into the trees.

TWO

It was as if the guardians of the galaxy had answered all Morgan's prayers at once. Not only did the dog handler arrive but minutes after so did Sergeant Al McNulty, the force Police Search Adviser, along with two other officers. Morgan watched them all begin to walk down the path towards them. She turned to Cain.

'You better tell that family to clear the area, and the ones in the other tent.'

He shook his head but made his way over to speak to them. Amy would be proud of her; she was getting better at delegating the crap jobs. Morgan waited on the path to greet them. It was Al who spoke first.

'All right, chuck, what's going on?'

Morgan smiled at him despite the grim situation. He was always so cheery and lovely. She pointed to Sara's tent.

'Sara Fletcher is camping here alone; she was supposed to meet her friend, Sofie, for lunch and didn't turn up, which isn't like her apparently. We checked her tent, and it looks as if there is a large cut in the rear of it. On closer inspection there are marks on the grass leading from the rip in the tent to the fence over there. It looks like she went into the woods.'

Al nodded. 'Do you think someone used force or she went of her own accord? Could she have crawled there, maybe woke up a bit disorientated and ripped the tent herself?'

Morgan shrugged. 'Maybe, either way she might be hurt or in difficulty. I haven't gone inside the tent but it looks as if there is a bloodstained eye mask on the sleeping bag. I left it for CSI. She isn't answering her phone – it's going straight to voicemail.'

'Right, I agree with you something isn't right. Let's get a cordon on this area. No one is to cross it or go into the tent except for the dog and obviously you, Cassie, then it's CSI.'

Cassie looked around; her golden Labrador, Brock, was straining at his leash, raring to go. She crossed the grass and looked inside the tent for an item of clothing for him to sniff. Picking up a discarded T-shirt, she held it under his nose so he could begin sniffing for scent cones in the air that might be flowing downwind from Sara and tracking the ground for any scent trail she would have left behind. He took off in the same direction as the tracks in the grass with Cassie following behind. Cain turned to watch.

'Sarge, should I follow just in case she finds anything and needs help?'

Al nodded, and Cain began to follow. Morgan was relieved he was taking one for the team. She didn't know if she was fit enough to keep up with Cassie and Brock. She was eager enough to go in and search, but not at that speed. They stood watching as first Brock, Cassie, then Cain all disappeared over the fence and into the thicket of pine trees.

'Anything?'

Ben's voice startled Morgan. She had been so focused staring into the forest she hadn't seen his arrival. She turned to see Amy standing by her boss and shook her head. 'Not yet.'

Al pointed to the trees. 'Let's hope that Brock finds her,

otherwise this is going to turn into a major operation. Can someone go and wait with her friend, so she can update us if she hears from Sara so we're not chasing our tails?'

Amy turned and began walking back up towards the site office, where Sofie was waiting. Morgan's stomach was churning and she felt sick. She hoped that Sara was okay. She couldn't imagine anything more terrifying than being lost in the woods and needing help.

More and more vehicles began arriving. The CSI van was directed down the track towards where they were all gathered. She recognised the 4x4s Mountain Rescue used; Al was on the phone summoning up as many hands as he could muster. He ended the call.

'That was Lowland Search and Rescue. They are scrambling a team together; the forest rangers have been made aware of the situation and are sending every available resource to help out. I'm tempted to call in air support if the dog doesn't get a hit.'

Morgan felt helpless; she wanted to be in that forest searching herself. Wendy, the CSI, got out of the van and slid open the door. Taking the heavy bag and camera out she nodded at them all.

'Well, this is different. I take it that's the tent?'

Al nodded. 'Yeah, can you work your magic, Wendy, please?'

'I'll do my utmost.' She began to suit and boot ready to document the scene. John, the site manager, walked towards them and passed Al a map of the area, which he spread out on the bonnet of the van. He took in the scene. His face had lost all of the colour he had earlier when Morgan had arrived; his ruddy cheeks were now pale.

'You think something bad has happened to her?'

Morgan watched him closely. 'We can't say, and we can't

take any chances. It's better to do this by the book so we can preserve any evidence.'

Morgan wished she felt as confident as she sounded. She glanced at Wendy who was photographing the large cut in the fabric of the tent. Wendy looked up and beckoned Morgan over, and she crossed as near to her as she could without contaminating the scene. Wendy shuffled over to her and spoke in hushed tones.

'That is definitely a cut, not a rip. It also looks as if there's dried blood on the inside of the sleeping bag and that eye mask, quite a significant amount where her head would have lain. I don't think she walked out of this tent of her own accord, Morgan.'

'Okay, thanks, I'll tell Ben. Wendy, this is awful.'

She nodded. 'It's terrifying is what it is. Does the site not have cameras? Someone must have seen something.'

'Not this far down, they're nearer the caravans and campervans.'

Wendy turned back to look at the tent. 'I can't even imagine camping here on my own. Look how far away she is from anyone else.'

Morgan glanced at John, forcing suspicion into her thoughts. She wondered if he'd purposely put Sara so far away on her own so she was easy prey. Morgan walked back towards Ben and Al, whispering what Wendy just told her to them both.

Ben nodded. 'Let's get John away from here then. I'll ask Amy to go back to the station and start running checks on all our systems for the owners of the campsite. Ask John for a list of staff, and let's see if anyone here has a record for violent assaults or any sex offenders; one of the workers could have slipped through the net.'

They heard Brock barking in the distance, and all stood still, hoping that he'd found Sara and she was safe. Cassie's voice echoed over the airwaves, and Morgan leaned in to listen to

Ben's radio, which he turned down in case anyone was listening to the conversation.

'*Brock has found something; I think it's a body.*'

Ben sighed as the hope of finding Sara alive was banished forever. Morgan let out a small gasp. She had been praying this wouldn't happen and they would have found her alive.

Ben answered her.

'What do you mean "you think"?'

'*Actually, it looks like a skeletal hand, partially sticking out from under a huge fallen tree trunk.*'

Morgan looked up at Ben, her eyes wide with surprise; a skeletal hand was not what she'd expected to hear Cassie describing and she wondered what was happening.

'It's not our missing person then. She wouldn't be skeletal yet.'

There was a slight pause. 'No, it's not our misper, but it looks as if whoever this is was hidden under a blanket of twigs and leaves. I'm going to need someone to come down here and take a look at this so I can continue looking for Sara. When you come into the forest walk to the left and keep coming downhill; I'm a good way down the hill. There's the tiniest path between the trees – follow that.'

Morgan was already clambering over the wooden fence, glad to have the chance to be doing something other than standing around twiddling her thumbs. Al and Ben began to follow her, but she took off not waiting for them. Her heart was racing, adrenalin forcing the blood around her body way too fast. Who could this be? And how long had they been there?

THREE

He'd waited in a nearby lay-by for the action to begin, purposely parking facing this way so he would see the police vans turning off onto the narrow road that led up to the campsite. He had his nose in a book about crime scene forensics and a cup of coffee on the dashboard, his feet stretched out on the front passenger seat. There was the occasional muffled thump from behind and a little jolt as his passenger hit the sides of the van, but he wasn't worried about anyone hearing her. He'd spent a long time soundproofing the small space behind him. He didn't know why she was so upset; it might not be very big, but it was at least comfortable. He'd upped his game from the first time around. It had been so close that time. The girl had almost got away, had to be knocked out a second time; he remembered the drive through the forest on the old logging trail to find a secluded place to put her. And it was the perfect place. Near enough to the campsite but not so near anyone would hear her screams. The next time had been close too; that girl had made a run for it, but had been stopped in her tracks. He had found it was a lot harder than he'd imagined, but he'd had a good teacher. He liked to keep his girls for seventy-two hours, enough time for the major searches, should there be any, to be scaled back. The police would spend forty-eight hours in a frenzy and then ease it off a little because of the manpower and the cost; after seventy-two hours it was relatively easy to sneak back into the forest and leave them a present. The thrill and the feeling of absolute power over both his victim and the coppers was one of undeniable pleasure. He was far better at this than he could ever have imagined, a natural, so he wasn't wasting these talents he'd been shown. They would have made a great team, but then he'd gone and got caught for something else, something he'd done on the spur of the moment without thinking about the consequences and, because he'd struggled to adjust to the prison rules, he'd ended up getting more time added on until he realised he was going to have to change his ways if he ever wanted to get back out and continue with the master plan, which was so much more fun.

He'd had a long time to get it all planned out, so it was perfect. The lasting memory of the first time had kept him going until he was able to do what he pleased.

There was another thump, and then he caught sight of the first police van in the distance. It didn't seem to be in a great hurry: no blue lights or sirens. He sighed, that was a disappointment, maybe they weren't going to the campsite after all. He'd waited here all morning, unsure if anyone would have even noticed she was missing, but he'd kept a check on her phone which had suddenly got a flurry of phone calls and text messages around one o'clock from someone called Sofie. It was at this point he had turned the phone off and had thrown it into the bushes.

The police van turned onto the narrow road, and he fist pumped the air. So far so good. Draining the last of the coffee from his cup, he got out and stretched. Folding up the deckchair he had placed to the side of the van he put it in the back. It was time to move on. As much as he'd love to hang around, he wasn't stupid. There was no point in drawing attention to himself. While he thought he was good, and his plan brilliant, he was also astute enough to know that he had to be very careful. Now he would drive as far away from Forest Pines as he could get. He wouldn't be back until the police had 'explored every avenue', wasn't that what they called it on the television? He figured they would search all of the forest, and then when there was no sign of their missing woman, they would scale it back and maybe have a few of those community officers dotted around the place. He would be bold enough to bring her back then and finish what he'd started.

He saw a flurry of cars racing in the opposite direction to him, including a police van with 'CSI' emblazoned across the side, boy they were taking this seriously. He was impressed he had chosen wisely this time; at least he'd had the experience to improvise when he'd needed to. It was satisfying beyond anything he'd imagined. He grabbed the silver crucifix around his neck and smiled, not quite sure God would approve of what he was doing but not giving a damn anyway. He liked the necklace because it held very special memories for him of the first time it had happened, when he'd crept back into the forest late at night in the pitch-black to find her grave, and taken it from her to keep as a reminder of those memories.

FOUR

Morgan didn't have the best sense of direction but Brock's barks in the distance were enough to help her go the right way. Al and Ben were behind her; they made a sombre trio as they crunched through the twigs and debris on the floor. Then Cassie was there, holding Brock's lead tight, her cheeks red with the exertion of trying to keep him from pulling away. She pointed to a huge fallen tree trunk. Morgan looked but couldn't see what she was looking for. As Ben and Al arrived, Cassie stepped a little closer. 'There, near the end where the roots are.'

And then Morgan saw it: a white skeletal hand, missing a finger and thumb.

Ben muttered, 'Jesus, how long have they been there?'

Al took a step closer, crouching down. 'A long time, that's for sure. It's not our misper.'

Brock was straining to get free, and Cassie asked, 'Can I go? He's desperate to follow the trail.'

'Yes, of course. Morgan, do you want to follow behind in case he finds anything else? Cain will guard the scene.'

Cassie was already heading off into the trees, and Morgan began to follow. She turned to look at the hand once more and felt a wave of sadness wash over her. Whoever that was had been left out here for God knows how long. At least they could reunite them with their family now. She kept on following Cassie and Brock, who seemed to be more excited than he'd ever been in his entire life, straining and jumping at the leash. It was warm and Morgan was beginning to get hot and sweaty. Her thrice-weekly fast-walking sessions that she labelled as a run to anyone who asked hadn't prepared her for such a rough terrain. She burst out through a trail of trees to see Brock sitting on the floor by a narrow dirt road and Cassie wiping the sweat from her brow.

'It ends here.'

Morgan looked at the dog. 'Did he just say that?'

Cassie smiled. 'If he could speak we'd be in the movies, not doing this for a living. No, he's adamant that the trail ends here.'

'Which means what?'

'My guess would be she was on foot or dragged until it got to this point and then she left in a vehicle.'

'Fuck.'

'Yeah, it sucks. Tell me again, what do we think happened?'

'Wendy has found dried blood in Sara's sleeping bag, and her car is still in the car park, so she didn't leave here of her own accord. Someone sliced her tent open, possibly hit her on the head to render her unconscious or to disorientate her enough she didn't put up a fight, and now it looks as if they had some kind of transport here to get her out of the area.'

'This isn't a main road. Look, it's a dead end further up there, where it stops abruptly, and there's a tiny turning circle.'

'Whoever took her must know the area well then because how would you even know to park here unless you were local or worked around here?'

Cassie shrugged.

'We need CSI to come and see if they can find anything. Blimey we need at least two more CSIs. There's three areas to process now, and the body in the forest is a little convenient, isn't it? What are the chances of someone abducting a woman from the same area where another body has been hidden?'

Cassie shrugged. 'You're the detective, I just find the criminals, with a lot of help from Brock.' She reached down and gave him a good old scratch behind the ears, and he looked up at her with such love in his eyes Morgan felt her heart melt. For a second she was overcome with the desire to get herself a puppy to help her not be so lonely all the time. She nodded.

'Yes, I am. I'll figure it all out.'

'Yeah, I think you will. It's terrible about whoever that is buried back up there, isn't it? What an awful way to be left. Are you going to be the bearer of good news and let control know exactly how many crime scene investigators we need?'

Morgan nodded and began relaying all the information she had to the control room; this was turning into the biggest crime scene they'd ever encountered. She requested as many patrols they could spare as well: this area needed a scene guard, as well as the path through the trees that Brock had followed to get to here and to the body. She closed her eyes wondering how they could even begin to manage something of this magnitude. Were they out of their depth? She thought about Sara; until they learned otherwise, Morgan would keep believing that she was alive and fighting to survive, and she would fight just as hard to find her.

FIVE

Ben looked at Al. 'I guess I'll take the body and you continue looking for the misper?'

Al nodded. 'This is bad, isn't it?'

'Really bad.'

'I need to go see where Cassie is and what she has, then I'm going to have to coordinate a full search. I'm going to bring in the Lowland Search and Rescue Team, Mountain Rescue and gather a team of police licensed search officers to deal with the direct area. I might even scramble the National Police Air Service helicopter to do a sweep of the forest, although they're going to be picking up heat signals from every mountain biker, walker and tourist out for a spot of exercise. Unless we cordon off a huge area and concentrate on that.'

'What about a drone?'

'Could utilise one of those. It's a little difficult with the trees, but we could definitely use it to search open areas. What I need is someone with extensive knowledge of this area, preferably someone who knows it like the back of their hand, to point out any hiding places, caves, disused areas that she could be hiding in or have been taken to.'

He began talking into his radio, asking Cassie what she'd found, and heading in the direction she'd gone. Ben watched him disappear through the trees and turned back to the partially hidden skeleton. He had no idea if they had stumbled across a hand or an entire body. Crouching down he picked up a stick to try and lift some of the twigs to look underneath them.

'Get the hell away from my crime scene.'

Ben jumped. Dropping the stick he stood up and saw Emma, the crime scene investigator for the south Lakes area, watching him like a hawk with a smirk on her face.

'Emma, thanks for coming so fast.'

'I'd say you're welcome, Ben, but what fresh hell is this? Wendy said there's a missing woman *and* a dead one.'

He grimaced. 'Well, we don't know if it's a man or a woman yet. All we have is a hand at the moment.'

She looked down to where he was pointing. 'Oh, you're going to have to call in a forensic anthropologist for that. Whoever that is looks as if they've been here awhile.'

'What else do you need?'

'For you to step away from there for a start, retrace your steps back if possible. I'll tape the area off, I think, until we know any better information. I'll photograph what we can see but there's not much else. This isn't a fresh scene; I can tell you that much.'

He knew that if he had to guess he'd say that the hand had been here at least ten years, probably a lot longer. He rang Morgan.

'Hey, what you got?'

'Brock followed her track to a small dirt road. She isn't in the area though; it looks like someone drove her away.'

'We're sure about that, the dog isn't just playing games?'

Cassie's voice was loud in his ear.

'No, it isn't. He's a highly trained search dog. In fact, he's

trained in cadavers and he already found you one today. How many more would you like?'

'I didn't mean it like that, Cassie, no more, please. I think we have enough to contend with at the moment.'

Morgan spoke again.

'Try not to upset everyone, boss, everyone is as bewildered as you are.'

'Who said I was bewildered? And what are you, my gran? She used to say stuff like that. I'm just trying to figure out where to start.'

'I guess we start at the beginning. Sara is our priority because as far as we're aware she's injured and has been taken away from here by someone. We need to find her before something awful happens to her. I have a bad feeling about this.'

'And there it is, the official seal of doom from Morgan. Do you want to check with your crystal ball and see if there are any other disasters coming our way?' The line went dead, and he realised he'd just taken his fears and frustrations out on Morgan. That had been uncalled for. He typed out a message.

Sorry, that was shitty.

She didn't answer, and he figured he had earned her giving him the silent treatment for a little while.

SIX

Amy was in the site office with Sofie and John. The woman was in shock. Her skin had a pale, clammy tinge to it and she was wide-eyed, looking around. John, on the other hand, was looking decidedly dodgy. He was pacing up and down, running his hand through his hair.

'What's the matter, John?'

He turned to glare at her. 'What do you think is the matter? One of my campers is missing and I don't know what else is going on in the forest, but this isn't good for us.'

Sofie's eyes fixed on him. 'Sorry, did I hear you say that my friend who might be in serious trouble might be bad for you? What you, the campsite? I don't give a damn about your campsite right now. Why would you put her where you did anyway? You may as well have told her to go camp in the forest on her own. What were you thinking?'

Amy nodded, damn Sofie was good, and had just blatantly said what everyone was thinking.

John's cheeks, already flushed, turned a deeper shade of crimson.

'I didn't mean it like that.'

'How did you mean it then?'

Sofie was standing defiantly, staring straight at him, and Amy was enjoying watching him squirm. The door opened, and Ben walked in, his cheeks almost as red as John's but through exertion and not embarrassment.

'How well do you know the forests around the campsite?' He was staring directly at John.

'I've lived here most of my life. I was brought up around here.'

'Have you got a map of the area, a detailed one?'

John nodded and disappeared out to the back office behind the counter. He came back with an Ordnance Survey map, and he spread it out across the counter. Ben bent over it then lifted his head.

'We need to know if there are any caves, shacks, disused shelters that kind of thing, where a person could hide out or be hidden in. Is there anything like that round here?'

'No caves nearby, the nearest are Rydal and there are Millican Dalton's Caves in Borrowdale. It's a big forest though, there are probably a million hiding places.'

John looked at Ben, avoiding Sofie's glare. 'I don't know of any shelters or shacks. The rangers at the visitors' centre for the forest might know more, but like I say it's a huge area.'

'For now, we are concentrating on the area directly around the site. We believe Sara has been taken through the forest to an old dirt track and has possibly left in a vehicle.'

There was a gasp from Sofie, and Ben realised he should be careful how he worded his next sentences. Amy was patting her arm which was very un-Amy like; she was usually quite reserved when it came to human interaction.

Sofie whispered, 'Whose vehicle?'

He turned to her. 'We don't know that yet but we're working very hard to find out.' He turned back to face John.

'That dirt track is a dead end at one point. Where does the other end lead to?'

John bent down over the map and took a red pen from the overstuffed pen holder on the desk, and he marked an X where the road finished, then drew a line along it until it reached a wider road that opened onto the B5292. 'There, once you're out on that road you can make a pretty fast escape.'

Sofie crossed towards him, her eyes wild with fear and frustration. 'And how would you know that, John? Have you tried it? Where is she? What have you done with Sara?'

Ben looked at Amy, who was looking at Sofie in awe. 'Amy, could you take Sofie back to where she's stopping, please?'

Sofie placed her hands on her hips. 'Why, am I asking too many questions and doing your job for you? This is my friend. I heard that CSI say there was blood, I want to help.'

Ben nodded at her. 'I know you do, and I would be exactly the same if it was one of my friends, but we have to do things a certain way. We have to be methodical to make sure we don't miss anything important. I really need you to go back to your house and wait there in case Sara contacts you.'

'No, you don't, you want me out of your way.'

'Yes, I do, because I can't concentrate with you taking over.'

Sofie opened her mouth to argue back then nodded, seeming to deflate in one sudden movement. 'Okay.'

Amy led her out to the car park as Morgan walked in.

'We need a mobile incident unit here, Ben, there's too much going on and too much to talk about with too many people around.'

He nodded. 'You're absolutely right, Morgan, great idea. I'll sort that out.'

John looked at them both. 'You can't just bring a mobile police station and set up camp here. You're going to scare my tourists away. I'll never recover; they'll want their money back, and once word gets out about what's going on this place will be like a ghost town.'

Morgan looked at him. He was older than her – she'd guess in his late twenties. 'Are you saying we can't do that? Because to be totally honest with you, John, this is serious beyond all comprehension. We might have to close the site and move people off anyway.'

'You can't be serious.' He turned to Ben. 'Who is she? She's not serious? This is my livelihood you're ruining.'

Morgan stepped closer to him. 'I'm deadly serious. There is a dead body in the forest not far from the perimeter of your campsite, and there is a missing woman who was taken from her tent in the middle of the night, abducted and injured. Do you want to explain to me why you thought it was acceptable to put a woman camping alone so far from the rest of the site? That pitch is like the last stop to hell.'

'What are you insinuating? I had nothing to do with this, that was the last pitch I had left and she said it was okay. I always leave that one until last and give campers the choice of the better pitches. I can't help that the site was fully booked. Don't you dare come in here, throwing your accusations around.' Spittle flew from his lips as he growled at her.

Ben stepped between them. 'She isn't saying anything, John. But I'm saying that it's better for everyone if you coop- erate with us. Otherwise, you'll get locked up for obstructing the course of justice and we don't want it to come to that. I appreciate this is an awful time for you, but our hands are tied. I'm sure you would rather we put all our resources into recov- ering the body from the forest and finding Sara. The quicker we get it dealt with the sooner we'll be out of here and, let's face it, you'd rather be known as the helpful campsite who couldn't do enough to assist the police in a search for a missing camper than an obnoxious prick who ended up getting arrested.'

'You can't talk to me like that.'

'I just did, seriously have a think for a couple of minutes. Take yourself outside and breathe in some of that fresh, woodland air. It might help you to come to your senses.'

A woman walked in with a Louis Vuitton Neverfull tote bag thrown over one arm and Selfridges bags in the other. John looked at her and groaned.

'Want to tell me what the fuck is going on, darling? I leave you alone for a day and there are more police on site than campers.'

She turned to Ben and Morgan. 'ID, please.'

Ben looked as if he was about to lose his cool big time, but he fished in his pocket and pulled out the Cumbria Constabulary lanyard, passing it to her. Morgan's was tucked under her shirt and she tugged it out and off her neck, also passing it to her. As she did, she asked, 'And who are you?'

'I'm Eleanor, that poor bastard's wife. Now, be a dear and tell me what has happened before I lose my shit. The officer at the entrance wouldn't tell me anything.'

John, whose face was getting a deeper shade of red by the minute, shouted, 'There's a missing woman and a dead body.'

She turned and stared at him, incredulous. 'What? I'm sorry, what did you just say?'

Morgan stepped in. 'We have a lone female camper who we think has been abducted from her tent, and while we were searching the woods for her, we stumbled across a body.'

Ben was nodding his head. 'It's a bit complicated.'

'A bit complicated? It's a disaster is what it is. Whose body have you found, the missing camper? I don't understand what you mean.'

He shook his head. 'No, we think she's been taken away from the area. I'm sorry, there isn't much more I can tell you because I don't know myself yet what is happening. We are in the very early stages of what is going to be a huge investigation, and we're going to need your help; it'll be far easier for everyone if you're cooperative.'

She looked at her husband and shook her head. 'Fine, what do you need?'

Morgan spoke. 'Somewhere for our mobile incident unit to set up, access to your CCTV systems, a list of all the visitors who were here at the same time as the missing camper, especially any that might have checked out this morning. In fact, what time is check out?'

'We ask them to leave by eleven, but we don't go chasing them out until it's an hour before the next camper is due to arrive. I'll print out the guest register for you and anything else you need.' Then she turned to her husband. 'John, I'll be needing a word outside, please. I can't have a night away without all hell breaking loose.' She dropped her bags behind the counter then walked out of the door back into the open air. John followed her, leaving Morgan and Ben staring at each other.

'This is going to be a logistical nightmare. How's Al getting on?'

Morgan shrugged. 'Busy organising search teams to come in and do a full sweep. What about the campers on site at this moment? We can't let anyone leave; they all need speaking to.'

Ben shouted Cain's name into his radio. 'I need you at the entrance, no one comes in or out.'

'*Already here, boss, I figured I'd better let that woman who owns it in though. She lives here on site.*'

'Thanks, Cain, as soon as we get some PCSOs here they'll take over.'

Morgan whispered. 'John lives on site; he was alone last night, and he also put Sara at the furthest pitch away from everyone he possibly could. We should search his house just to make sure she's not in there. Have any intelligence checks been done yet?'

'Amy has gone to take Sofie home, then she's going back to the station to do them and any others once we get a list of visitors. I think you're right, but he's not going to be happy about it.'

'He might not be, but as long as he hasn't got anything to hide, he's got nothing to worry about. From where I'm standing, he could have taken her to his house or he could have dragged her through the forest to a waiting vehicle and then taken her to his house so no one could see him.'

'Morgan, I like your way of thinking. I'm not going to enjoy breaking the news to him. He's already angrier than Amy when she's hungry.'

She shrugged. 'While the cat's away... he had the opportunity to do it while his wife wasn't here.'

The door opened, and Eleanor walked in with John following behind. She smiled at them both.

'Right, now that my husband has calmed down let's see what we can do to help find this missing woman. It's just awful to think that something may have happened to her while she was here. Are you sure she hasn't just wandered into the forest and hurt herself?'

Ben shook his head. 'It's unlikely, although not impossible. But the dog has searched for her trail, and it ends at a small dirt road.' He paused, and Morgan knew he was wondering how to ask for permission to search the house without upsetting them. She thought again about Sara's tent sliced open and didn't feel quite so bad about it. She spoke up.

'Is it okay for us to do a quick search of your house, garage and any sheds, storage areas, that kind of thing you have on site?' She smiled at them and watched as Eleanor placed her arm on John's forearm, stepping in front of him as if to block his face from Morgan so she couldn't see the expression etched across it.

'Of course, it is. John will take you up there now while I'm accessing all the records and getting them printed off for you.'

John grunted something so low and unintelligible she couldn't make it out and then he left. Morgan and Ben followed, leaving Eleanor staring after them. Morgan popped her head back through the door before it closed.

'How many staff work here? Can you gather anyone on site here so we can figure out how to search the campsite thoroughly?'

Eleanor already had a walkie-talkie in her hand. 'I think there's only Luke working today; Miles has been a bit off colour, so we've been a bit short.' She sighed deeply. 'I shouldn't have gone to Manchester yesterday, but it was already booked and paid for. John was supposed to come but he had to stay here once we'd sent Miles home.'

Morgan thanked her for the information and went back outside; Ben and John were heading uphill and quite some distance away. She began following, thinking all the while about Sara. She wondered whether her abduction had been planned, or whether it was a spur-of-the-moment crime. They reached a large slate house secluded from the campsite by a perimeter of laurel and rhododendrons that had grown enough in size to give it lots of privacy. It wasn't a pretty house but she supposed you could call it practical. John unlocked the door, and Morgan watched to see if Ben was going to glove up, but he didn't, so she didn't either. Inside, the house was much cooler than outside. There were wooden shutters at the window, and it was all in darkness. John stood in the doorway, the heat from his body radiating waves of anger into the space.

'Could you open the shutters or put some lights on, please?'

Morgan wasn't sure why Ben was being so polite to this guy who up to now was doing nothing but make her feel he was their number one suspect. He actually stomped across the wooden floor in his heavy work boots, throwing open the shutters, transforming the dark shadowy room into a light and airy open-plan living space that was very minimalistic and not at all what she'd been expecting.

'This is lovely.'

'What were you expecting, the shack from *Friday the 13th* at Camp Crystal Lake? A few animal skins hanging from the ceiling, the missing camper chained to the wall?'

Ben smiled. 'Not at all, do you want to give us a guided tour?'

He shook his head. 'Nope, I'm too tired to take these boots off and if I go any further Ellie will kill me, and she's far scarier than you lot.'

Morgan glanced at him. Suddenly the angry man looked more human, and she realised that he was probably nervous and annoyed at the sudden implications he was facing, under the scrutiny of the police. He certainly wasn't doing himself any favours with his behaviour though.

'Go on and look around. Please try not to mess the place up too much though, because as you know I'm having the shittiest of days and if I have to listen to Ellie complaining all night about the state you've left the house in, then you might have to come and take me away before I explode and kill someone.'

Ben nodded. 'Yeah, sorry, mate, this is tough for all of us. We're not purposely trying to make it look like you had something to do with this; it's just protocol. There's a checklist of actions we have to take in these situations, and it's tough but done with the best of intentions.'

John nodded. 'I suppose so, I'll wait outside for you.'

He left them alone and gently closed the door behind him on the way out.

SEVEN

Morgan looked at Ben. 'Change of heart, realised just how much of an arse he's been, or scared of his wife?'

Ben laughed. 'Scared of the wife for sure. Come on, let's put him out of his misery and do a full search. Do you want to go up or down?'

'Down, I always end up having to look in the bedrooms.'

He smiled and made his way to the stairs. Morgan looked around, down here was pretty open-plan. There were a couple of doors and she made sure to open them all, determined never to make the same fatal mistake she had when searching for the missing Potter family. One door led to a storage cupboard full of coats and shoes. Morgan pushed the coats to one side, making sure there wasn't anyone tucked behind them. She knew there wasn't because the house smelled clean, like fresh linen, and the air wasn't tinged with the underlying, stomach-turning stench of blood or decomposition. Satisfied, she shut the door and crossed to the other one, which led into a huge kitchen that looked brand new. It still smelled of fresh paint and wood. She opened every cupboard, looked in the pantry and checked the huge American-style refrigerator that was well stocked with enough wine and champagne to throw a lavish party. Eleanor liked the high life, whereas John appeared to be the opposite. But that was hardly a crime, and there were no bloodstained hammers in the sink or dishwasher to point to anything more serious. She picked up a large gilt photograph frame from the kitchen windowsill and stared at the wedding party. She recognised a much younger John and Eleanor as the bride and groom. There were two men standing to the side of Eleanor and another man standing next to John, who must be the ushers, she thought as they all looked very smart in their top hats and tailcoats, even if they did look very young. She carefully put the photo back, wondering if she'd ever marry; probably not: it wasn't something she'd ever thought about if she was honest. Morgan carried on with her search, thoroughly checking everywhere, but found no hidden doors leading to a cellar containing the missing woman.

She heard Ben's footsteps above her. He was walking around upstairs, opening and closing wardrobes and cupboards too. She tried a door which opened onto an empty drive at the side of the house, where there was enough room for a couple of cars. There was a garage and a shed further back. She walked around to the front of the house, where John was sitting on the front step smoking. She hadn't pegged him as a smoker; he hadn't smelled of cigarettes.

'You have a lovely home.'

'It's all Eleanor, nothing to do with me. Fancies herself as one of those Instagram Influencers, so spends a fortune on making the house look as if there's nothing in it.'

He smiled at her, and she realised he looked much younger than she'd thought he was when he wasn't exuding a cloud of black smoke from his ears. Clearly the cigarette had settled him.

'That's an art form in itself, she's good. What about your stuff though, surely you have things?'

'See that shed and the garage.' He pointed to them. 'They are my domain. I keep all my treasures in there that aren't allowed in the house, and before you ask, no, the missing woman is not in there. But yes, you can go take a look.' He held out a large keyring.

'Ben was right, this is tough for everyone, most of all Sara though. It's our job to find her, it's what we do. I know this is awkward, but it's not personal.'

He nodded. 'I guess not, sorry about before. I was being stupid, well more stubborn really, and panicking. We can't afford to close or lose visitors, especially after the last year, and with Eleanor living her life as if she's a EuroMillions lottery winner, it's a lot of stress.'

'I can imagine; hopefully, we'll find her soon and be out of your hair.'

'What about the body in the forest?'

'We can deal with that from the dirt track. We don't need to utilise the campsite to remove whoever the poor soul is. Hopefully, we'll only need the mobile incident room for the next twenty-four hours while we organise the searches for Sara. We are going to have to speak to everyone on site though. It's vital that we gather any information that might help find her.'

'I never realised what a tough job you lot did. I see a uniform and always used to think "jobsworth". You know, giving out speeding tickets and what not. This is something I've never had to deal with, and I don't envy you all one little bit.' He stood up. 'Come on, I'll show you my man caves.'

Morgan smiled at him, following him to the large, detached garage. He unlocked the door and stepped inside. It smelled of oil and paint, no underlying smell that might arouse her suspicion that something bad had happened in here. She looked around. There were the usual shelves of tools, paints, lots of cardboard boxes and crates. She stepped inside, and John flicked a light switch. The whole place was illuminated with bright fluorescent tube lights; there were no dark corners. Morgan knew with certainty that Sara wasn't in here and never had been. She turned and walked outside towards the large shed. John shut and locked the garage door, then came over to unlock the padlock on the shed.

'We might be in the middle of nowhere, but you just can't be too careful with the campers. A few years back I had some tools stolen out of the garage and a knackered old lawnmower that didn't work. The thieving bastards went to all that effort to nick a broken lawnmower.' He shook his head. 'At least it saved me a journey to the tip, but I've kept everything locked up since.' He laughed and pushed the door open.

Morgan opened her mouth. 'Wow.'

'Aye, wow all right. This is my space. I get to keep all my stuff in here, and Eleanor is not allowed in here, no matter what.'

Morgan stepped inside what looked from outside like a rather ordinary shed into a completely different room. It was kitted out like a sleek bar with a dartboard, pool table, large beer fridge fully stocked with cans of lager and cola. There were strips of pork scratchings and nuts pinned on the back wall. As well as bar stools, there was a large leather sofa, a fifty-inch television with an Xbox console underneath it and wall-to-wall shelves of DVDs and games.

'The lads come round once a week for a drink and whatever takes their fancy; I come here when I can. It's the only way I could live in that house with nothing on show, drives me mad it does. It's not like she has neighbours to impress. Spends all her time taking photos to put on Instagram or something like that. Still, it makes her happy, so I leave her be. She's a good woman underneath the desire for expensive stuff.'

Ben walked into the shed at that moment. He stopped short and then sighed with delight.

'This is amazing. I have serious shed envy, and I live on my own with no one to tell me where to keep my crap.'

Morgan nodded. 'Isn't it?'

Ben nodded. 'Come on, job here's done. Thanks for being so cooperative, John, makes things much easier.'

'Yeah, I hope you find her soon. I'm just going to go lock up the house. See you back down at the site.'

They walked off, leaving him standing in the shed. When they were out of hearing distance, Ben asked, 'So, what did you think?'

'Sara hasn't been in the house or the outbuildings. She would have been bleeding heavily from the head wound, and there were no telltale traces of blood or anything to arouse my suspicion that we needed CSI to do a full sweep. Plus, he admitted he'd been an arse and was sorry. I don't get the impression he had anything to do with her disappearance.'

'Unless Amy brings up a criminal record that gives us reason to bring in a search team and take him in for questioning. We can't rule him out because he has the best man cave I've ever seen.'

Morgan smiled. 'Obviously. I'm just going off what I saw and my instinct, Ben. Has Al sent an update?'

'Yes. Pathologist and forensic anthropologist have been called out to deal with the body in the woods. All the extra officers have arrived, so if we gather the PCSOs in the office and take a look at the site map, we can give them an area each to speak to the visitors. Everyone must account for their whereabouts last night, and if they're on their own, pay them closer attention. Not that it couldn't be someone with a partner or family, but it would be rather more difficult to sneak out, assault and abduct a woman from her tent without being noticed.'

'Who's to say a couple couldn't have done this? It would be easier if there were two of them, don't you think?'

'Morgan, why do you do this to me? Yes, I suppose it would.'

They walked down the hill back to the campsite, which was now flooded with lots of officers wearing luminous yellow body armour. From the distance it looked to Morgan as if there were lots of life-sized glow sticks walking around.

EIGHT

Everyone gathered inside the site office. Morgan found it hard to breathe and felt as if she'd walked into a sauna. It was so warm with the heat radiating off the bodies packed inside that Eleanor had to throw open all the doors and windows, so that what little air there was could circulate. The Chief Super had arrived with DCI Tom Fell in his Land Rover. The car looked as if it had been in a mud bath, making Morgan wonder where on earth he'd been in it. Everyone liked Tom, he was a decent boss, but the Chief Super was new to this area, and no one knew her very well. She seemed okay and smiled at everyone which Morgan took as a good start. First impressions counted in such a small community, and if she'd walked into this cramped, stuffy office breathing fire and exhaling smoke everyone would have instantly been put on edge. Ben leaned over and whispered, 'That will be you one day, mark my words.'

She shook her head. 'Don't be ridiculous.'

'You'll have to move on at some point. You don't want to be held back working with me forever, and besides, I'll be retiring in another seven years give or take. Depending upon whether you kill me off before then.'

'I'll think about moving on when you do, now shut up.' She pushed her way through the officers to the counter where Eleanor had spread out a large map of the campsite and surrounding forest. Ben followed, so did Tom. The Chief Super held back though, which surprised Morgan and made her like the woman even more. She wasn't wanting to push in and take over which was unusual. No one seemed to be doing much of anything, except chatter amongst themselves and the noise was quite deafening in the confined space.

'Can I have your attention?' She shouted a little louder than she'd meant to, but it worked, and everyone turned to stare at her.

'Sergeant Matthews is going to give out your instructions as to which area of the site he wants you to cover.' She smiled at Ben.

'Thank you all for coming. What we have is a lone female camper, Sara Fletcher, who we believe was abducted from her tent in the early hours of the morning. There was a rip in the side of the tent, and a significant amount of blood in her sleeping bag to suggest she has a head injury. The dog has traced her scent through the forest to a dirt track, where it ends. It looks as if she may have been taken away in a vehicle, but we can't discount the fact that she could still be here or may have hurt herself and be in the forest somewhere. Lowland Search and Rescue and the forest rangers are going to tackle the forest when they arrive. We are solely concentrating on the campsite; someone must have heard something. I want to know who they are, who they're with, how long they've been here, where they're from, if they have heard or seen anything, if they saw anyone suspicious hanging around. If they have dashcam footage in their vehicles and anything else that might be relevant.'

A hand went up and Morgan smiled at Cathy, one of the PCSOs.

'Is there a body in the forest? What's the craic with that?'

Ben nodded. 'To further complicate matters, there is a skele-tonised body in the forest, discovered while searching for Sara. It seems to have been there a long time; a forensic anthropologist is on their way.'

'Is it suspicious?'

'I'm treating it that way until I know more about it, yes.'

'That's a bit uncanny, isn't it? A missing woman and a body in the same part of the forest. Do you think they're connected?'

'It's too early to say but, yes, it's very strange and I'm not ruling anything out.'

Cathy turned to look at the PCSO standing next to her, and Morgan knew they were thinking about the number of days they were going to be out here on scene guard.

'As you will be aware, the first forty-eight hours are the most imperative of a missing person's investigation. Let's get out there and try to find some answers as to what's happened and bring Sara back.'

Morgan was bent over the map. She had a red pen and was circling areas to send officers to start their enquiries. Eleanor was hovering in the back office.

'Have you got a photocopier?'

She nodded.

'Please can you copy this map?' She did a quick count; there were eleven officers and PCSOs, thirteen including her and Ben. Al was still in the forest with the body, waiting on the pathologist to arrive. 'Seven copies, please.'

She disappeared and came back with sheets of paper that Morgan passed out. 'If you go in pairs and cover an area that's numbered.' She assigned each pair a number, so they knew which circle on the map was theirs, and then they all filed out into the fresh air leaving Morgan, Ben, Tom and the Chief Super looking at each other. Morgan realised she didn't actually know the new Chief Super's name and wondered how to ask it.

'Hi, I'm Melanie, but call me Mel.'

Ben nodded. 'Not ma'am?'

'God no, I hate that. Unless we have to make it formal, but Mel is fine.' She smiled at Morgan, who found herself warming to her instantly.

'I know who you are, Morgan, and I'm very pleased to meet you. You've had a busy time since you joined. I believe you've been keeping Rydal Falls officers on their toes.'

Ben laughed. 'She's certainly keeping me on my toes. I can't keep up.'

Mel nodded. 'That's good, in fact it's bloody great.' She looked over to Eleanor who was clearly listening. John walked in, an expression of pure misery on his face.

'Should we take this outside?'

Mel led them outside towards the police incident unit that was reversing into a space on the gravel at the far end of the car park.

'I want to know your thoughts about the body in the forest. Could you tell anything about it? I find it very hard to believe that whoever abducted Sara walked her directly past a body by pure coincidence.'

She was asking Morgan.

'Well, I have to be honest. I don't think it was. Hopefully, the pathologist and anthropologist will find a connection to them both.'

Ben was nodding. 'It could be unrelated, but unless whoever it is lay down, covered themselves in branches and leaves and then died, it looks like there's a lot more to it, and I have a hunch that they're both connected.'

Tom was staring off into the distance through the forest, and he turned back. 'Have we had any missing persons' reports for this area where they haven't been located? We need to go back a very long time, because I don't think there has been since I've been in the job and that's well over thirteen years.'

'Amy has gone back to check; I can't recall anything though, can you?'

Tom shook his head. 'No, not one, but I wonder if someone could have slipped through the net.'

'Sir, if this person was reported missing, there would have been some record of it. The owner of the campsite said he hadn't had any other campers go missing.'

Mel looked over her shoulder. 'Do you believe him? What about his whereabouts last night?'

Ben side-glanced Morgan, who answered, 'He was alone; his wife was away in Manchester. They were short staffed so he couldn't go.'

'Interesting.'

'Yes, Amy is pulling up his records too, if he has any. We're about to go over the CCTV footage from last night, to see if there is anyone who enters the site or is wandering around in the early hours. I'll show you Sara's tent and you can see for yourself. It's a bit off the beaten track, and to be honest I don't think he should have put her where he did, but he said it was the last pitch he had available and she wasn't bothered. There are no cameras that far down. They're centred around this part, the showers and where the motor homes are.'

'Lead the way.'

Morgan turned to walk her down, Ben too; Mel followed, and Tom stayed behind.

'Are you coming, sir?'

He shook his head. 'No, I'll leave that to the experts. I'm expecting an important call and might not get a signal down there.'

Morgan wondered what was going on. He seemed cagey, and then she wondered if he was feeling a bit put out because

Mel was interested in the case and also his superior, but then wouldn't he want to set a good example?

NINE

Declan Donnelly, the forensic pathologist for this part of Cumbria and Lancashire, arrived at the campsite in company with the only forensic anthropologist for the whole of the north-west, who just happened to be teaching a class at Lancaster University. Doctor Chris Corkill was a good friend of Declan's; they liked to listen to live bands and drink at the same pubs when they weren't working. As soon as the call had come through to Declan, he'd messaged Chris to see if he was available and had then downed tools in the mortuary to go pick him up. They made quite a pair; both of them were tall, both had shaved heads and tattoos. Chris, who had far more tattoos than Declan, always wore a shirt and tie though, while Declan preferred combat trousers. But from a distance you might think the pair of them were brothers they were so alike. Morgan and Ben were heading back to where Tom was standing, his phone glued to his ear. Ben grinned at them.

'Well, if it isn't the Kray twins in person.'

Declan laughed, running his hand over his recently shaved head. 'What's up, Benno, jealous of my dashing style and good looks?'

Morgan chuckled.

'Definitely not, although it suits you.'

'You know Chris, don't you? Our resident forensic anthropologist?'

Ben nodded. Reaching out he shook his hand. 'Chris, long time no see.'

Chris smiled. 'It's been a while.'

Declan pointed. 'This is the one and only Morgan Brookes. If you haven't met her, I bet you've read about her escapades around here.'

Chris laughed and reached out to shake her hand. Morgan took it and shook firmly. 'Ah, yes, the Morgan Brookes. I've definitely heard about you. It's great to meet you in person, although it would be nicer under better circumstances. So, what fresh hell have you called us to today? Your control room inspector said there were skeletal remains in the forest? Sounds like a plot of a Netflix movie.'

'I wish it was, at least then we'd get to know how it ends. What the dog found was a hand sticking out. I didn't look much further.'

'Only because I stopped you; honestly, he was crouched down poking at the pile of leaves with a stick like an eight-year-old child.'

Ben's cheeks flared red, and he turned to face Emma who was smiling.

Declan was shaking his head. 'He never changes, do you, Ben? So how are we getting to the body? Is it better to go on foot or drive, and more importantly, is it far?'

It was Morgan who spoke up. 'I'll walk you both down there if you want, but it's quite some way. There's a dirt track: you could drive there, but you might get your car scuffed, Declan, it's a narrow, rough track.'

'In that case we will walk and follow you, then we'll come back for the car if needs be.'

They went back to the car and began to suit and boot. Declan took his heavy case out and Chris did the same.

Ben leaned over and whispered in Morgan's ear, 'They look like a pair of hitmen.'

She smothered the laughter wanting to escape her mouth with the palm of her hand. Humour was what got them through on days like this when the weight of the responsibility they were feeling was heavy on their shoulders.

As they reached the end of the path that branched off towards the tent, now sealed off with blue-and-white crime-scene tape, she pointed to it.

'Sara was alone in the tent and there's been no contact with her since yesterday. We think someone sliced open the side of the tent, maybe knocked her out and then took her through the woods.' Before either man could ask, she answered, 'There was a significant amount of blood inside her sleeping bag; she was definitely injured.'

Declan was staring at the tent. 'That's a little bit out of the way from the other tents. Is that the way the campsite is laid out, or was it intentional, do you think?'

'I don't know, but it really bothers me that she was put so far away. A tracker dog followed her scent into the forest but didn't find her. The forest rangers and Lowland Rescue are doing a search of the forest, and air support from Lancashire is on its way. They're going to use thermal imaging to look for her around the area, just in case she's unconscious somewhere. However we need you for what *has* been found.'

They walked single file through the trees, Morgan leading the way down to where the remains lay. Police tape had also been run around the trees here, keeping a separate path down there. A single figure was waiting outside the cordoned-off area. Al looked up from the hand to see them heading towards him and nodded.

'I need to go meet the search and rescue team up at the incident room. Is it okay to leave this with you? Claire went back to the van for a tent to cover the body with.'

'Yes, of course. Ben's up there waiting.'

'Thanks, Morgan, this is turning into an absolute nightmare.'

Declan looked at the hand and turned to them both. 'Yep, death pronounced. No doubt about that.'

Chris ducked under the tape. Morgan stayed back and, to her surprise, Declan waited with her. He turned to her. 'Not really my area of expertise. This one is going to be in Chris's hands until he needs me.'

Chris was crouching down. 'Has the area been fully documented? I don't want to disturb anything until it has.'

Morgan used her radio to phone Claire, turning it onto loudspeaker so Declan and Chris could hear. 'Can they touch anything?'

'*Yes, they can. I've photographed, filmed and documented everything. Evidence-wise there is nothing to note apart from the area directly around the remains.*'

'Thanks, I'll take it from here.' Chris gave her a thumbs up as he studied the hand and fingers. He picked up the stick nearest to him, using it to lift the leaves and branches, poking through the mound of detritus that covered it just enough to see underneath. Taking out a torch from his pocket he shone it on the skeletal remains underneath.

'Wow, considering it's been out here a very long time it looks remarkably intact. It's not in a grave, just left on the ground and covered, parts of it may have sunk down into the ground. I'm surprised the bones aren't scattered more by animals. There are a few missing metacarpals but until we get it to the mortuary I can't really say much more. I want to get it recovered as soon as possible. When Claire comes back, we'll get it photographed in each stage of recovery and take plenty of soil samples. We'll be able to get a good idea of how long it's been here. Are you still using the undertakers to recover remains?'

Morgan nodded.

'Right, let's get them here on standby ready to take it to the hospital. I'm not anticipating a long, drawn-out recovery process for the remains.' He stood up.

'How long do you think they've been here?'

'Good question, from what I can see it's completely skeletal. It doesn't look as if there's any soft tissue left. At a rough guess they have been here a long time, ten, fifteen maybe twenty years; this is by no means recent. A body can be fully skeletonised in a matter of weeks depending upon the environment; but judging by the colour of the bones and speaking from experience, I'm leaning towards fifteen years plus.'

Morgan looked down at that lonely hand, an overwhelming aching of grief in her heart for whoever this was lying dead on a forest floor, covered in branches and years of fallen leaves for a burial site and not somewhere their family could visit. Someone somewhere must have reported this person missing. There had to be some record of it. She vowed to find out everything she could about them and reunite them with their loved ones no matter where this investigation took her.

TEN

He was parked in the busiest car park in Keswick. He'd
managed to snag a space just big enough to squeeze his van
into. A little old woman with curly white hair, who had been
stooped over the steering wheel of her Mini Cooper, had
beeped furiously and given him two fingers when he'd beaten
her to it. Normally he would have been raging at such bad
manners, but he'd laughed, mouthing *sorry Grandma* as he
turned into it, and she'd beeped again, mouthing what he was
sure had been *Go eff yourself*, which had made him chuckle
even louder. There was a loud thud from the back of the van,
and he wondered if he was doing the right thing by parking
here. It was busy. He wound the window down and listened. It
was also market day and very loud. There were lots of people
passing through, so he figured no one was going to pay any
attention to the odd muffled thump coming from the back of
his van, or so he hoped. He believed that hiding in plain sight
was the best thing to do, no one expected that, and it had
served him well before he'd been sent to prison. He was a free
man now though; he could travel where he wanted and pick
up who he wanted, and no one would be able to stop him or

tell him how to live his life. His stomach groaned and he realised he was hungry; he hadn't eaten since yesterday evening, and the breeze was carrying the aroma of fried onions this way. He jumped out of the van, not bothering to buy a parking ticket. So what if he got a parking fine in a few weeks? If it all went to plan he'd be long gone from this area. He liked that he was a free man and could do whatever he pleased. He led a simple but wholly satisfying life. What more could anyone ask for?

He wandered through the busy stalls that stretched from the top of Market Square, above Moot Hall, all the way down to Bryson's Bakery. He was particularly fond of their pastries and made a point to visit whenever he was up this way. The stalls were bustling, and he found some of the goods they sold quite eye-opening; was there much call for incense, coloured rocks, bath salts and jars of herbal teas? He wondered if they did much business, but there were plenty of people around so he assumed they must. He found the stall with the frying onions that had drawn him in and waited patiently to order himself an artisan burger with the full works. It sounded pretentious, but as long as it contained cheese, onions and burger sauce he'd be a happy man.

After collecting his order, he wandered down to the bakery, chewing slowly on his burger, savouring each mouthful. He had basic food in the van to last him a few days should he need to find a place to go off grid, but he was hoping he wouldn't have to. He didn't want to be too far from where he'd left her in the van. He bought some fresh bread, pies and a couple of short-bread biscuits from the bakery and headed back to his van. He'd been long enough; he better go back and check on her.

As he walked back through the car park, he saw the old woman near to his van and wondered for a moment if she was going to pull a knitting needle out of her bag and stab one of his tyres, but then he saw the van move slightly and heard a dull thud. He jogged back towards it, realising that she was making quite a commotion. The old woman stared at him.

'What's making that thumping sound?'

'My dog, it's probably needing to pee. Why are you bothered?'

She stared at him, squinting over the top of her glasses, and he realised that she wasn't quite as old as he'd thought.

'Strange dog, it hasn't barked once.'

'She's very well trained, but huge; she's a Cane Corso and not very people friendly. I better take her somewhere for a walk. You can have this parking space now.'

'I don't want it; I found my own.'

She turned to walk away, but he got the feeling she wasn't happy with his explanation, and he got into the van, throwing the paper bags on the passenger seat. He gripped the steering wheel and his hands slipped; they were slick with sweat. His breathing was much faster than normal and he inhaled deeply to get control again. Wiping them on the side of his trousers he started the engine and began to reverse. He needed to get away from here. He had been far too full of himself believing that she was going to behave herself. This one was obviously a fighter. He slammed his fist against the wheel. She would pay for this. Who did she think she was trying to get him in trouble?

As he drove towards the exit, he saw the woman staring after his van. She was on the phone. He memorised her number plate and kept his cool. He knew that it didn't matter what she told the coppers; they were never going to find him.

ELEVEN

Amy threw open every window in the office. It was far too warm in here, or was it just her? Des had gone to the campsite to help with the search. She was glad she didn't have to; there wasn't anything worse she could think of than trekking through the forest in this kind of weather and getting bitten to death. The phone on Ben's desk began to ring and ring. She stared at it, willing it to stop because she was busy and she couldn't be bothered moving again to answer it. After what seemed like forever it did stop, and she looked back down at her screen to see if it had loaded the pages for John Winder, because from what information Morgan had passed on he seemed to be their main person of interest. The phone began to ring again. She stood up and walked into Ben's office, snatching it from the cradle.

'CID.'

There was a slight pause and then a voice said. '*Is this Sergeant Ben Matthews?*'

Amy rolled her eyes, wondering if she sounded like a man.

'No, it's Detective Constable Amy Smith. Ben's not here, can I help?'

'*Oh, I hope so. Would it be possible to get a message to him?*'

'Yes, no problem.'

'*Good, that's good, I suppose he's out at the crime scene.*'

Until this point, she had been picking at her fingernail, the phone in the crook of her neck. She stood up straight and grabbed the phone with her hand.

'Who did you say you were?'

'*I didn't, but my name is Detective Inspector Brian Walter; actually I'm retired now but before I left, I ran the CID department in Herne Bay, Kent.*'

Amy sat up straighter, he was one of them and a DI; he instantly had her attention and her respect.

'What can I do for you, boss?'

He laughed.

'*Brian is great, no need for formalities now, DC Smith. I'm phoning about the current investigation you have ongoing; I know you can't disclose anything to me, but I'd really like to talk to whoever is running it and from what I've heard it's DS Matthews.*'

'Amy is fine, Brian. Which investigation?'

'*The missing camper.*'

'How do you know about that? Surely it's not in the news yet; it's only been a few hours.'

'*I'm afraid it's headlines on the internet, no idea about the news. Your police force has issued a missing person's report with a request for information. Look, I know you must be rushed off your feet, but I really need to speak to your supervisor.*'

'Don't worry, Brian, I'll let him know. Give me your contact details and I'll get him to give you a ring as soon as he can.'

'*Thank you, that's very much appreciated, Amy.*'

She took his name, phone number, rank, collar number and station details, in case Ben wanted to check he was real and not some crank caller. Then he hung up, and she stuck the washed-out lemon Post-it note onto Ben's computer monitor and went back to her intelligence checks. There were only a couple of arrest disposals on John Winder's PNC record and they were for fighting in the late 2000s. There wasn't anything on there that raised a red flag with her. Her phone rang, and she heard Morgan's voice.

'*Anything on John Winder? Enough to bring him in?*'

'You should be so lucky, couple of bare-knuckle fights in his younger days. Nothing recent or of concern. Have you got me a list of the visitors on site so I can begin checking those out?'

'*Yes, Eleanor has emailed them over to you, but they might take some time to arrive. There's quite a few and you know how slow the email system is.*'

'Are you near Ben?'

'*No, he's at the incident unit. I'm at the grave site with Declan, why?*'

'There's a guy phoned to speak to him, a retired DI, can you ask him to ring me when you see him?'

'*Yes, of course.*'

'Any sign of Sara?'

'*Nothing, it's like something out of a nightmare; to think she was happy camping when someone came and took her, it gives me the chills.*'

'I know, it's awful. Hey, ask Ben if he knows this is public knowledge as well; apparently the press office issued a release about Sara.'

'*How?*'

'No idea, did her friend go public with it?'

'*Probably, you took her back home. Did you tell her not to speak to the press?*'

'Of course I did. Well, if it's out in the public you better be ready for an influx of volunteers turning up to help search. If there's one thing Rydal Falls is good at it's pitching in to search for anyone in distress.'

'*Thanks, Amy, I'll go tell him the good news.*'

Amy hung up.

* * *

Morgan opened up the Facebook App, which she rarely used. Logging on again she waited for it to load and the first image on her page was a photo of Sara laughing and smiling, captioned 'Missing: Have You Seen This Woman?'

A sharp pain between her eyes reminded her that she was beyond tired and getting a headache from hell as she began the trek back through the woods to inform Ben that this had gone public.

Chris and Declan were inside the white crime-scene tent that had been erected over the remains. Ben was standing at the entrance. The undertakers had arrived along the dirt road, and the van filled it. She wondered how they were going to turn around and get out of here, but that was their problem, she had enough to worry about. Ben turned to her, and she gave him a small smile that immediately told him she was bringing bad news.

'What's the matter?'

'Amy rang, said John Winder has very little on his record: a couple of fights back in his late teens and nothing since.'

'Oh, well, we still have the guest list to be checked off. Has she started on that yet?'

'I think she's still waiting for the email. I've come down to tell you that news has already broken: it's all over Facebook, and the press office released a statement too. Did you tell them to?'

He nodded. 'Yeah, I phoned them when you went back up to the site. I figured we better get Sara's photograph out there, far and wide; it might just save her life.'

She nodded. 'That's okay then; she said some retired DI phoned for you too.'

'Right, well, I'll sort that out when we get back to the station.'

Morgan peered behind him to see what they were up to in the tent and muttered, 'If we ever get back to the station.' It didn't look as if much was happening inside the tent.

'I'm going to get a couple of officers to come here then they can accompany the...' He paused and she knew he was struggling to think about what to call them. 'The remains to the mortuary and get them booked in, so we don't mess anything up procedure wise. Then we'll concentrate on Sara and look into any potential witnesses the PCSOs have picked up.'

Morgan stared up at the path through the trees. She had been up and down here more times than she could count today, and her feet were beginning to ache. 'Sounds good, do we have to come back down here when they move?'

Ben was shaking his head. 'No, I'll send Cain. He's the most experienced; he knows exactly what to do.'

She didn't say the words *thank God* out loud because that would have sounded disrespectful, but she definitely thought them.

TWELVE

Ben and Morgan left Al behind at the site and made their way back to Rydal Falls station, to speak to Tom and Mel. Both of them were red-faced, grubby and tired, and neither spoke a word to each other. When they reached the station Morgan disappeared into the ladies. Bending over the sink she ran the cold tap until it was freezing, then splashed handfuls of water over her face and the back of her neck to cool down. Her shirt was sticky, and she wanted to strip off and have a long, cold shower. Instead she went to her locker and grabbed a clean T-shirt, then sprayed herself everywhere with a can of Dove deodorant someone had left by the sinks. She felt slightly better. She was torn between thinking about where Sara Fletcher could be and who the remains in the forest belonged to. It was information overload, and the pounding in her head signalled that she needed to drink water and scrounge some painkillers from somewhere. Her cheeks were burnt from the late-after-noon sun, and she realised that she hadn't put any sunscreen on before she left for work, which was why she now had the headache from hell. She probably had her first sunstroke of the year. Being a redhead seemed to guarantee it every time the sun shone for more than a few minutes at a time. Damn it, she couldn't afford to be ill now, there was far too much to do. For the first time in her entire time working at the station she didn't even attempt to walk up the stairs and pressed the call button on the lift. Stopping at the first floor she went to the canteen, where there was a vending machine, and bought two bottles of ice-cold water. Holding one against her forehead she got back in the lift to go up to the next floor, not caring how lazy or hot and bothered she looked. As she walked into the office glugging the water, she heard Amy say.

'Oh, Morgan. Tell me you didn't, you haven't?'

'What?'

'Forgot to put sunscreen on. You look like a lobster. You're gonna pay for that later.' She opened her drawer, took out a bottle of green gloop and launched it in her direction. 'Go plaster yourself in that and don't go back out in the sun today.'

Morgan caught it and turned around, walking straight back out. Amy followed her, heading in the direction of the printer. She could hear Ben talking to Tom and Mel, but she went into the toilet and began rubbing the cooling aftersun gel over her cheeks, neck and the parts of her arms that were red. She looked awful, and her freckles had erupted like a volcano all over the bridge of her nose. Taking a deep breath, she went back in the office and asked, 'Has anyone got any paracetamol?'

Ben turned to look at her and nodded. 'In my top drawer. Are you okay?'

'Fine, just realised how much I've caught the sun, thanks.'

She went into Ben's office, which was much cooler than the main office because he kept the blinds shut all the time. Sitting down on his chair she opened the top drawer and moved a stack of pens and Post-it notes to see a blister pack of tablets with four left in it. She popped out three for good measure and took them, noticing the Post-it stuck on his monitor, which she peeled off and took to Ben.

'Did you see this message?'

He nodded. 'Yeah, I haven't got time to ring him right now.'

'Do you want me to?'

'If you want.'

Amy came back in with a stack of papers and caught the conversation. 'He wanted to speak to the boss.'

'Well, I'm too busy. Didn't you ask him what he wanted, Amy?'

She shrugged. 'He asked for you.'

'Morgan, please phone him back and give him my apologies, see what he wants. Is that okay?' He turned to Amy. 'I can't believe you didn't ask him.'

She shrugged. 'Well, I'm sorry. I've been a little bit busy, you know.'

'It's fine, I don't mind. Can I use your office, Ben, it's cooler?'

Ben waved her away, and she ducked back inside, glad to be here. She sat down and sipped at her water; her head felt as if it was on fire. Picking up the phone she dialled the number on the note and listened to it ring. It was picked up after the second ring.

'*Hello?*'

'Oh, hi is it possible to speak to Detective Inspector Brian Walter?'

'*Speaking, well I'm retired now so Brian is fine. Can I help you?*'

'This is DC Morgan Brookes from Cumbria Constabulary; my colleague left a message for our boss to call you back. I'm really sorry but he's tied up for the foreseeable and asked me to ring you back on his behalf.'

'*Well thank you for getting back to me, that's much appreciated, DC Brookes.*'

'Morgan, please. How can we help?'

'*I don't want to sound rude, but this is important, and I need* to know that it will get passed on and that you will take me seriously.'

'I promise that it will. We are a very small, close team, Brian, and anything you tell me I will go and directly pass it on to Ben myself.'

There was a slight pause and Morgan wondered what an earth he was about to disclose to her.

'I call him The Travelling Man.'

'Who?' As she said it, a cold chill settled down the full length of her spine.

'The man who has your missing woman.'

He didn't speak, allowing Morgan time to digest what he had just told her, and she grabbed a notepad off the desk and a pen. She scribbled it down, looking up to see if Ben was still in the office, but he had gone, along with Tom and Mel. Amy was nowhere to be seen.

'Are you still there, Morgan?'

'Yes, I am. Why do you call him that?' As the words left her lips she didn't know if she wanted to hear his answer.

'Good, I need your attention because this is important. I think that he takes them and keeps them for up to seventy-two hours before killing them in a wooded area. I retired six years ago, but back in 2004 when I was a DS there was an unsolved murder of a young woman who to this day has not been identi-fied. It haunts me, and I am going to be honest with you I have never got over the fact that we didn't catch him or find her family.'

For once she was speechless and wished that Ben or Amy, anyone, was here to listen to this, but they'd all disappeared and she was on her own with it.

'Can you give me any more information, please?'

'I have a lot more information, but I'm not sure I want to pass it all over the phone. I'd rather do it in person.'

'I'm sorry but that's not going to be possible. We are a small team and now we're working flat out to locate the misper and identify the remains.' She stopped herself, wondering if she had said too much.

'*You found skeletal remains? In a woodland area?*'

'I'm sorry, you know how it is, I can't say anything else.'

'*I would bet you that it's all connected, that you didn't find those by accident. He is clever, cunning and the evilest person I have ever encountered, and I've met a few over the years. I'll tell you now that I think he's been doing this for a very long time.*'

Morgan's stomach was rolling around just thinking about it. She had to remind herself, though, that all they had on this theory so far was one retired detective's word. 'I'll go and find Ben now, get him to call you.'

'*I can go one better than that. I've been meaning to come for a trip to the Lakes since I retired. How about I bring everything I have to you? I'll load up my campervan with the files and research I kept. I could probably be there this evening, although it would be pretty late, but if I set off now, we could meet first thing tomorrow morning.*'

'Are you sure? That would be amazing. Where are you going to stay the night?'

'*Which campsite did he take this camper from? Could you see if they have room for me for a couple of nights? I'd like to be as close to the investigation as permitted.*'

'It's called Forest Pines and yes, I'll arrange that for you now. Are you travelling alone, Brian?'

'*Yes, my wife is on a week-long break to Portugal with her sister. I don't want her involved in this in any way, shape or form so it's just as well. All I need to do is ask my lovely daughter, Jo, to pop in and feed the cat and everything will be fine.*'

'Thank you, Brian, this is very kind of you.'

'*Not really, it's entirely selfish of me. I need to find this sick bastard. The fact that I didn't while I had the chance has been eating away at me since the day I hung up my boots. I'm doing this as much for myself as for anyone else.'*

'That's as good a reason as any. Is this the best number to phone you on?'

'Yes.'

'I'll text you my mobile number, you can ring me anytime. See you tomorrow.'

'Yes, I will.'

The line went dead. Morgan felt as though she was going to throw up. She couldn't get those words out of her mind: *The Travelling Man*; they were whizzing around in her head making her feel dizzy. It sounded so ominous, not to mention downright terrifying.

THIRTEEN

Ben opened his office door, took one look at Morgan and asked, 'What's wrong?'

'The Travelling Man.'

'What are you talking about?'

'That's what he calls him.'

He sat in the chair opposite her. She took a mouthful of water and swallowed it in a gulp.

'Morgan, do you need to go home? Have you, like, completely fried your brains? I don't have a clue what you're talking about.'

She shook her head. 'Yes, I feel like crap. I think I have sunstroke, but I don't need to go home. I've had some paracetamol. The retired DI, Brian Walter, said he thinks this is a killer who he named The Travelling Man. Christ, just saying it out loud makes me shiver.'

'Can you explain more, please?'

She did; she repeated the conversation word for word and watched as Ben's face paled.

'He's on his way to speak to us in person and said he'll bring what files he has.'

'Okay, that's good, that might be a big help. Who is he, can you please do some checks to make sure that there is a retired DI with Kent police and we haven't been talking to some delusional, crackpot wannabe?'

'Yes, I will. Oh, I accidentally mentioned that we'd recovered some remains. I didn't say anything else, sorry about that.'

Ben closed his eyes for a second, and she felt awful. He looked at her. 'That's okay, look, do the background checks then go home, Morgan, and cool off. I'm getting sunburn from the heat radiating off your face. We'll have an early start tomorrow.'

'What about you?'

'I have a lot to do. I'm going back to the campsite. Amy and Des have gone to interview Sofie and meet with Sara's parents, who are also on their way here.'

'Then I'm good. I'll go back with you to help with whatever needs doing.'

'No, you're not good. I have all the help I need today. There's a whole host of searchers out combing the forest. If she doesn't turn up, then tomorrow will be a long day and you also have Brian to take care of. If I need you, I'll phone you, deal?'

She nodded, her head still aching despite the tablets she'd taken earlier. 'Deal.'

He left her to it, and she began to google Brian Walter's name and collar number, to get as much background information on him as possible. She also rang the campsite and asked Eleanor, who was still manning the phones, for a pitch for him for the next few days. A picture of a man in a smart suit, walking out of a wooded area, a phone clasped to his ear and a look of despair on his face filled the screen. The headlines said, 'Skeletal Remains found in West Blean Woods'. She sent the article to the printer and the few more that were linked under it. Then she googled the telephone number for Herne Bay police station and phoned.

'*Herne Bay front office, can I help?*'

'Hello, I hope so. My name is Detective Constable Morgan Brookes from Cumbria police, and I was wondering if you knew of anyone who could confirm if a detective inspector called Brian Walter worked there.'

'Brian, oh yes. He's a lovely man but he retired a few years ago now. Why are you asking?'

'I'm just making enquiries, thank you.'

'Is he in trouble?'

'Oh, no, definitely not. Thank you for your time.'

She hung up before she got sucked into a conversation she didn't have time for. She was satisfied that he was who he said he was, as long as he looked like the pictures she'd printed off, and she'd found a fair few. She was going home for the cold shower she'd been dreaming about and would continue looking at the news reports of any high-profile cases that Brian had covered so she could quiz him tomorrow.

Morgan had never been so glad to kick off her boots and strip off. Bolting the front door behind her she went straight to the bathroom.

After a long, cool shower she used the remains of last year's aftersun and slathered it all over her face, neck and arms. She wasn't hungry, but she grabbed a bottle of water from her fridge and two ibuprofen for good measure, then threw herself on top of her bed. She hadn't opened the blinds this morning, so it was cool in there and for that she was grateful.

As she lay down, she could swear she heard a voice whisper *The Travelling Man* and opened her eyes suddenly. Fear lodged inside her throat as she turned her head from side to side to see who had said it. There was no one in the room with her and she realised it must have been her own voice, or one inside her mind. She had no idea why but the thought of some guy taking women from their tents then keeping them alive for seventy-two hours before brutally killing them terrified her beyond anything she'd ever known. Closing her eyes once more she began to inhale deeply through her nose, exhaling through her mouth to calm her nerves and relax her body. She felt terrible that she was here, at home, on her comfortable bed knowing that Sara might be out there terrified and hurt. But her head felt as if it weighed more than the rest of her body, and her skin was on fire it was burning so bad. Just a few hours' rest, she told herself, let the painkillers kick in and the aftersun cool her scorched skin enough so that she could get dressed and go find the bastard who had taken Sara away.

As she lay there, Morgan wondered if that was why she was so scared. Was it because she knew that somehow, no matter what happened, whoever had taken Sara had brought this to her on her own doorstep, and she would find him despite the danger it may pose to her?

FOURTEEN

Morgan opened her eyes to the vibrating of her phone from underneath her pillow. She felt around for it groggily. Her skin felt too tight on her arms where the sun had caught it, and she flinched. Grabbing her phone she answered the call with a muttered, 'Hello.'

'*Morning, are you ready to go?*'

She sat up. Her head felt much better, but her arms, face and neck were still on fire. It was light outside, much lighter than she expected.

'Did you find Sara?'

Ben paused, and she knew she was putting him under pressure.

'*Not yet, but we will, I'm sure of it.*'

She sighed. 'Yes, we will. Where do you want me?'

'*The station, please. I believe we have a visitor who is already waiting at the front desk to see us both.*'

'Already, wow he's keen, and I'm impressed.'

'*You're impressed? You must have sounded like you knew what you were doing when you spoke to him. It's me who's impressed.*'

'Well then, let's give ourselves a clap. Aren't we all bloody brilliant.'

Ben laughed. *'You're still a moody morning person.'*

'Listen who's talking. I'll be there soon.'

She hung up. Peeling herself off the top of the duvet she surveyed the damage. Her face looked like a beacon and there were freckles everywhere. She tutted at her carelessness and this time, after she'd washed and cleaned her teeth, she smothered herself in factor 50 sun cream. Stan used to laugh and tell her she needed factor 5,000 especially for gingers. She smiled at the thought of his cheeky grin. She had never thought she would miss him this much, but his death had come out of nowhere before she'd had time to make her peace with him properly, and it pained her heart every time she thought about it.

By the time she left the house in record time, her scalp had been sprayed along with every piece of skin on show. She didn't bother with a suit today; the material would stick to her. Instead she wore a black T-shirt and a pair of cropped linen trousers. She still wore her boots because if all else failed and she needed to protect herself, a good kick in anyone's groin with her Docs would give her time to make her escape.

As she drove to work it bothered her that all she kept thinking about was being able to defend herself should the need arise. What exactly was her subconscious telling her? Was it a warning or just self-preservation? She wasn't sure, either way she was on edge far more than any other case she'd worked since she'd joined the police. If Brian was right about the seventy-two-hour window, they had no time to lose.

* * *

She entered the station through the side door, making a beeline for the front office and the CCTV monitor in it. She wanted to take a look at Brian Walter, just to make sure he looked like the guy in the newspaper articles. There were two women, and a man sitting alone clutching a briefcase. His hair was a little shorter than on the newspaper photographs and greyer, but he still had the same style glasses.

Brenda looked at her.

'Who are you checking out?'

'Is that Brian Walter?'

'It is, he was so polite, and he's been here since I opened the doors and hasn't grumbled once.'

'Bless him, thanks.'

She opened the double doors into the reception area, and all three heads turned to stare at her. She made eye contact with Brian and smiled. 'Brian, would you like to come this way?'

He stood up, nodded his head and gave her the warmest smile that practically melted her heart. As he got closer to her, he asked, 'Morgan?'

'I am, and I'm glad you made it here. I can't believe you drove all this way.'

She reached out her hand, shaking his.

He laughed. 'You have no idea how happy I was to drive here; believe me, this is something that is worth travelling for.'

She led him through into the atrium, wondering where to take him. It might be a little early to thrust him straight into the investigation and show him around the office. There was a small room with a sofa, coffee table and couple of armchairs that they tended to use for runaway teenagers that needed supervising until someone came to retrieve them, so she decided on that until Ben had met him. As she opened the door the lights flickered on, and he nodded.

'This is much better than my old nick. It was falling to pieces.'

'This one has recently had a full refurb and modernised; thankfully I didn't work here before that.'

He looked at her. 'How long have you been in the job?'

She knew her cheeks were turning pink, but it didn't matter because her face was already burnt so he couldn't tell.

'Almost two years.'

'And you're a detective, not just any detective either, you have an amazing success rate with solving high-profile crimes.'

She realised that Brian had also been checking her out on Google and this thought made her smile.

'I was literally thrown in at the deep end; actually it was more like being thrown off the end of a cliff on my first day on independent patrol. It's been a whirlwind of a couple of years.'

He nodded. 'Yes, I could imagine it has. Well done, that's amazing, Morgan. Dare I ask if you've located the missing camper?'

She shook her head. 'As far as I'm aware not yet, but we will.'

'I'm sure you will, you have that confident air about you. It's a rare thing, the sort of thing you usually see in seasoned detectives.'

'Would you like a drink, tea, coffee?'

He laughed. 'Tea would be great, milk no sugar, thanks.'

She left him there and went to find Ben, who was in the briefing room talking to Tom and Al.

'Boss, Brian's here. He's waiting in that little room with the sofa.'

'What little room?'

She pointed down the hall. 'Just grabbing a tea.' She didn't ask if anyone else wanted one. She wasn't brewing up for the whole station, only Brian.

She opened the door to the room, and Ben was already there, sitting on one of the chairs. She placed the only mug she could find without a chip in it that wasn't an actual health hazard on the small table in the middle of the room.

'Thank you, Morgan.' He smiled at her, and she knew

immediately that she liked Brian Walter and would have guessed he'd been a great DI, not to mention boss.

'I'll get straight to the point, Brian, we have limited time and even fewer resources. Can you tell me why you think that this man has taken Sara Fletcher?'

'Of course, and I call him The Travelling Man. You're right, I'll show you what I have.'

He began to unclasp the worn leather briefcase and pulled out a thick brown file. He passed it across to Ben, who opened it and began to flick through, then picked up the mug and began sipping the tea, not grimacing once.

Morgan asked, 'Why do you call him The Travelling Man?'

Brian looked up at her. 'Good question, I've spent a lot of time searching the net for any cases of the same nature, and up to now I've found ones with similarities to the body we discovered in Kent in Scotland and France.'

She glanced at Ben, unable to help herself. 'What similarities?'

'It happened in my jurisdiction in 1998: a lone female camper disappeared from her tent. No, sorry that's not right, was taken from her tent. We found a long slit in the fabric when we got our hands on it. Did your misper's tent have a cut in it?'

Morgan looked at Ben. It wasn't up to her to disclose this information.

Brian nodded. 'Sorry, I know you're limited in what you can tell me, but if it did then I think we are definitely up against the same man. It's his MO. It's how he works. This victim was, is still to my knowledge, unidentified; the people in the tent next to hers reported an incident that happened in the night. They said they heard a scuffle and dragging sounds but were too scared to go outside and look. They told the campsite owner, who phoned us. He played it down big time to the response officer who attended, told them he wasn't worried, and that people get up and leave to get out of paying the site fees. The officer, much to our disgrace, was, for want of a better word, a lazy bastard who did nothing with it. Until a few years later, when the skeletonised remains turned up in the woods.'

'How did you trace it to the missing camper?'

Brian nodded at Morgan. 'Her clothes were tattered, but there was a folded, faded map of the campsite in her pocket, no ID on her whatsoever. I went to see the owner and asked if he'd had any campers go missing. He mentioned the woman who had disappeared in the night. He'd kept her tent, sleeping bag and toiletries out in a bag in the storage unit. We took it away and discovered the cut in the tent. The forensic databases never brought up any DNA or fingerprints on any of the systems.'

'Wow, that's so sad.'

'It was, it still is. Then another camper was reported missing in Scotland early 1999. I've got copies of everything if you need them.' He passed them a much thinner file from inside the folder he was holding.

'Thank you so much, Brian. You told me that he keeps them for seventy-two hours. How do you know this?'

'The body in Scotland was discovered seventy-two hours after she was reported missing. Same again, lone female camping. Her boyfriend had missed his train and was joining her the next day. He arrived at the campsite to find his girlfriend missing, a cut in the back of the tent and blood inside. A huge search of the area was carried out and no sign of her until a walker discovered her naked body in the woods covered with branches. He didn't do a very good job of hiding her, so he was either disturbed or this time he wanted her to be found. I still haven't quite made my mind up which it is.'

'Yes, thanks, Brian, this is very helpful. We'll take a look into it and be in touch. Are you staying here for a few days?'

He nodded. 'I certainly am. If you need me, obviously, I'm available whenever.'

'I'll show you out.'

She led him back to the reception area.

'You have my mobile, don't you? Thank you for coming all this way.'

'You're welcome. Please, whatever you do, Morgan, catch this bastard and be very careful he doesn't catch you.'

She smiled at him, but there it was: that cold fear spoken out loud by a stranger whom she'd spoken to twice.

'Did you ever get close to catching him? Have an idea, named suspect?'

He shook his head. 'No, he was like a ghost. We think he planned everything meticulously and carried spare number plates with him to swap and change, so there was no tracing him through the ANPR cameras should anyone have noticed him looking or acting suspiciously.'

'That's scary and clever. Don't worry, I will be careful. I've been in some sticky situations and made it out of them so far.'

She left him and let the door close. Her knees were trembling, and she reached out, pressing the palm of her clammy hand against the cool plaster of the wall and hoping that Brenda wasn't watching her on the CCTV. Inhaling deeply to calm herself down, she opened the doors and went over to the lift. She needed to make sure she didn't make a habit of this because running up and down the stairs all shift long was her most productive workout routine. One that didn't rely on her actually leaving the comfort of her apartment when she really couldn't be bothered.

'Morgan.'

She looked up. Ben was standing at the door to his office.

'What?'

'Do you think he's onto something? This Travelling Man, do you think he's real? I'm not so sure, I mean he seems like a nice guy and was a decent copper, but it's all a bit far-fetched and there are some tenuous links in his way of thinking. Not to mention it's mainly circumstantial, there's no hard evidence.'

Her eyes began to roll, and she caught herself in time. 'Yes, I do, why would he waste years gathering information if he didn't and, I'm not going to lie, the thought of it scares the crap out of me. It's like something the FBI would be investigating. Should I go and get a map of the area to pin up and we can pinpoint everywhere we've searched and look for any possible hiding places he may be holed up?'

'Yes, please, that would be great. I'll read through the rest of his notes and see what there is.'

'I could also go and relieve Amy if you want?' She didn't know why she didn't just tell him she wanted to speak to Brian again, but for some reason she felt as if he'd want to know why. She wanted to ask Brian what he thought and show him the map first. She wasn't convinced that Ben was going to take him seriously, and she didn't think they had the luxury of time on their side. Every lead deserved her full attention, including Brian's.

'If you really want to give them a break, you could go for an hour then I'll get someone else to come man it. If no one has come forward with anything by then, I think we'll get PCSOs to take over. I could do with Amy back here to carry on viewing the CCTV that has been seized from the campsite entrance and office.'

Nodding, Morgan stood up, grabbed her laptop bag and left before he changed his mind. She wanted that brown file that lay open on his desk so bad, but Ben was in charge, not her, and he was probably still looking at it. There were sheets of paper spread across his desk, and she strained her neck to see what they were.

'Oh, Chris said he will have finished excavating the site this afternoon. He's had a couple of students helping him. Do you want to come with me to the mortuary to see what he's got? The latest update was that they've recovered the whole body, and the victim was female.'

'Yes, of course. Let me know and I'll come back.'

'Great, I need to speak to Wendy about the samples from the tent and see how the search of the forest is going. I know they completed an initial one yesterday, but Al and a team were going back out at first light.'

He ducked back into his office, and she left him to it, so many burning questions filling her mind. She needed to find a map of the area and get back to Forest Pines before she forgot any of them.

FIFTEEN

The post office didn't have any maps. Morgan walked into the newsagents and spied a faded, torn map stuck in the corner of a display unit.

'Is that a map of this area?'

The man behind the counter, who was reading the paper, peered over the top of it to look and see who had disturbed him.

'I believe so, do you want to buy it?'

'Yes, please.'

'It's a bit outdated, it's been there forever. The bookshop might have some modern, more up-to-date copies.'

'I'm in a hurry, this will do.'

He stared at the laptop bag slung over her shoulder and then the blue lanyard around her neck that had 'Cumbria Constabulary' printed along it in white.

'Is this official police business? If it's to help you find that missing woman, you'd do better to get one off Mountain Rescue. Aren't they handling this?'

She bit her tongue. 'Lowland Search and Rescue are, I just need the map, please.'

'Take it.'

'How much?'

'It's yours, anything to help.'

He went back to reading his paper, and Morgan plucked it out of the cabinet with a *thanks*. The front was faded, and she just hoped the inside was okay.

She needed coffee and crossed over to the café where she used to come for lunch regularly with Dan. She swallowed the lump in her throat. He'd been a good tutor, and a pretty decent copper, she'd thought. How wrong she'd been about him. Taylor, her brother. She hadn't even guessed they were related. It had been a while since she'd thought about him and wondered if he thought about her; and her childhood, when her name was Skye, before Gary Marks killed their mother and they were separated into different foster homes, he probably did. There wasn't much else to think about in prison other than the person who put you there. Picking up a latte and a sandwich, she got back in the car and began driving to Forest Pines.

* * *

As she parked next to the large mobile blue-and-white livered police unit she saw a lad who hadn't been here yesterday disappear along a footpath. He was wearing a dark green polo shirt which said *Staff* in bright yellow on the back. Morgan wondered if anyone had spoken to him yet as she grabbed her stuff and opened the door of the van. The heat from inside washed over her like a sauna, and she left the door open. Des was in a chair, feet on the desk, head back and eyes closed.

'Busy?'

He pushed himself forwards, his eyes opening wide. 'Yeah, no, not particularly. Are you on your own?'

'Yes, aren't you glad Tom or the Chief Super weren't with me? Sleeping on the job, Des, whatever next?'

'I'm knackered and Amy has done nothing but complain

about being stuck here. Have you brought me something to eat? I'm starving.'

'No, well, I've brought myself something. You can go and get your own. I'm taking over for an hour.'

'Really, you're not winding me up?'

She shook her head and walked across to the two small windows, pushing them open.

'No wonder you're tired, there's no air in here. It's like a hothouse. Anything to report?'

'No, a lot of the campers left this morning. We took details of everyone who checked out and their vehicles, that's about it.'

'Any news? Who is that kid walking around in a staff polo shirt?'

'No idea, didn't see him, sorry.'

'Have you brought coffee?' Amy's voice sounded hopeful as she entered the unit, and Morgan felt bad; she could have brought them one.

'Sorry, just my own. You can get off now though. Ben said I was to take over. He needs you back at the nick to view the CCTV.'

Amy walked inside, grabbed her bag and keys off the desk. 'Right, well, brill. I'll forgive you for not bringing me coffee. Come on, Des, what are you waiting for? Did you fall asleep again?' Amy didn't even wait for his reply. She was outside and striding towards the white Focus in the car park.

'Thanks, she's scared in case you change your mind.'

Morgan smiled. 'See you later.'

Des waved and hurried after Amy, and she left the door open so that what little breeze there was could flow through. Putting her sandwich in the top drawer of the old desk, she took a couple of sips of coffee then went out to see if she could find the lad she'd spotted earlier and then Brian.

. . .

She walked into the office and saw Eleanor moving around in the back office, and she waited at the counter for her to come back. A walkie-talkie crackled into life, and she heard Eleanor's voice.

'*Miles, did you manage to clear up that mess by pitch twenty-seven yet?*'

Silence greeted her and she muttered, '*Rude.*'

Morgan leant over. 'Hello.'

Eleanor came through and smiled at her. 'Hi, any news?'

'Not that I'm aware of but we're doing everything we possibly can.'

'Good, those two earlier this morning were miserable. Are they still here?'

She smiled to herself. 'No, they've gone. I've taken over. Who is that walking around with the staff shirt on?'

'Miles, he's neither use nor ornament but John has a soft spot for him, and he's come back to work after being ill so I can't complain too much.'

'Would you ask him to come and speak to me? I'm over in the incident unit.'

'I will. I don't want to sound ungrateful but how long is that ugly thing going to be taking up most of my car park? You're welcome to clear a space in the corner over there, and I can get Miles to bring you a table and chair.'

'I'll speak to my boss, thanks for the offer.'

Eleanor picked up the walkie-talkie. 'Miles.' Silence apart from the odd burst of static. She rolled her eyes at Morgan. 'He has the worst case of selective hearing you ever did come across; I'll get John to hunt him down.'

Morgan smiled at her, but as she left the office she replayed the words in her head, *I'll get John to hunt him down.* They sent a shudder down her spine, and she glanced back over her shoulder. She knew it was just a saying, a phrase, and it didn't mean anything, but the choice of words struck her all the same.

. . .

Instead of going back to the van, Morgan headed down towards the area where the campervans were parked. She could have asked Eleanor which pitch Brian was camped on, but for some reason she didn't want her to know about him. What had she told her when she'd phoned up to see if they could squeeze him in? Nothing, because she knew very little about him. She'd asked if there was a pitch spare for a friend, she was sure that was all. Morgan felt fiercely protective over Brian, as if his coming here was her responsibility, and she wondered if it was because he was around the same age as Stan. His grin was similar to Stan's, and maybe she was doing what she could to keep him safe because she hadn't been able to save Stan. A voice whispered, *why would you need to keep Brian safe? He's not in danger.* She shrugged that off, too, her mind was working overtime today. Any minute now she was going to have a pounding headache with using it far more than she usually did.

'Morgan.' A deep voice called her. Turning, she saw Brian sitting in a camping chair in the sun, and she waved, hurrying towards him.

'Hi, what do you think?'

'About what, this place or the case? This place is amazing, looking down at those swathes of evergreens spread across the side of the fell and the mountains in the background is breath-taking. It reminds me of one of those national parks you see on TV in the US. I can't believe how beautiful it is. I didn't bother speaking to your colleagues in the van; they looked hot and bothered when I peered through the door, and I thought it might be best keeping it between us, my reason for being here.'

'You have no idea how great that is. I was wondering, do you have a copy of the stuff you gave my boss?'

He nodded. 'I certainly do, come inside.' He pushed himself up from his deckchair, and she followed him into the compact living area. 'Take a seat; I don't really want to talk about this outside where people can hear.'

She squeezed behind a laminated table. Brian disappeared into a small room and came back with a brown card file much thicker than the one he'd brought to the station that morning. He passed it to her.

'I wasn't sure how you were going to take to me, so I gave your boss a condensed version. I didn't want to give him all my files to be left sitting around on a desk gathering dust for days. I guess it all sounds a little far-fetched, like some twisted serial killer thriller on the television, but it's not. Or at least I wholly believe that it's not, this is real, and The Travelling Man is very real. My colleagues in Kent were happy to brush it away when they found no other lines of enquiry; no one else was taken from the area, no more missing campers, so they didn't want to stir the pot so to speak.'

'But you did?'

'Let's say I decided that I'd gather my own evidence and prove that I wasn't talking rubbish.' He pulled a photograph album from the storage area above her head, passing it to her.

'I scour newspapers, search engines every day looking for anything on missing campers. That file is what I've managed to collate up to now. I definitely believe it's the same killer. There's the case in Kent I investigated, then the woman from Scotland. I found a report of a missing camper in France, but it's hard to say whether that's connected or not with so little information on that case.'

She opened the cover and looked at the newspaper cuttings; there were pages of them. Lots about the case Brian covered and some from Scotland and France. She scanned them all, digesting the information. They were all reports of lone female campers, missing from their tents in the middle of the night.

'That makes four with Sara Fletcher?'

'That I know of. I think the remains you found in the woods

may make it five. Who knows how many bodies he has hidden in other forests or wooded areas around the country? What I do know is that your missing woman isn't his first.'

'No, I think it's too sleek and well executed to be a first attempt. He's confident, skilled and bold as brass but he's taken the wrong person this time. The others weren't reported missing straight away, except for the victim in Scotland, even years later. Sara's friend, Sofie, reported her on the first day. We have a head start on him; I think he won't have been expecting us to jump on this so fast. Maybe he's panicking and if he does that, he may slip up.'

'Let's hope so, Morgan, God knows we need to catch a break. Someone has to put a stop to this, to him.'

Morgan nodded, that unsettling feeling washing over her once more. She would do whatever it took to catch this man. 'Can I borrow these and read through them? I'll return them tomorrow; I promise to take good care of them and not share them.'

He paused for a moment. 'Yes, you can. All I ask is that you ask me before you show it to anyone else. If your boss decides that it's all relevant after reading what I gave to him then it's all yours to keep. I can breathe a sigh of relief that I've passed it on to someone who cares and wants to put a stop to this. My job will be done, and I can go back to my retirement with a clear conscience.'

Morgan stood up, gathering both the file and scrapbook under her arm. 'Brian, I swear we will end this. Thank you for trusting me with these. I'll return them tomorrow.'

She stepped out of the van, glad to be out in the fresh air. A flash of dark green, in the distance, caught her eye: Miles, finally. She hurried after him, in the direction of the office.

. . .

Morgan followed the boy, making sure he didn't veer off the path and disappear, but he kept on towards the reception area.

Satisfied that he must have got Eleanor's message, Morgan went to the police car she'd arrived in and opened the boot. Taking a quick glance around to make sure no one was watching her, she took out a brown paper evidence sack and dropped everything she'd received from Brian inside before sealing it closed. Then she locked the car and went back into the incident room. She'd left the door open and did a quick check to make sure no one had been in and helped themselves to anything, but in all honesty the only thing of any use in here was her now cold coffee and lukewarm, soggy sandwich. She was desperate to read the files, but she would speak to Miles first.

Heavy boots thudded against the temporary metal steps, making the whole van vibrate, and there was a knock on the open door.

'Come in.'

John was followed in by Miles, who looked uncomfortable, his eyes shifting around taking everything in.

'This is Miles.'

Morgan looked at the boy. He looked much younger than John who was standing behind him. 'Hello, Miles, I'm Morgan. There's nothing to worry about, I just need to ask you a few questions. Let's start with your age?'

'I'm thirty-two,' came the surly response.

John nodded in agreement. 'Yep, he just has a baby face, don't you, Miles? He can't even buy a packet of condoms without getting his ID checked, can you?'

John was laughing as he turned and left. Miles's cheeks had flared deep red, and he gave John's back the finger. Morgan felt sorry for him. He was clearly uncomfortable, but she'd needed to check he wasn't underage and needed an appropriate adult.

She glanced in the window at her reflection, wondering if she looked as young too.

Before she could make that decision he asked, 'What do you want me for? I wasn't here when the woman went missing.'

'Please have a seat. I know you weren't. John already confirmed you had been sent home. I just want some more information about the campsite.' She took out her notebook, uncapping the pen.

He dropped into the chair opposite her, head down, shoulders slumped like a sullen teenager.

'Before we begin, I need your full name and date of birth; is that okay?'

A single nod of his head. 'Miles Gilbert, twentieth December 1989.'

'Did you see Sara Fletcher when she arrived?'

A shrug.

'What does that mean, Miles? Is it a yes or a no?'

'I might have, I'm not very good at faces.'

She stood up and unpinned the missing poster with Sara's face on it that the force had issued county wide and passed it to him.

'It was only two days ago; she's been all over the news and social media.'

'I don't watch the news or have Facebook. Yeah, I think I saw her. She didn't say much.'

Morgan breathed in deep, searching for patience.

'Where did you see her?'

'Taking her tent down to the pitch. I was clearing the pitch a few over from hers. It was messy; they'd left their rubbish behind.'

'Did you see anyone nearby, was anyone paying her much attention?'

'I was busy. I glanced up and saw her putting her tent up. I think she was laughing on her phone about how hard it was.'

Morgan leaned forwards, that was a lot of detail for someone who a minute ago couldn't remember if he'd seen her.

'Did you offer to help her?'

He shook his head. 'No, too busy for that, and by the time I'd bagged up the rubbish, she had it up anyway, and was drinking a can of those cocktails you can buy in the off-licence. She was staring into the forest.'

'Then what did you do?'

He shrugged. 'Took the rubbish up to the bins, then helped John the rest of the afternoon until I felt sick, and he said I could go home.'

She scribbled down what he'd said, not sure what to make of him.

'Where were you on Thursday night?'

'Why? I didn't do anything wrong; I was at home sick. I told you I never saw her.'

'It's just a general question, Miles, we're asking everyone including John, Eleanor and anyone who was on the campsite.'

'Ellie was in Manchester, John was here, I was at home probably on my Xbox or asleep.'

'Do you live with anyone?'

She was expecting him to storm out any moment: he was getting fidgety and rubbing the palms of his hands against his trouser leg. 'My mum, she's always home.'

'Thank you, Miles, that's great.'

He leaned forwards. 'Is that it?'

'Yes, you can get back to work now.' She flashed him a warm smile.

'Oh, yeah, right. Thanks.' He stood up and walked out of the narrow door. There was a damp patch of sweat on the back of his shirt. It was hot and stuffy in here, but there was something not quite right with his behaviour. He walked slowly up the path back towards the office, and Morgan wondered if he'd turn around, but he didn't. He walked straight in and let the door slam behind him.

She phoned Amy.

'Are you back at the station?'

'Yes, just.'

'Can you do me an Intelligence Check on Miles Gilbert, twentieth of December 1989, please?'

'*Is that the lad that works there? He's avoided us all morning. How did you get hold of him? What did he say?*'

'Denied seeing Sara, then went on to describe her struggling to put her tent up, on the phone to someone and drinking a canned cocktail when she was finished.'

'*Blimey, that's a lot of information for someone who didn't see her. I'll do it now.*'

Amy hung up.

SIXTEEN

Florence Brown, or Florrie as her friends liked to call her, couldn't stop thinking about the creepy guy in the van yesterday. She liked to think she was a good judge of character, and he had shown exactly what kind of man he was by driving into the parking space she'd been waiting for. She was a pensioner for God's sake, people like that were what was wrong with this country. She'd made a note of his registration number and passed it on to the police because the banging on the side of that van hadn't sounded anything like a dog. A dog would have barked and growled, especially in this heat. They had been very clear thumps, almost as if someone was banging to get out. The more she thought about it, the more convinced she was. The police were useless though; forty minutes she'd waited for an officer to turn up: forty minutes the weirdo was probably on the motorway escaping before they'd even bothered to turn up. She had tossed and turned all night, fretting over what to do. The policeman who had turned up hadn't been the slightest bit interested in what she'd had to say. He hadn't even got out of the van; he'd just put the window down and chatted to her from there. He'd told her he would have a drive around, looking for the van, but didn't hold out much hope of finding it because it was market day, and it was busy. He'd said it was probably some market trader. She pointed in the direction the van went, and he'd thanked her and driven off in the opposite direction. Idiot.

All morning she'd tried again to forget about it, and then she'd turned the news on and seen about the missing woman. She had gone missing from Forest Pines; Florrie knew that campsite well: she used to take her grandchildren there when her knees were a lot less painful than they were now. It was only a few miles away. She could feel the certainty of it in her bones that something was terribly wrong, and it all had to do with that man yesterday in the van. Picking up her phone she rang her granddaughter who worked for the police but it went straight to voicemail. Florrie sighed, she wasn't mad because this meant she was very busy and would ring her back as soon as she could because she always did without fail, she was a good girl like that. As she sipped her mug of tea, she knew she had to do something. She couldn't let this go. What if that girl had been in that van? She'd never forgive herself. She stood up, tipped the rest of the tea down the sink and decided to go back to the car park. She could have a look for his van, maybe take a slow wander through the market and see if she could spot him. If she saw him again this time, she would dial 999 immediately and tell them she was in trouble; that should get a faster response, and what could they do at her age, throw her in prison? Much better to be wrong than sit here dithering and doing nothing when that poor girl was in serious trouble.

* * *

The car park was even busier today: there was no chance of a space, but at least she got to circle it a few times, checking out any vans that were the same navy colour as the one yesterday. It was hot today; she was getting warm and realised she was going to have to park in one of the side streets. As she exited the car park, she didn't see the man from yesterday slowly crossing the road behind her.

He'd noticed the white curls of the annoying woman from yesterday straight away as she'd driven her green Mini around the car park at a snail's pace. But he was confident she hadn't seen him: his hood was down and he had a navy baseball cap on today. The woman's head was going backwards and forwards studying the cars, paying particular attention to the vans, and he swore. Though he'd returned for another burger, he'd parked in a much quieter place today, so she wouldn't have seen his van, but he had no doubt that she was looking for it. Chewing the rest of his burger slowly he watched as she drove out of the car park, then he crossed the road, hurrying to get back to his van.

Florrie decided to have a little drive around. She wasn't giving in that easily and she needed to find somewhere to park her car. As she drove along the narrow street behind the main road, she passed the small private car park for the estate agents and saw a navy van. A surge of excitement rushed through her veins. Smiling to herself she muttered, *Blimey girl, that's the biggest thrill you've had for years* and chuckled. It was the same size as the van from yesterday, and she was sure it was the one she was after. But she didn't want to make it too obvious she was looking. Instead she carried on driving until she found a space before the double-yellow lines on Poplar Street, which wasn't too far to walk for her knackered knees. She got out of the car feeling like Nancy Drew, confident that she was going to nail this creep. She hobbled back the way she'd driven to get to the rear of the estate agents, praying the van was still there. She hadn't been able to get the number plates because she'd driven past too fast, but she had her phone tucked in her pocket and thought she might just remember how to use the camera on it. As she reached the corner of the small back street she peered around and smiled. Head held high, she hobbled on towards it. That awful man wasn't getting away from her today. There was a narrow gap between the van and the wall. Florrie had to squeeze herself into it. Sucking in her breath she shuffled towards the passenger window. Suddenly a shadow passed over her from behind. A cold feeling of dread came over her and she knew he was there, watching her. She hadn't been as clever as she'd thought. Her fingers reached inside her pocket for her phone and she pulled it out and turned around. He was leaning against the van, wearing a baseball cap today, his arms folded across his chest so she couldn't see his eyes. He was blocking her exit onto the street, and she knew what a fool she'd been. Who did she think she was, some kind of Supercop? She scolded herself: she was eighty-two and knew better.

'And just what do you think you are doing?'

'My dog ran up here.'

She lifted the phone to her ear, two could play at his game but still, a chill had come over her that made her cold to the bone.

'Did it now?'

Florrie nodded.

'Where is it now?'

She shrugged.

'I think you're telling lies.'

'My daughter is on her way to help me search. Yes, darling, that's right, I'm just behind the estate agents on Main Street.'

He was smiling at her, and she knew that he knew there was no one on the end of the phone. She began shuffling back towards him; better to act bold as brass than show fear.

'Excuse me.' There wasn't enough room for the both of them. She couldn't get past him unless he backed out.

'Sorry, I can't do that.'

'What, why?'

'Because you are snooping around in my business and I don't want that.'

'I told you, I'm looking for my dog. I don't know who you are.'

He shrugged then stepped backwards, and Florrie tried not to let the relief she was feeling show. Instead she hobbled past him out onto the deserted street. She could hear the voices and sounds from the market square not too far away, vibrant and full of life. She didn't turn to look at him and took another step away, then she was jerked back as his arm wrapped around the crook of her neck, and he dragged her backwards into the tiny gap. She gasped. He had her in a choke hold. But she wasn't going to die like this, so she lifted up her foot and threw it behind her, kicking him in the shin with all her might.

'Garr, you bitch.'

But the pressure eased on her neck slightly and she clamped her mouth down on his arm, hoping the denture fix she'd used this morning kept her dentures in place. He was pulling her from side to side, but she wasn't letting go, and then he threw a punch with his other arm so hard it knocked her to the ground as it hit the side of her temple, making her vision blur. Florrie let go, and he began to rain down blow after blow on her head and face. She cracked her head against the cement floor and the edges of the world began to turn black. Fading out of consciousness she was helpless as the metallic taste of blood filled her mouth, and she knew she was dying.

SEVENTEEN

Morgan was staring out of the window; Miles hadn't come out of the office yet unless there was another door. Her phone vibrated, and she answered without checking the ID. 'Hi.'

Ben's voice spoke in her ear.

'*Do you want to come to visit Declan and Chris?*'

Morgan smiled. He was waving an olive branch at her, the only way he knew how to get back on good terms after their earlier disagreement.

'What about the incident room?'

'*Lock it up. If everyone has been spoken to, we're not going to get anything else useful. I'll send Cain to drive it back when he's available. Have you found anything?*'

'I've spoken with Miles, the other staff member. Amy was going to do a background check on him.'

'*Yeah, she mentioned something. Do you think he's a person of interest?*'

'At this point anyone is, although judging by Brian's notes he would have been nine when the camper from Kent disappeared.'

'*Not impossible though. Let's get him checked out and see if he ever lived in the area.*'

'But he wouldn't have driven a car or van at that age? Ben, don't you think it would have been a bit hard for a nine-year-old?'

'*Not legally, but who knows? Any lead is worth checking out at this point and yes, it's highly unlikely, but at least we can rule him out.*'

He hung up, and Morgan stood up, grabbing her laptop which wouldn't connect to the server here anyway. She pushed it back into its bag. She thought about dropping her sandwich wrapper and coffee cup in the small bin then changed her mind; it was likely this thing would get driven back to the station yard and dumped there until something else major cropped up, which could be in a month or two years. She made sure the door was secure, not that there was anything to steal except maybe some out-of-date leaflets on neighbourhood policing and a half-decent desk chair.

There was a bin near to the campsite office, so Morgan headed towards it. The door was ajar, and she could hear animated voices filtering out. Depositing her rubbish, her curiosity got the better of her and she opened the door, the bells above it tinkling. The voices stopped, and she waited for someone to come and see her. It took a few moments but eventually a red-faced John appeared.

'Can I help you?'

'I just wanted to let you know we're moving the van; someone will come and get it later.'

'Thank God, it's scaring campers. I've had two leave before they'd even booked in.'

'Oh, that's not good.'

'No, it isn't. Have you found her yet?'

'Unfortunately, not.'

John glared at her; his anger was rolling off him in unseen waves, but she could feel the heat radiating between them and she wondered why he was so angry again when earlier he'd seemed fine.

'I'm sorry you're having a hard time, but it's not the police you need to be blaming.'

'No, who is it then?'

'Well for a start whoever thought they had the right to enter this campsite and abduct Sara Fletcher. I also think you need to be taking a good hard look at your pitches and the responsibility you have to the people staying here.'

'What do you mean by that?'

'I'm all for equality, but do you honestly believe that it's safe putting lone females so far away from the rest of the campers that it gives whoever this sick bastard is the perfect opportunity to do as he pleases? I'd be utilising desolate spots for couples at the very least, and even better, groups of friends.'

John's face was contorted in anger, and she knew she had royally pissed him off.

'Just an observation, you know, to maybe prevent anything of this nature ever happening again. We'll be in touch if we find anything.'

She turned and walked out of the door before he exploded. She was torn between believing he was innocent or maybe had more to do with this than they currently knew.

Morgan got into her car feeling better that she'd got that off her chest. She had a niggling feeling about John; he and Eleanor had obviously been arguing before she'd stepped in, and the woman had hidden in the back office out of sight.

Her radio crackled in the glove compartment, and she realised something was going down. Leaning forwards she took it out, turning the rotary dial so she could hear the conversations between the control room and response staff.

'*Control we need an ambulance now, elderly female uncon-scious on the floor behind Main Street Estate Agents.*'

Morgan hated these kinds of calls.

'*Is she injured or collapsed?*' the control room operator asked.

There was a pause.

'*She's bleeding, serious head injury and oh God she's black and blue around her head and face. She's been severely beaten.*'

There wasn't an estate agent in Rydal Falls, which meant they were talking about Keswick which was only four miles away. Despite the search for Sara she couldn't ignore this, and CID would get called to a serious assault, so she might as well go in the first instance then pass it on if needed.

* * *

Morgan put her foot down and began to drive faster, wondering who the hell would beat up an elderly woman in broad daylight. Her phone began to ring. Glancing down she saw Ben's name but didn't answer it, her priority was reaching the scene. She drove past an old blue van not noticing that the driver had turned to take a long hard look at her. She knew she should be slowing down, not speeding up – she was in an unmarked car and was taking risks – but for Christ's sake who would do such a thing?

Luckily for Morgan the roads weren't congested with tourists or cyclists, and she made it through the narrow, one-way street system to where a police van was parked across the road blocking the entrance. Abandoning her car, she got out and jogged to where she saw Cain kneeling on the floor next to the victim. He looked up at her and his eyes betrayed his feelings. She felt a wave of nausea. Morgan looked down at the battered, bleeding woman. Cain's jacket was rolled up underneath her head to support it from the cold cobbles she was lying on.

'Is she breathing?'

'I don't think so, I can't find a pulse.'

Morgan couldn't tear her eyes away from the large pool of blood surrounding her head.

'Who would do this, Cain? This is beyond evil.' She clasped hold of the woman's cold hand, squeezing it. 'You're safe now, lovely, there's an ambulance on the way.'

He shrugged and whispered, 'I don't think she can hear you.'

Morgan sat down on the floor, her knees unable to support her. She had seen awful, awful things but this woman looked like the kind of grandmother you saw on the sitcoms, a head full of white-grey curls underneath the dark, sticky, cloying blood.

Sirens turned into the street and an ambulance parked next to the van. Morgan heard the clatter of the doors opening and the sound of heavy boots running towards them along the cobbles. She looked up to see Nick, one of the paramedics who she often ran into, approaching with a look of horror that mirrored hers.

'Jesus, what's happened here?'

She knew he wasn't asking her medical opinion. 'It looks as if someone has battered her.'

They both knelt down and began ripping open packets of dressings. Nick checked her pulse and started going through basic first aid training. Placing one hand on her forehead he gently tilted her head back slightly, while using two fingers from his other hand to support her chin. He checked her airway to make sure it wasn't blocked, then he placed his ear near to her mouth and stared down at her body.

'She's not breathing. How long has she been here?'

Cain shrugged. 'I got the call around ten minutes ago. She wasn't breathing when I got here.'

Nick nodded. His partner had the defibrillator out and he was ripping open the woman's shirt ready to place the patches on. Attaching them he pressed the button on the machine to run a line and see if there was a heart rhythm. The electronic voice told them not to administer a shock: there was nothing and they all knew that, but you had to try.

Nick shook his head. 'There's nothing we can do, sorry, Morgan. Official time of death 15.17.'

Morgan bit her lip to stop the tears welling in the corners of her eyes from falling. What an awful, brutal way to die, alone and bleeding to death on a cobbled backstreet. Cain reached out a hand to her, pulling her to her feet. Another car turned into the street. She knew this would be Ben and didn't turn to look at him because she couldn't take her eyes off the body. He ran towards them. She didn't know the last time he'd run but his feet pounded against the cobbles. She heard him suck in his breath.

'Oh shit, is she...?'

'Yes, Nick called it.'

'She was DOA, probably had been for some time.'

She glanced at Ben; his hand was running over his head like he did whenever he was stressed.

'Thanks, right let's get this done properly then. Was there any ID on her?'

Nick shrugged. 'Sorry, I didn't check, would you like me to now?'

Ben nodded. 'Yes, please, if you've already touched her it's better if you do it.'

He bent down and began patting her trouser pockets with his gloved hands. Her sky-blue blouse that was open exposing her chest, had no pockets.

'Sorry, nothing.'

'Right, let's clear the area then. If you could all leave the way you came in, no touching anything else. We'll find out what the hell happened here.' He turned to Morgan, who was already walking to the van, where Cain was now taking a roll of police tape out ready to seal off the street.

'Morgan, let's get suited and booted. I'll call in the troops.'

'Cain, have you got any stuff in the van?'

He nodded and pointed to a bag full of protective clothing, gloves and evidence bags. She rooted through it for a packet containing overalls that would fit her best and proceeded to tug them on, followed by foot covers and double gloves.

Morgan looked around; they needed a tent to cover the body but luckily for now very few properties overlooked the crime scene. It was hard to tell if anyone lived in those first-floor properties above disused shops. Her back to everyone, Morgan let the tears flow that she'd been struggling to keep inside. Sara Fletcher was still missing, they had unidentified skeletal remains and now this poor, poor woman. She wasn't sure how much pain her heart could take and prayed that Sara was alive, and the remains would be identified and reunited with their loved ones, and this woman would be avenged.

EIGHTEEN

Wendy arrived twenty minutes later, bringing with her a tent to cover the body. Morgan greeted her from her place leaning against the side of Cain's van.

'It's awful, this poor woman.'

Wendy nodded. 'Do you know who she is?'

Morgan shrugged. 'She had no ID on her and we haven't found a handbag yet.'

'Robbery gone wrong?'

'Here, in Keswick?'

'Travelling criminals, wrong place at the wrong time or she saw some drugs shit going down.'

Morgan glanced towards the body. 'I don't know, maybe.'

Wendy passed her the tent, and Morgan tucked it under her arm while she got her camera out. As they got closer Wendy stopped dead and murmured, 'Oh no.'

Morgan looked at her; the blood had drained from Wendy's normally rosy cheeks, leaving her with a pallor the same colour as the body, and she realised Wendy knew her.

'Wendy, are you okay, do you know her?'

Wendy hurried towards the body. Placing the bag on the floor she knelt down and let out a sob. 'Nan.'

Morgan rushed after Wendy. Reaching down, she grabbed hold of her arm. 'Oh, Wendy, tell me this isn't your nan.'

Wendy let out a loud, hitching sob, and Morgan yelled for Ben. He was on his phone, but he turned to see what was happening, and immediately rushed towards them.

'It's Wendy's nan.'

Ben bent down, gently taking hold of Wendy's arm and motioned for Morgan to take the other. Between them they lifted her to her feet and turned her around.

'I'm so sorry, we had no idea. Let's get you away from here.' Ben's voice was shaken and Morgan thought that it was about to break. She could feel Wendy's whole body trembling as they led her to Cain's van and helped her inside. Morgan followed her in, and Ben shut the door to try and block out the scene in front of them and to protect Wendy from seeing any more.

'Her poor face, they beat her to death. Why? Why would someone do that to an old woman?'

Morgan wished with all her heart that this wasn't happening. It was all far too close to home. An image of Stan's body inside the doorway to his flat flashed before her eyes. It was like déjà vu. She knew how painful it was to lose someone so violently, how those awful images would plague her at night, just before she closed her eyes.

'Wendy, look at me, I just need you to answer two questions, okay? What is her name? And who should we call to come and pick you up?'

Wendy sniffed. She used the sleeve of her white paper suit to blot her eyes. 'Florence Brown and I don't need picking up, I'm fine, it's just the shock. I can do this, Morgan. I want to do this, please.'

'I'll speak to Ben, but I don't think that's a good idea. It's not my decision though.'

'Who else are you going to get? Claire rang in sick, and there's been an arson in Barrow, so the rest of the team is tied up. I can do it. I'll process the scene so we can get her moved. I can't bear the thought of her lying out here on a cobbled floor, covered in blood, for hours. Would you want your nan to have to suffer that too?'

Morgan shook her head. She didn't have a nan; she didn't have any family – they were all dead, well, the ones she cared about. Except for Ettie but she was a long-lost aunt who probably hadn't forgiven her for Ben arresting her not that long ago. When Stan had died Ben hadn't let her anywhere near his body or the crime scene. She had been whisked away to the station by Amy, and she remembered all too well the feeling of helplessness.

'I'll go speak to Ben.'

Reaching out, Morgan wrapped her arms around Wendy who was sobbing into the crook of her elbow. She wasn't very touchy-feely in general, but she thought about the time Cain had hugged her out of the blue and how it had comforted her. Wendy clutched hold of her much harder than she'd imagined, fiercely holding on to her. The van door opened, and Ben stood taking in the scene before him. He nodded at Morgan who smiled back. She extracted herself from Wendy's arms and squeezed through the small gap. Walking towards him she lowered her voice.

'She wants to work the scene.'

Ben arched an eyebrow at Morgan, glanced in Wendy's direction and whispered, 'No, absolutely not. She can't do that, it's unethical and the evidence wouldn't stand up in court should she be called to give testimony. More important than either of those things she would never, ever get those final images of her nan out of her mind, and she doesn't deserve to have to remember her like this.'

'Well, you're going to have to tell her then because I'm not.'

She realised that never in a hundred years would he have lain that responsibility at her door, and also he was right, it would be far too traumatic. He nodded, his blue eyes cast downwards. She knew that he was tired and feeling just as bad about this as everyone else. Her fingers reached out and clasped his arm.

'Thank you, I know the last few days have been a nightmare, but you're doing great.'

He lifted his head and looked deep into her eyes, and for a moment she felt something deep inside her soul that made her want to reach out and hold him forever. Some unforeseen force passing between their locked eyes until Morgan broke his gaze.

Shaking his head, he walked towards Wendy, and Morgan took out her phone to ring the control room to find them another CSI. When she turned around, Wendy was arguing with Ben, but it was all one-sided. She was angry, sad and confused; he had his palms up facing her, trying to calm her down, and then suddenly she crumbled and let out a large sob. Ben didn't hesitate. Wrapping his arms around her he pulled her close, turning her away from the tragic scene.

Morgan saw the bag on the floor near to the body with the pop-up tent inside and headed for that. Unzipping the bag she took it out. Cain came over to help her and between them they managed to erect it over the body.

Ben glanced over and nodded at her. He still had an arm around Wendy and at the same time walking her towards his car. He beckoned Cain over and passed him the car keys. Morgan continued watching as Cain got into the driver's seat, and Ben gently helped Wendy into the passenger seat, reaching over and fastening her seat belt. Giving her shoulder one last squeeze he closed the door and gave Cain a thumbs up for him to drive away.

'I sent her home, to go and see her parents and break the news to them,' Ben said when he was back at Morgan's side.

Morgan nodded. 'Wise decision.'

'Right, let's get this done. Have you had any luck finding me a CSI?'

'Control have phoned Liz from Barrow, who is off duty but has agreed to come and take over. Pathologist is on the way; hopefully, Declan will get here after Liz has had a chance to arrive and document the scene.'

'Thanks, and thank you for covering the body.'

'It's the least I could do. I felt terrible enough when I arrived and saw that poor woman beaten to death, but to know that it's Wendy's nan is just...' She couldn't finish her sentence.

'More than your heart can bear. Too much unnecessary violence. What the hell is going on here? Everything has gone to rat shit in the space of thirty-eight hours. I mean it's been terrible before, but this is like a whole new level. Now we've got three different investigations and we're getting nowhere fast.'

'Do you think this is all connected?'

'How?'

'Sara Fletcher was abducted from her tent, marched through the trees past the skeletal remains that have been there a long time, years according to Doctor Chris. And why, after all this time, has it suddenly been discovered? The forest borders the campsite, there must have been hundreds of campers clambering over that fence to go exploring in there. How come we only discovered it now? And now this, we have never as far as I know had an old age pensioner beaten to death in broad daylight in a back alley.'

'Are you saying you think that whoever abducted Sara knew about the remains? And for some reason also attacked this woman?' He pointed towards the tent. 'Why?'

Morgan sucked in her breath, releasing the biggest sigh ever. 'Yes. What if she came across him? According to Brian, The Travelling Man likes to keep his victims alive for seventy-two hours before killing them. If we're going to take this as a real possibility, maybe he was here, parked up somewhere and Sara tried to escape, or something caught Florence's eye that made her get too close for his comfort and he lost it.'

'The Travelling Man. Look, I like Brian he's a nice guy and all that, but...'

'But what? Have you looked at the evidence he's collected? It makes sense, and while we're chasing our tails wondering if he's real or a boogey man, Sara is running out of time. It's all too much of a coincidence. We need to figure out if he was here.'

'Say he was. We don't even know what kind of vehicle he's using.'

'We can find out, we only need someone to go and check out the main street CCTV cameras. They're ours, aren't they? We'll have access to them. Any large van, camper or caravan leaving the area is surely going to be a lead, and if we get a number plate, we can track it down through ANPR and find Sara. Please, Ben, you know this is a real possibility. How else can you explain this madness?'

'I'll leave those enquiries with you. Get hold of Amy and tell her I need her here; you go do what you think needs doing.'

'You won't regret this, Ben, thank you.'

She almost broke into a jog to get to her car, where she ripped off the suit, shoe covers and gloves. She had Brian's files in the boot and she was desperate to read them, but first of all she was going back to the station to check the camera footage herself. She didn't know if she was even on the right track, but it felt as if it was. Her instinct was screaming at her and who was she to go against that?

NINETEEN

Morgan steamrolled into the station faster than she'd ever walked in before. She passed Amy on the stairs, on her way to the scene.

'Is it true it's Wendy's gran?'

'Yes, it's awful. Cain has taken Wendy to go and tell her parents. She wanted to work the scene still.'

Amy nodded. 'Yeah, well I think we can both relate to that. I know I would want to, and you wanted to with Stan, didn't you?'

'I did, but no one let me.'

'For your own good, kid; some day you'll be glad you didn't. What you got there?' She pointed to the thick brown file tucked under Morgan's arm.

'Oh, just some stuff I found in the boot of the car. I thought I better bring it in.'

Amy carried on walking, and Morgan ran up the stairs feeling bad for that little white lie, but Brian had trusted her with this, and she wanted to read it fully. Putting it into the bottom drawer of her desk, she went to the small room where the CCTV monitors for the joint police and council-owned

CCTV cameras were for Rydal Falls, Keswick and Ambleside, allowing officers to view them and monitor areas if needed. They used to have a full-time operator, but budget cuts meant they had been shipped off to work from headquarters, and a few officers and staff were sent on training how to access the local cameras and download the footage from them. Morgan technically didn't have any training, but it wasn't going to stop her. She'd been on the list to attend before she'd had to miss it, so had been given passwords and a printout of the process. She had missed the training because she'd been in hospital after almost being strangled to death from the banister in the hallway of her apartment building after letting a killer into her home. A shudder ran down her spine. She was pretty good at pushing traumatic events to the back of her mind but occasionally they broke free of the box she stored them in. For a moment she felt as if she couldn't breathe, reliving the noose around her neck, cutting off her circulation, and then she gasped. *Focus, Morgan, this isn't about you, get a grip. It's about Sara Fletcher and Florence. This is about finding The Travelling Man and putting an end to his reign of terror, even if no one except Brian believes in him. And me, I believe it too.*

Pressing her pass against the electronic keypad, she watched as the door swung open, and she stepped into what was basically a 1990s time warp. The monitors were huge bulky things and all of them had dark screens covered in a thick film of dust. It didn't look as if they'd been used for a few years. Stepping in she let the door close and saw a large modern computer monitor in the corner. Morgan sat at the desk and logged on to the system. It asked for her password, which she typed in and then, bam, the screen filled with small squares of live CCTV footage. She grinned and let out a small whoop. Now all she had to do was to figure out how to rewind the camera that covered the main street in Keswick. If the killer left in a vehicle, they were going to have turned out onto Main

Street, or so she was praying because God knew they needed to catch a break. She studied the monitor, focusing on the camera she needed. Camera thirteen. She smiled quietly to herself, unlucky for some but not for Morgan. She liked all things black, and the number thirteen was her favourite. She played around with the controls until she managed to get just the right camera angle on the full screen. She checked the time. What time had she arrived at scene? She wasn't sure. Grabbing her radio again, this time she used it to input Cain's collar number onto the pad and pressed the green button. His radio began to ring.

'*Go ahead.*'

'It's me, Morgan. What time did I arrive at scene?'

'*No idea, but I can tell you exactly when I did.*'

Of course; he was there first. 'Yes, please that would be great.'

'*At 15.09 to be precise, how's that?*'

'Perfect, when you arrived did you see any vehicles leaving the area?'

'*No, definitely not.*'

'Thanks.' She ended the transmission.

After some faffing around she managed to rewind the camera to 15.00, and she picked up the radio again.

'Control, who phoned the log in for the sudden death?'

There hadn't been any witnesses when she arrived, and Cain hadn't mentioned anyone either.

'*It was anonymous, Morgan, no details left, but the call came in at 15.01.*'

'Can you run a check against the number, please, and see if it's on our system at all?'

Who had rung it in? Surely no one in their right mind could walk past Florence lying there bleeding to death on the floor and carry on with their day? Only a monster would do that. She nodded her head, a monster, a killer and what was the likelihood of two monsters being in this area at the same time? Very small, impossibly small. It was him, she was sure of it: it was The Travelling Man. She wanted to phone Ben, but he'd be back here at some point to hold a briefing. Instead she considered the killer. He had Sara, what was he doing still hanging around in a busy Lakeland tourist spot? The best she could figure, he liked to be close to the action; he thought he was clever for hiding in plain sight. Morgan's stomach was churning. This was sick beyond belief. But now to figure out if it was the same guy and, if it was, why had he killed Florence? She was about to get her answer. Her phone began ringing; it was an unknown number, so she answered.

'*Morgan, it's Pam in control. I ran a check on that number and it's for a phone number we have on the system from a log from yesterday.*'

'Really, what was the log?'

'*A woman phoned up to report a suspicious male in the main car park at Keswick. She said he was rude and aggressive. He stole her parking place, and there was banging coming from inside his campervan.*'

The churning inside Morgan's stomach turned into a vicious, clenching feeling of utter despair.

'It was Florence wasn't it, the dead woman?'

'*It was Florence Brown, yes.*'

'Oh God. What happened, did an officer attend?'

Morgan's skin was clammy, and the room was beginning to blur around the edges. It was so hot and stuffy in here.

'*I've sent the details of the log she put on yesterday to the Force Incident Manager to take a look at, and forwarded a copy on to Sergeant Ben Matthews who is at the scene.*'

'They didn't go, did they? The officers fobbed it off.'

'*It was a grade two because she said he was driving off and leaving the car park. An officer attended but it was forty minutes later. The van had gone. They spoke with the caller and updated the log with area search negative, caller spoken to.*'

'Fuck, who attended?'

'*Collar 2923, what a mess.*'

'And now Florence Brown is dead, beaten to death, probably by the same male she had a run-in with yesterday. Thanks, Pam.'

Morgan hung up. If the call came in from Florence's phone there was a good chance that she wasn't able to make it. So did the killer call it in? She needed to think carefully and discover if they'd found the phone at the scene, she hadn't noticed it but that didn't mean that it wasn't there. Where was this all going? Her headache from yesterday was back; she'd need to find some painkillers after this. She managed to rewind the camera footage to play from 15.00 onwards, and at 15.02 a dark blue van nudged its way out of the side street onto the main road. Morgan felt a buzz of excitement. She tried to zoom in on the number plate but it wasn't very clear. She needed someone who could work this system better than she could.

She went down to the parade room where there were three officers sitting working.

'Hey, does anyone know how to operate the CCTV system?'

Three heads looked up at her. She waited for an answer, and they just stared.

'Anyone? Did you hear me, can you speak?' She was experiencing a whole host of emotions, and her fingers clenched into fists. She pushed them behind her back. 'I need to know if you can work the camera system. Are any of you trained?'

They all shook their heads in unison, and she walked out furious.

Patrol Sergeant Mads was crossing the atrium floor.

'Morgan.'

'How do you work with them?' She threw her head in the direction of the parade room.

He shrugged. 'It's a barrel of laughs I'll tell you that much. Did you get much conversation out of them?'

He laughed too loud, and it echoed around them both, making her smile. 'Not a peep. Hey, I don't suppose you can work the cameras?' She wasn't sure whether it was the pleading in her voice, or the look of desperation etched across her face.

'I can, I'm actually a superuser so I guess it's your lucky day.'

She wanted to throw her arms around him; instead she opted for, 'Oh God, you're a lifesaver.'

Mads grinned. 'Now then, let's not go that far. Come on, what do you need?'

He began walking up the stairs to the dusty, stuffy room, and Morgan looked up towards the ceiling and bowed her head *thank you, God, universe, whoever for sending him my way.*

Within a few minutes he had not only zoomed in on the van's number plate, he had also sent stills to her email address. Unfortunately, they only had a blurry image of the guy driving, enough to tell that he was wearing a cap of some kind. But it was something, it was a lead.

Thanking Mads, Morgan ran down to the CID office to log on to her computer and send the images to print so she could show Ben. She printed out a spare copy to show to Brian too, because as far as she knew this was the closest anyone had come to finding an actual image of The Travelling Man. Taking the sheets of paper from the printer tray she stared down at him and whispered, *I'm coming for you.*

TWENTY

Ben was leaning against the side of Cain's van when he saw Declan picking his way towards him. He stood up straight and lifted the tape up for him to duck under.

'Ben, why is it either I don't see you for months on end or I end up seeing you more than my current date?'

'Trust me I'd be happy never to see you again.'

Declan looked hurt. 'Thanks for that and here was me thinking we were friends.'

'You know what I mean, professionally obviously, not personally.'

'I know, I know. So, what have you got for me today?'

'I have no words; you need to look for yourself.'

'That awful?'

They walked towards the white tent, and Ben lifted the opening flap to one side. Declan placed his metal case on the floor and whispered, 'Oh no, who would do this?'

'You want to know what else? She's eighty-two, and Wendy's gran.'

'Dear Lord, this is an abomination.'

Ben didn't disagree. He watched as the forensic pathologist began to unclasp his case.

'Wendy didn't see her like this, did she?'

'Yes, we've had to send her home to break the news to her parents. We didn't know until she arrived that it was her gran, there was no ID.'

Declan was shaking his head. 'This is terrible, poor woman and poor Wendy, what is this part of the world coming to? Has this been documented?'

'Yes, you turned up just as CSI finished. You're all good to go.'

He bent down. Reaching out a gloved hand he took hold of the elderly woman's chin and gently opened her mouth. 'I'm sorry this happened to you. What's your name, darling?'

Ben whispered, 'Florence.'

'Well, I'm sorry about this, Florence, but let's get you sorted out and off this cold floor. Now where are your top teeth?' He looked up at Ben. 'Her top teeth are missing; I'm assuming she wore dentures. Do you think she left the house without them? Because she is very smartly dressed, aren't you, Florence? You don't come across as the sort of person to go out in public without your teeth.'

Ben looked around on the floor to see if they had fallen out, but Liz, the CSI, would have bagged them up if they had. He went to go and speak to her then came back; Declan was taking her body temperature.

'No teeth here.'

'Can you find out if she wore them? Because if she did and you can't find them, you're going to have to be asking yourself where they are. Judging by the marks on her hands it looks like she put up a bit of a fight. Good for you, Florence, I hope you hurt the bastard.'

'You think the killer took her teeth? Why would he do that?'

'Well, either he's got a bit of a fetish for false teeth, or they may be incriminating; I have a feeling that Florence may have bitten him.'

Ben's eyes widened. 'I bloody hope she did.' He looked down at the woman and smiled. 'I hope you bit a huge chunk from his arm and left us a nice bite mark to identify him with.'

Morgan appeared behind them. 'I think I have him on CCTV.'

She looked as if she'd just driven around Silverstone race-track, her eyes wide and her hair was falling out of its usually neat topknot.

'Really? Bloody hell, Morgan, you little superstar.'

She passed him a still. He took it from her, holding it close then further away. 'Blue van, blurry guy wearing a cap, is that it?'

'How about, wow thanks, Morgan, this is a vital piece of evidence, and all of that jazz?'

'You know what I mean, we need a little more.'

She plucked another still from her pocket. 'How about this?'

He took it from her and read the number plate out then looked at her. Reaching out he grabbed hold of both of her cheeks and kissed her forehead with an extra loud smacking noise. Declan looked up and smiled. Morgan turned as red as the blood staining Florence's blouse and pushed him away.

'Idiot. Don't get too excited when it comes back to an address in Manchester or somewhere not local.'

'But we pass this on to the cops there, they go pay him a visit, get him in custody and hopefully find Sara, then we'll pick him up and escort him into our custody, job's a good one.'

'Life would be a breeze if things worked out so neatly. Did anyone find Florence's phone? I think the killer may have called it in so it's possible that there may be prints on it if he did. And we still have those skeletal remains to identify remember, and what if he hasn't gone home and is still in the area? Which, if you ask me, is more likely.'

'Then we'll bring him down; we'll find him and take him out. I know it's sad but the remains aren't our first priority at the moment. We have to find Sara, then hopefully link Florence's murder to him. If we could also link the body in the woods that would be a hat trick.'

Declan let out a groan and stood up. 'My back is getting worse; I need a good massage. I can't do any more here. Her phone is tucked underneath her if you're looking for that, and you can see that it's clearly a homicide. An educated guess at cause of death would be massive head trauma but the PM will clear that up. Her poor heart may have given in before the head injury caused her to bleed out. Let's get her moved to the mortuary. It's not exactly a five-star hotel, but it's better than having her lying on these cobbles. Unless you need to leave her in situ for any reason.'

Ben shook his head. 'No, she needs to be moved and we need to get that phone sent off for analysis and fingerprinted in case he left us a nice print to identify him with. We can manage the scene without her body here. Damn it, I'm going to punch whoever did this to the side of their head so hard they won't know what's hit them.'

Declan reached out, patting his friend's arm. 'You're better than that, just find the bastard and lock him up before he goes around hurting anyone else. I have a full load at the moment. I left Chris working on the bones. Are you going to have time to come to the mortuary today for an update? Would you like me to squeeze Florence in? I can jiggle my schedule around a little and work late if you do, but you will have to be there before five and' – he lifted the sleeve of his paper suit up and stared at his watch – 'that gives you an hour and half to get there.'

Ben turned to look. They would keep the scene secured and locked down until tomorrow at least. He didn't want to waste any time. Now they had a vehicle to look out for, the details would be passed out on a countrywide bulletin for observations, and the number plate put into the automatic number plate recognition database. When it next passed through an ANPR camera it would ping, and they'd be able to send patrols to pick him up. It should all work like a dream, and for the first time since he arrived at Forest Pines, he felt hopeful they were about to catch a break. Ben grinned. Once again it was down to Morgan's tenacity. Maybe Brian was on to something, Morgan definitely thought so. He was going back to take a proper look at the file Brian had given him.

'We'll be there. Need to go back to the station for a briefing then we'll set off.'

Declan saluted him, then strode back towards his car.

Morgan looked at Ben. 'You seem hopeful.'

'Let's get this organised and see how I'm feeling then, but something has got to give. He's got to have made some mistake.'

She pointed towards the tent covering Florence's body. 'Yes, he did. A huge one, poor Florence wasn't expected or planned. He likes to take his victims and spend time with them alone, keeping them terrified in the back of his van. This was sudden, unplanned and unorganised, he is going to be furious with himself. I only hope he won't take it out on Sara. I've got to believe she's still alive.'

She got back into her car, and Ben watched her. She was right, of course she was, but he was praying that they could find him and Sara before it was too late. He didn't want to see another person lose their life because he hadn't been quick enough to figure it all out.

TWENTY-ONE

Morgan wanted more than anything to find somewhere quiet to read all of Brian's files. She wished Ben would let him come in and work alongside them. It would be beneficial to have his expertise, telling them what he already knew instead of leaving him at the campsite twiddling his thumbs. As they arrived back at the station, she was pleased to see the car park was empty. Good, that meant the patrols were out and there was more chance of them coming across the blue van. She went upstairs to the briefing room. Amy and Des were already there, as was Tom. Morgan was followed in by Mel. CSI were still finishing off at the scene in Keswick. Al and a couple of task force officers sauntered in looking a formidable sight dressed all in black from head to toe. If Morgan hadn't found herself thrown in over her head and drafted into CID on her second day, she would have definitely applied to be a task force officer; wearing all black was her favourite colour of choice. Finally, Ben walked in and nodded at everyone.

'Thanks for coming, we have a lot going on at the moment so let's get everything as clear as possible.'

'You're all up to speed on the misper, Sara Fletcher. A

couple of hours ago the body of Florence Brown was discovered behind Main Street in Keswick. Unfortunately she is Wendy's gran, so I'd ask you all to be mindful of this and sensitive with her.'

Loud murmurs of shock and surprise went around the room, and Mel spoke, 'Poor Wendy, where is she now?'

'Cain took her home to break the news to her parents, ma'am.'

'I'll contact her and see what support we can offer her.'

'Thank you, I'm sure she'll appreciate that. Florence's cause of death is currently believed to be massive head trauma. The pathologist will confirm this during the post-mortem. But it looks like whoever did this beat her to death. The poor woman died in a puddle of her own blood all alone. She was eighty-two.'

This time it was audible gasps.

Ben continued, 'Morgan has managed to trace a blue van leaving the area around the time the call came in from Florence's own phone which was found at the scene. It's being sent off to the forensic services lab as we speak.' He passed the photograph to Tom who looked at it then passed it around. 'Even better than that, we have the number plate, which has been run through and comes back to an address for a Daryl Harper, in Manchester. I'm waiting on the area commander for Manchester Metropolitan to get back to me and get it all arranged. They're going to send a team to the address to see if the suspect is there. Amy, I want you to do a full PNC check on Harper, and also check our systems to see if he's reared his ugly head on any of them. I want to know if he's had a speeding ticket or fixed penalty notice while in this part of the country.'

'Yes, boss.'

'There is a high chance he won't be at home and could still be in the area. The number plate has been put onto the ANPR system with a warning marker, and he's going to be circulated as top wanted. He's smart, but we're smarter. No one kills a pensioner on my watch and gets away with it. I want every blue van stopped and searched. I don't care if it's a man or woman driving, stop them anyway.'

'Myself and Morgan are going to Florence's post-mortem, which has been pushed forward due to the urgency of the case, and I'll update you in due course as to the results from that. Let's do our best to locate that van. This man is dangerous and obviously has no qualms about who he kills, so I don't want anyone approaching him single crewed. All stops are to be carried out by taser officers at the very minimum, armed officers would be better. Is that okay with you, Al?'

Al nodded; he was in charge of the task force team as well as his role as the PolSA lead. 'Fine by me, the armed response vehicle has been deployed. We're ready to bring him in whenever you are. I can't believe he beat an eighty-two-year-old to death in broad daylight. What the hell would he get out of that?'

No one could answer because it was beyond even the seasoned officer's scope of comprehension.

'Who knows? but he's one sick bastard and the sooner we bring him in the better.'

A flurry of heads all nodded in unison, and then they were out of the cramped room, everyone focusing on their given tasks. Morgan was torn between wanting to go and hunt him down or attending the post-mortem, but she didn't have a choice. She walked out into the car park, Ben close on her heels.

* * *

The drive to Lancaster was uneventful. Despite them keeping their eyes open for a blue van they didn't spot one. What was reassuring was the number of police vehicles out on the roads. Morgan slowed as she drove past one of the busier car parks in Ambleside.

'You know he's not stupid, he's going to be so angry with himself and I'll bet he has a hiding place, somewhere secluded he's tucked away in, waiting for all of this to pass.'

Ben was staring out of the passenger window, and he turned to look at her. 'I know, but we've got to keep on hoping he's not that clever and might think he can get away with hiding in plain sight. The fact that he drove into Keswick on market day tells me that he's either brazen and doesn't care or he's very stupid, which kind of makes him even more dangerous.'

'Brian said that the murder in Kent happened twenty-four years ago; and the remains we've found in the woods look like they've been there quite some time. I was thinking, what if this man *was* caught and put in prison? Obviously not for abducting and murdering women or they wouldn't be out now, but something serious enough to give them a good stretch inside? That would explain the huge gap between the skeletal remains and Sara being abducted.'

'It definitely would and it's something to bear in mind.'

'I read an article on the FBI website about them ages ago.'

'About who?'

'Serial killers, and it states that most serial killers have defined areas of geographical operation they like to kill in, areas they know well. Or at least when they first start out, they do. They only start to move away from their comfort zones when they have gained confidence or to avoid detection. If we knew who his first victim was, maybe we could narrow down his comfort zone, and focus on offenders who lived in or worked near the area of the first body dump.'

Ben stared at her, his mouth open as she carried on.

'Just say that the remains we found the other day were of his first kill. That would mean he would be or would have lived in or around this area. He would know it well because it's his comfort zone. What if he got caught for an offence serious enough to put him in prison for a long time, like rape? What if he progressed from rape to murder, but got caught for the rapes first?'

'And?'

Morgan glanced at him. 'This might seem like a long shot, but what about Gary Marks? He was sent to prison probably around the time of these murders but not for these murders. He got sent there for the rapes of those two women by the riverside and for killing my birth mum. He somehow managed to escape and has kept a low profile for months, but I know how evil he is, and he would only be able to suppress those urges for so long before they began consuming him enough to make him act on them. Maybe that's why we haven't found him yet; he's got himself a van that he moves around in. He was brought up in this area and he knows these roads. He was a tree surgeon at one point; I read that somewhere too. So, he would know all the little forest roads around here. He may even have moved around the country and ended up in Kent working as a tree surgeon. Anyway, it's just a thought...'

'Wow, that's some thought, Morgan. I am seriously impressed at this line of enquiry.'

'But?'

'But nothing. It's worth looking into definitely. If we get Amy to pull up everything possible on him and get a file together, it will give us another line of enquiry to follow.'

'She won't need to do that. I've been researching him since he escaped.'

'Why am I not surprised about that? I guess if that murderous maniac was my dad, I'd do the same. Look, it's a good shout, Morgan, and it's definitely worth pursuing it. We have nothing to lose by following it up.'

'He's not my dad, he never was, he just happens to be the sperm donor. I might be totally wrong, but I can't see him just giving up and living a quiet life. Even as a teenager he was in and out of trouble. One woman said she caught him staring in her windows late at night when he was only sixteen.'

Ben screwed his eyes up, his forehead crinkling, and smiled at her.

'There's not enough coffee in the world for this conversation. Do you think Marks is The Travelling Man then?'

She shrugged. 'Who knows? That's what we need to find out and pretty sharpish too before anyone else dies. Especially for Sara's sake, we have to save her from that.'

'I'm praying with all of my heart that we do, but honestly, we need to find this bastard soon if we're going to be in time to save her life.'

'Good, I think so too. We can't give up on her. We need to find her and save her from an awful death.'

They hurried towards the entrance where Declan's assistant, Susie, let them in to the mortuary. She was sporting dark green hair today which Morgan really liked. 'Nice hair.'

'Thank you, do you like it? Declan keeps saying I'm in my witchy phase, whatever that means, but I like it.'

Ben arched an eyebrow at Susie, and Morgan laughed. 'He's a bit old-fashioned, aren't you, Ben?'

'No, it's very nice. It's just also very green.'

'Green's the in colour. Come on I'll take you through, it's like Euston Station in there; Dr Chris is working on the skeletal remains, and Declan has Florence waiting for you both. I've never seen him move so fast, apart from when it's been a kid. He hates working on kids, we all do. But I think with Florence he keeps thinking about his nan; she isn't well. I've never seen him so agitated about dealing with a body. He's usually mister calm and collected.'

'Yes, he is but if his nan's not well it's understandable.'

Morgan and Ben went into their respective changing rooms

and came out of the other doors that led into the mortuary, ready to watch. There were two CSIs she didn't recognise waiting to deal with the samples and photographing the body. Declan was chatting to them, but Morgan could tell by the way he was holding himself he wasn't as relaxed as he usually was. The steel table containing the body bag in which Florence Brown was waiting looked a formidable sight.

On the opposite side of the room Chris was working. The full skeletal remains of the unidentified body were laid out on the steel table in front of him. He waved them over.

'Would you like an update while Declan is getting ready?'

Ben nodded. 'That would be great.'

Chris smiled. 'Well, our Jane Smith here is pretty intact considering she's been out in the woods so long. I expected a lot more surface scatter, especially after twenty plus years of being exposed.'

Morgan stepped closer. 'Jane Smith? She's female and surface scatter?'

'Jane Smith is the British term for unidentified females, the equivalent of Jane Doe in America. And surface scatter, that's when animals help themselves and scatter the bones over a wide area. I think the fact that she was covered by those branches must have helped to contain the body. There are a few missing small bones but that's totally to be expected.'

Morgan nodded. 'You said she? Is that completely confirmed now?'

'Yes, you see the pelvis area here?' He pointed to it. 'The female pelvis is designed with optimal space for the birth canal. In other words they're much larger than a male's pelvic area. When you've been doing this as long as I have you can tell just by looking, but scientifically the presence of the ventral arch, the shape of the greater sciatic notch and the pelvic girdle are all significant elements confirming the diagnosis that this is a female. She hasn't, however, given birth.'

'How do you know?' Morgan was fascinated.

'Can you see how smooth the inside of the pelvic bone is? If she had given birth, there would be a series of shotgun-pellet-sized marks all along the inside of the pelvic bone here.' He pointed a gloved finger towards the area, and she leaned even closer.

'There aren't any present, but if there were they would be caused by the tearing of ligaments during childbirth. Those bone impressions are a permanent record of the trauma of childbirth.'

Morgan grimaced at the thought of her insides tearing enough to leave permanent marks on her pelvis. 'Ouch.'

'Yes, ouch indeed.'

Ben was also staring. 'Do you have an idea of age?'

'That's a bit trickier. She's approximately one hundred and thirty centimetres in length and has all of her adult teeth, so she's not a child. She also has good strong bones – there isn't a single break in any of them, no childhood injuries that could help with identification. I would hazard a guess at somewhere between the age ranges of nineteen to thirty-six. I'm sorry I can't be more specific than that. Judging by the overall shape of her skull, I'd also say she's of white European ethnicity.'

'That's great for looking through missing persons' reports. What about cause of death?'

'Now, that I can help you with. Do you see the mark here?' He pointed to the vertebrae at the top of the neck.

'This lesion was made with a non-serrated blade. I can tell you this because of the shape and its well-defined edges. A serrated blade would cause deeper and larger injuries to the bone surface.'

Morgan was staring intently at the area he was pointing at, but she wasn't quite sure what she was looking for.

'The blade had a width greater than one centimetre and the incision had been provoked by the blow involving only the inferior edge of the blade. Non-serrated blades are more superficial, and no bone fragments are produced.'

'What was the actual cause of death?'

Chris looked at her. 'Definitely the cut to the throat. I would say that he sliced her neck open and left her to bleed out, which wouldn't have taken too long but it is not a nice way to die. Judging by the rounded edge, near here, that indicates the direction of the fatal blow. The shape of the sharp edge is indicative of the point where the blade stopped, and it also tells us the direction of the wound. There are no other incisions on any of the nearby vertebrae, so it was a single wound. I would say that your suspect had done this before or, if he hadn't, he was very confident because there are no hesitation marks, which you would expect if it was someone's first time slicing someone's throat open. The blade went in near the back of the victim's neck, moving from the posterior to the anterior side of the vertebrae.'

Ben was standing closer than Morgan, and he looked at Chris. 'So, the killer attacked her from behind and slit her throat open with one movement?'

Chris nodded. 'Yeah, he did, what a guy. I've managed to extract DNA samples.'

Morgan shuddered at the thought of whoever this was being killed so brutally without a moment's hesitation. And it was likely that this killer had Sara Fletcher too.

TWENTY-TWO

Declan and Susie had X-rayed Florence's body and were waiting patiently for Ben and Morgan to tear themselves away from the skeleton. Declan looked across at the clock on the wall, then decided to change the radio station to Classic FM; he figured that Florence would appreciate some soothing music instead of the full-on rave fest that was currently playing. He looked at Morgan and Ben as they walked over and felt a searing sadness wash over his heart for both of them. They looked exhausted, not to mention stressed to the max. He wished they knew how much of a perfect match they both were for each other. It was painful to see them so close, yet not close enough.

Susie coughed, loudly, next to him, then whispered, 'It's rude to stare. What are you gawping at?'

He roused himself back into the room and smiled at the faces who were all watching him.

'Am I okay to begin, Chris? Are you finished explaining?'

'Yep, you're good to go.'

Declan nodded. 'Right, now it's my turn to have your attention. Let's see what Florence can tell us about the vile person who did this to her.'

He picked up the plastic name tag that was sealed across the zipper and read out her name and date of birth. Susie snipped the plastic tag off the body bag and began to unzip it, and between her and Declan they managed to roll Florence out of it. Their years of experience made it look easy, but after a rocky start in their professional relationship he and Susie were now working not only as a team but as firm friends. The atmosphere inside the mortuary was one of calm ambience despite the gravity of the tasks everyone in here faced.

They weighed, measured and recorded everything that needed to be done. The two CSIs worked effortlessly alongside them as they removed Florence's clothing then photographed and bagged it up to be sent off for forensics. When Florence's naked, battered and bruised body was laid bare, all of them took a moment to acknowledge the horror this elderly woman had been put through in the last minutes of her life. Her upper body was a mass of bruising from the injuries she'd sustained while her heart was still beating, and Declan found it hard to find any words. Usually, he managed to conduct an examination with a little conversation, but somehow, he didn't have the heart for anything other than statements regarding the process today. He'd witnessed far too much violence and its fatal results since he'd become a pathologist, but there was something so distressing and personal about this crime that he was struggling to concentrate on anything other than the body in front of him. When Florence had been photographed and washed, he began his external examination.

Morgan opened her notebook, ready to write down his observations.

'Well, Florence, you are of a good nutritional status. There is rigor mortis over the whole body and there are no signs of decay yet.'

Reaching out a gloved finger he gently lifted a swollen eyelid. 'There is blood vessel dilation and petechial haemorrhages on the right and left eyelid mucous membranes. The mucous membranes of the upper and lower lip look cyanosed.'

Picking up her hand he studied it. 'The fingertips and nails of both hands look the same, can see the bluish discolouration of the skin, which is due to the deficient oxygen in the bloodstream.'

Placing the hand down, he moved back up to her head. Florence had curly white hair that was thinning, making it easy to see the extent of the injuries. 'There are multiple bruises around the left side of the head as high as the ear canal. They are irregular shaped, blueish in colour and measuring approximately' – he held out a hand as Susie passed him a ruler – 'eight by two centimetres; they look to me like the kind of marks the knuckles on a fist would leave. On the forehead there is a three-centimetre bruise left of the midline and another four centimetres above the inner corner of the eye, which is a bruise that is irregularly shaped, reddish in colour, measuring six by five centimetres. There is an irregularly shaped bruise on the left upper eyelid, reddish in colour, measuring six by two centimetres. Damn it, he didn't care that she was old, he kept on punching her.'

He looked at Morgan, who had stopped writing and was staring at the injuries on Florence's face, and she lifted her eyes and met his. He needed to convey the horror of this to someone, and he knew Morgan would be the one to take all of this to heart; she would be the one who would bring this bastard to justice because she was made of something more than your average copper. She acknowledged his distress, a silent nod between them, and he felt a tiny bit better. Inhaling deeply, he looked back down and carried on.

'On the cheek four centimetres to the left midline, two centimetres below the outer corner of the eye are bruises that are irregularly shaped, blueish red, measuring seven by five centimetres. There are bruises on her forearms which suggest to me she was trying to defend herself.'

He continued to list the injuries that seemed to go on and on.

As he pressed on her chest area he tutted. 'I can't believe this, look at that visible deformity.' He pointed to the area. Pressing it there was palpable rattling of the bones in the right ribs. 'Did anyone commence CPR when they found her? That could explain the cracked ribs. The older we get the more brittle our bones are.'

Ben shook his head. 'That's a definite no, the officer could tell she was dead, and paramedics ran a line but that's it.'

When Declan finished the external examination, Susie gently lifted Florence's shoulders enough to slide the thick, rubber block underneath her back ready for him to begin the internal examination, and when he picked up his scalpel to make the Y-incision he realised that his fingers were trembling. Bad enough this woman had been murdered the way she had and now here he was about to cut her open from shoulder to shoulder and down to her pubic bone. He silently asked her for her forgiveness, not wanting the audience watching him to think he was losing it so publicly. No one spoke, all eyes were on him. He nodded. 'Right then, Florence, let's get this over with.'

Declan made the incision much more smoothly than he'd anticipated and relief washed over him. He was okay, he was good to continue. Peeling back the skin, muscle and soft tissue with a scalpel he then gently lifted the chest flap up over her face. Exposing her ribcage and neck muscles, he whistled.

'Look at that broken upper chest bone. There is also a second rib fracture to the sixth and seventh ribs. There is a lot of blood absorption in the chest muscles.'

He was back on firm ground and held out his hand for the

cutters to snip the ribcage so he could remove the breast plate and expose the internal organs. Ready to remove them, weigh them and take the slices of tissue samples needed to examine. When he had a clear view of the heart, he shook his head. 'There is a significant amount of blood in the heart cavity. There are also two penetrating wounds with uneven edges and blunt angles. Can you see where her broken ribs pierced through the heart?'

He worked deftly. All his worries and fears had been taken over by the primal need for him to do this to the best of his ability quickly and professionally, so that he could let Susie sew Florence back up again and leave her in peace for the time being.

'Well, I wasn't expecting that but there you go. The manner of death was most definitely unnatural, namely, the result of Florence being murdered, which we can all agree on. The cause of death is injury, and the mechanism of death was due to that injury which contributed to the death of the victim due to the blunt-force trauma in the chest, which resulted in a fracture of the chest bone and the ribs that tore through the ventricles of the heart. This caused bleeding in the heart cavity which led to suffocation.'

Ben was open-mouthed. 'Whoa, I thought it might have been the head injuries. I wasn't expecting that.'

'Me neither, my friend, and take it from me this wasn't an instant death. This poor woman suffered horribly and unnecessarily. Your man is a monster, there is no doubt about it, and if Jane over there also died at his hands, then you have a major problem. One that isn't going to go away anytime soon because he quite obviously enjoys what he's doing.'

He was addressing Morgan directly, who had tucked her notebook into her pocket and was staring at him.

'Thank you, Declan, we will find him.'

'I know you will, that's what I'm afraid of. Morgan, be very careful but do what you are so adept at doing and fast before I end up with any more bodies that should not be here.'

He smiled at her, and he watched her cheeks flush pink. He hoped she would catch this killer but not at any cost to herself.

TWENTY-THREE

The journey back to Rydal Falls was silent. Both Ben and Morgan were too absorbed in the post-mortem results and what that meant for Sara Fletcher. Ben's phone began to ring, making them both jump. Morgan was driving, and she glanced at him as he answered.

'Matthews.'

'*This is Glenn Shields, Force Incident Manager at Greater Manchester Police. Is this Sergeant Matthews?*'

He sat up straight. 'Yes, speaking.'

'*I have some good news for you. We have your suspect in custody.*'

'You do, really? That's brilliant work, thank you.'

'*What are you planning on doing with him?*'

'We need to interview him as soon as possible; can we drive down first thing in the morning and speak to him?'

'*Be my guest. I have to warn you he was claiming he had no idea what we were talking about when we arrested him. Then again, don't they all?*'

Ben laughed. 'Yeah, most of them do. Thank you; which station is he being held at?'

'*He's currently at Stretford on Talbot Road. If you go there, someone will meet you at the front office. Have a safe journey down.*'

The line went dead before he could say anything else. 'Did you hear that?'

Morgan nodded. 'Are we going right now? I'll let Tom know we're going to speak to Daryl Harper and maybe bring him back with us.'

Ben looked down at his watch. Where had the time gone? It was almost eleven.

'I feel as if we should, but it's been a very long day and I think maybe we should get some sleep and have an early start, if that's okay with you. We could meet at the station at five.'

Morgan nodded. 'Whatever you think.'

They left the car at the station, getting straight into their own vehicles, and Ben wondered if this was the wrong thing. Should they go to Manchester now? Morgan let out a huge yawn and he copied her, realising that although time wasn't on their side they'd be no good to Sara Fletcher if one of them fell asleep at the wheel on the motorway. They needed to rest even if it was just a few hours and hopefully the traffic would be lighter on a Sunday.

* * *

The next morning, as he arrived at the station yard, he grinned to see Morgan already in one of the unmarked vehicles, engine running, waiting for him. Opening the door he got in, reaching forward, and began typing the address into the satnav.

'Good morning, boss. Let's hope this is him and that he has that bloody awful van parked outside his house, and that Sara is still alive.'

Ben nodded. 'I have everything crossed, Morgan, and morning.'

They arrived at the police station two hours later. Traffic had been busy on the M61; they had crawled for a couple of miles past roadworks until Morgan reached the A56 and finally Talbot Road.

'Oh, wow this is nice, there's trees and everything.'

Ben started laughing for the first time in what felt like days. 'There's trees and everything; you're so funny. What were you expecting, Morgan?'

She shrugged. 'Well obviously not this. I don't know, I imagined some big concrete block somewhere on a busy street.'

She parked the car and they got out. Pulling her lanyard out from underneath her shirt so it was on display, and Ben did the same.

'I've been thinking, our man obviously hates women, so I think you should take the lead.'

'Why? Won't he relate to you better if he dislikes us so much?'

'He might, but if you start with the questions, we'll be able to see what pushes his buttons. If he clams up, I'll take over, but he might enjoy making you feel uncomfortable and think he's got some kind of power over you, even though we know there is no way on this earth that could happen. Only if you feel comfortable with it though. It's entirely up to you.'

She didn't even pause. 'Well then it's fine by me too.'

Ben smiled. He wished he could tell her how proud he was of her. No, that wasn't it, there was something more than that, those words seemed highly inadequate for his feelings. As she walked on ahead of him with her head held high, striding confidently towards the front desk, his heart tugged inside his chest. He inhaled deeply, the smell of freshly cut grass and diesel fumes filling his lungs, and he smiled. Exploring that was going to have to wait until it was the right time, they had a job to do right now: finding Sara Fletcher was their priority and he wouldn't jeopardise her safety.

. . .

Inside they were signed into the visitors' book and issued with lanyards then ushered through the double doors by the front desk into the back of the station, where they were greeted by a man around the same age as Ben. He smiled at them. Reaching out his hand he shook both Morgan's and then Ben's.

'Welcome to my humble abode. I'm DS Jihan Dacre. You made it in good time.'

Ben pointed at Morgan. 'She's a bit speedy, but an excellent driver.'

Jihan grinned. 'Good, exactly what you need. This is a bit of a situation, isn't it? Come into my office and I'll explain where we're at.'

He led them along a narrow, thin corridor that smelled faintly of curry, and Morgan said, 'It doesn't matter where you go, every single station always smells of stale curry.'

Jihan laughed. 'We have an excellent takeaway just down the street. I think most of the response staff live off their menu. If you get hungry let me know and I'll order for you. They are always happy to serve the police no matter what time of day or night it is.'

'Thank you, that's very kind.'

They followed him past several wooden doors, until he reached one with a brass plaque outside that read 'CID'. He shoved the door and it flew open, crashing into the wall and making Morgan jump. There were detectives sitting around the room and not one of them even blinked.

He turned around. 'Sorry, the door is knackered but it's good practice for breaking down doors.' He smiled again, and Morgan realised that she liked Jihan; he was funny and reminded her of Ben.

'Come in, please. You lot, this is DS Matthews and, I'm sorry, Morgan, I didn't catch your surname.'

'Brookes, DC Morgan Brookes.'

'Welcome to our department, the both of you. We are very pleased to have you here.'

There were a few nods of heads and mumbled hellos. 'Believe it or not they do have tongues, but it's been quite a few days for us. Two armed robberies in two days and a serious assault.'

He led them into his office, which was even messier than Ben's. 'I know what you might be thinking, but I can assure you this filing system works perfectly.' He laughed again, and Morgan joined in.

'Please take a seat if you can find a space. Let me tell you what happened after we got the request from yourselves to arrest Mr Harper.'

He waited until Morgan and Ben were both seated. 'Can I get you any refreshments?'

'No, thank you, we're good.'

'Let me know, won't you, if you do want some? Right, where was I? Ah, yes, Mr Harper is well known to us. He's been in and out of prison regularly. Apparently though, he found God while he was inside HMP Manchester this time, which was nice for him, and he's been helping out at the local Methodist church with the food bank and other such good causes.'

'What was his last sentence for?'

'He has a bit of a problem with thieving; in fact, he's gone from strength to strength there and his last little job, which landed him with a lengthy spell, was armed robbery.'

'How long? And is he a suspect for any current investigations, the armed robberies over the last few days?'

'Not at the moment. For one thing he has an alibi and for another, witnesses state the robber was white, whereas Mr Harper is mixed race. His last stretch was for eight years.'

Morgan felt a sinking feeling inside her stomach. The

blurry photograph of the man driving the van had looked white. 'Oh, then there is a good chance he won't be our suspect either.'

Ben passed Jihan the still of the man in the van, and he lifted it close to his face to study it.

'I'm afraid that doesn't look like him. Well, you're here now, you may as well interview him.'

'You said he had an alibi for the armed robberies, has that been corroborated?'

'It has. The local vicar and church warden have both given accounts of his whereabouts at the time of the incidents. He was at the food bank boxing up parcels on both occasions.'

Morgan looked at Ben. 'Then he definitely couldn't have killed Florence Brown; that was yesterday morning.'

Jihan lifted his hands. 'But the vehicle that you traced came back to one registered to Mr Harper, yes?' They both nodded. 'Maybe he has a van that he loaned to a friend; he does have an unsavoury bunch of characters who he calls his mates. That could be a real possibility. It's too early to give up hope just yet. Come on, let's get you introduced, and you can figure it out as you go along.'

He stood up and led them down to the custody suite, where they were buzzed in and shown into a large, sterile interview room.

Jihan waited until Daryl Harper was led in and sitting opposite Morgan and Ben.

'Good morning, Daryl, these detectives have travelled all the way from the Lake District to speak to you. Isn't that nice?'

He turned to Morgan and Ben, smiling. 'I'll leave you to it.' Then he left. An officer was standing against the back wall. Daryl was glaring at them both in turn.

'So, it's your fault they banged me up, is it? What the fuck am I supposed to have done now?'

Morgan smiled at him. 'Yes, sorry about that, Daryl. I'm Detective Constable Morgan Brookes and this is Detective Sergeant Ben Matthews. Are we okay to ask you some questions about some incidents that have happened in Rydal Falls and Keswick?'

'Do I need a brief?'

'That's your choice.'

He looked at Morgan, his eyes slowly moving up and down from her head to her chest.

'Nah, I don't think I do.'

'Why not?'

'Because I've never heard of Rydal whatever, so I haven't been there, have I?'

Ben passed her the still of the blue van, and she placed it in front of Daryl.

'Can you tell me if this is you?'

He looked at the photograph and laughed. 'Not a very good likeness, is it? No, it's obviously not. Apart from the obvious reason, I don't own a blue van, I never have.'

He crossed his arms and sat back in his chair grinning. A cold chill settled down the full length of Morgan's spine. She didn't glance at Ben despite wanting to, needing to. She wanted his reassurance that this was the right thing, that they weren't wasting precious time on a wild goose chase.

'Do you know anyone who owns a van like this?'

He shook his head.

'What was prison like this time around?'

'What does that mean?'

'I'm just curious, did you make any close friends? You were in there much longer than you usually are.'

'I made lots of friends, I'm a friendly guy.'

'Who did you share a cell with? What were they like? Did you get on with them?'

'What has that got to do with anything?'

'Well, if you haven't driven a blue van to Rydal Falls then someone who you know has.'

'And how exactly do you figure that one out?'

'Why else would someone register a van in your name, at your address? You tell me, Daryl. If I was you, I'd be pretty pissed that someone was trying to set me up. Aren't you the least bit annoyed that someone is committing serious crimes in Cumbria, crimes that will send them away for life when they get caught, and they're putting you forward as their fall guy? I'd be furious, especially for tarnishing your name now that you have your act together. Yet here you are, smiling and thinking this is all some big joke when really the joke is on you.'

Daryl threw himself forwards, his chair scraping along the floor. The copper standing behind him stepped towards him. He leaned across the table, staring directly into Morgan's eyes.

'If this is true, then I'll find out who it is and sort them out myself, but I'm no grass.'

'I never said you were, but it would be a lot easier if you gave us some names and let us take care of it. They are never going to know it was you. Why would you be grassing someone up who yesterday morning battered an old lady to death so hard that he broke a bone in her chest that pierced her heart and left her bleeding to death on a cold, cobbled street?'

He sat back; all the fight left his body as quickly as it had taken over it. 'He killed an old lady?'

She nodded. 'Brutally. Have you got grandparents, Daryl? Would you like to see your gran die in so much pain for no reason?'

'I'd kill him with my bare hands if he hurt my nan, that's not on. You don't go around killing pensioners.'

His shoulders were slumped as he looked down at his hands which were in his lap. He looked up at Morgan. 'I shared a cell at one point with a guy called Marks. He was a sick bastard. He told me he was in for killing his woman, but I found out that he was a rapist as well. He managed to escape a few months back, and no one has seen him since. We got on okay until I found out about the rapes. I never spoke to him again after that, then I got released.'

Morgan could taste the bitter service station coffee welling up in the back of her throat like acid. Ben took one look at her face, blanched at the mention of Marks, and took over.

'Is there anyone else you can think of who might have used your details?'

He shrugged. 'I don't know anyone sick enough to kill an old lady for the sake of it, even scrotes have morals. Marks is the only name I can give you.'

Ben stood up. Leaning forward he reached out to shake Daryl's hand, and Morgan was surprised to see the man take it and shake it. She didn't offer him her hand; she needed to get outside and breathe in some fresh air because the room felt as if it was closing in on her, and the last thing she needed was to pass out in front of everyone.

TWENTY-FOUR

Outside, Morgan leaned against the back of the car, breathing in huge gulps of diesel-filled city air, trying to clear her lungs and her mind. Ben was inside speaking with Jihan. She felt rude, but she didn't trust herself to speak. She looked around the busy street for something to take her mind away from the horrors that were playing out inside. She'd been so hopeful that they'd caught their killer with Harper; hopeful that her theory about Gary Marks had been wrong. Now it seemed more likely than ever. The man who had killed her mother was out there torturing another woman.

'Hey, I said goodbye for you to Jihan. He sends his best wishes.'

She turned to look at Ben who was already getting in the car, and did the same.

'Thanks, sorry, I kind of freaked out.'

'Yeah, I got that impression. Are you okay, Brookes?'

She nodded. He sometimes called her Brookes when it came to personal stuff, real people feelings and not police talk. 'It was the shock of hearing his name. I know we talked about him, but I didn't actually expect anyone else to bring him in to it. What do you think?'

'Is he even in the area? Do you think he could be here and so brazen enough to hide right under our noses?'

A look of pure misery crossed her face. She thought he was; in fact, she was sure she'd seen him twice. Fleeting glances that were lost in the blink of an eye, and she'd been so bloody stupid and pig-headed enough to think that she would find him and bring him in single-handed when she should have notified Ben and everyone else. They would have scrambled a team and gone looking for him. What had she been thinking? Now Florence Brown, and they were running out of time for Sara Fletcher because of her.

'What are you thinking?'

She looked at him and couldn't stop the tears that were welling up in the corners of her eyes and whispered, 'This is all my fault.'

'What? What are you talking about?'

'Sara, Florence, I may as well have killed them myself.'

'What are you talking about? They had nothing to do with you. Did you drag Sara from that tent? Did you beat Florence to death? No, you did not.'

She stared out of the window, blinking furiously. When she told him what she'd done, he'd never be able to look at her again. He definitely wouldn't trust her ever again or want to work with her. She would be back on section working response before the end of the shift, if she was lucky and he didn't report her to professional standards for withholding information. She closed her eyes and inhaled; the smell of Ben's aftershave wasn't as strong as when they'd started work this morning, but it was there, warm, comforting and safe.

'What are you doing, are you ill?'

She opened her eyes and looked at him. 'I'm storing a memory.'

He frowned, and if she wasn't so devastated at the realisation she'd thrown her entire life away by not passing on the information that she may have seen Britain's top wanted man, she would have laughed.

'I just wanted to remember what we had before it's lost, that's all. I love working with you, Ben, and the rest of the team, please know that but...' She saw the expression on his face change to one of concern and felt even worse.

'But?'

'I think I saw him, twice, but I couldn't be sure that it was him. It was a split-second glance and when I looked again, he was gone.'

'And you submitted the relevant intelligence reports on the system, asked for patrols to flood the area to flush him out?'

She wanted to stop time, go back and do both of those things. Why the hell hadn't she?

'No, I did not.'

'What did you do?'

His look of concern was morphing into one of quiet fury. She had seen this before only once and this time she deserved it.

'I wasn't sure it was him.' Her voice was low, not her usual confident self.

'We need to get back. Jesus, Morgan, what a complete and utter pile of crap this is.'

They never spoke another word the whole way home. Ben was busy on his phone asking for alerts to be put out for every blue van to be stopped, he didn't care who was driving. He also asked for Gary Marks's picture to be circulated to all patrols, and Morgan's stomach was a mess of churning knots. When they eventually arrived at Rydal, Ben addressed her for the first time in two hours.

'I need you to go home, Morgan, drive to your place and I'll take the car back.'

'What about the enquiries briefing?'

'You are walking on a cliff edge, and now that you've told me I'm hanging on there with you, I need to figure out what to do about this mess. Have you told anyone else you saw Marks?'

Her head shook. 'Thought I saw him, and no, I haven't.'

She drove miserably to her apartment, stopping the car on the gravel drive next to her neighbour, Emily's, Mini Cooper and hoped that her perfect, perky neighbour didn't appear in the next couple of minutes. Getting out of the car she left the keys inside and the engine running. Quickly opening the boot she retrieved Brian's file.

Ben got out and walked around to the driver's side. He didn't even look at her which hurt her more than him telling her off. She stepped back to give him some room, then turned and walked towards the entrance to her apartment.

The car tyres squealed on the gravel he reversed so fast, spraying tiny stones everywhere. She didn't turn to wave. She let herself inside ashamed and burning with anger at her own stupidity.

TWENTY-FIVE

He knew he had almost blown it; he had made a big mistake with the old lady, but she had been sneaking around the van. She'd known there was something unsavoury going on. He couldn't stop wondering how old she was, not that it mattered now, but she'd had something about her that he couldn't forget. More than the police at any rate, who seemed to be completely clueless. They couldn't really be that rubbish, could they? He laughed, and realised that yes, they probably were. After all, this was a huge rural area and they probably didn't have enough coppers to cover it, which was lucky for him. He had parked the van in a secluded lay-by deep in the middle of Grizedale Forest, way off the beaten track. It was very early. The rain had begun to fall an hour ago, which was good: bad weather was his friend. It kept all but the hardcore fitness enthusiasts at home, and with the rain came the best kind of cover; the sky was a mass of brooding dark clouds, and if he wasn't mistaken the smell of ozone was present in the air. A storm was coming, which was a fitting end for the woman who was reduced to a whimpering wreck under the false floor in the van.

She had given up the banging after he'd gagged her even

tighter and then refastened her arms and feet together. At one point, when she'd caught the attention of the old woman, she'd been headbutting the floor, which must have been painful for her because he'd given her quite a blow when he'd first rendered her unconscious with the hammer. She was tough though, and clearly a fighter, but her fight was almost over. Soon it would be time to move on. The girl was too high profile now; her photograph was plastered all over the newspapers. She had been a mistake. He had struck too soon; he had taken the first opportunity that had come his way without properly taking the time to gauge whether she was the right victim or not. Next time he would be more cautious.

Opening the back of the van, he was glad he had a stomach made of steel. The lingering stench of sweat, urine and fear was overpowering. He hadn't had the time for toilet stops with his captive, it was too risky. Picking up a newspaper earlier he'd seen the article about the Supercop who was hot on his heels and recognised her. How could he forget her? Then the other day when she'd hurtled past him, he had been sure it was her and now, after looking at her photograph, he knew for sure. She would kick herself if she knew she'd driven straight past the man she would most like to capture without a second glance, but he had been quite taken with her and was tempted to cut his losses with this one and go after DC Morgan Brookes instead. A bit of a reverse game of cat and mouse; instead of her coming to find him, it might be fun if he went to find her. He needed to get rid of the problem in his van first and bleach the hidden compartment to get rid of the smell. Turning on the ultra-bright head torch he lifted the trapdoor, lowering his head slightly so the light shone directly into her eyes and blinded her. The woman moved a little, turning her head away from the beam, and whimpered. He reached down, grabbing her under the arms and dragged her out of the small space. She was surprisingly heavy and making an awful low keening sound through the gag like a wounded animal, but there was no one around. Dragging her out of the back of the van he let her fall to the floor, and her body curled into the foetal position on a bed of pine needles. He looked around. He needed to get her away from the lay-by and into the forest, but she didn't look as if she was going to walk.

'Get up.' He kicked her thigh with one heavy tactical boot, and she let out a grunt but didn't move. Deep-seated anger filled his belly. He didn't like being disobeyed, not one bit. He reached down, roughly grabbing her arm.

'I said, get up.'

She was trembling; her entire body was shaking. He shook his head and began to laugh.

'You're not supposed to just lay down and die here, bitch. We have a plan to stick to and you giving up all hope right here isn't in that plan. I know that you can walk so move it.'

Cold, hot, white fury clouded his mind as he looked around. He couldn't do it here, it would leave too much blood. Even if it rained all day those fancy detectives with their forensics would find traces of her here, and he wasn't ready for that to happen, not now he had his next woman in his sights. The thought of capturing her made his spine tingle. If he was going down it was with one grand finale, and Morgan Brookes would provide him with that, he had no doubt about it.

'For Christ's sake, what's wrong with you?'

He bent down close to the woman's face. She threw her head back and headbutted him with so much force he felt his lip split, and a warm gush of blood flowed from his nose. He fell backwards onto the ground, clutching his face. As he writhed on the floor, the woman loosened and slipped out of the ropes tying her arms and feet, dragged herself up and took off running into the forest. He let out a yell so loud it echoed around the trees, sending nesting birds squawking into the sky. He stood up, spat out a huge glob of blood and mucous then began to follow her.

He drew the hunting knife from his belt. He was going to make her pay for this. She might think she'd outsmarted him but that was nothing compared to when he got hold of her. He didn't shout again or call out. He began to chase her into the trees, not panicking that she'd got the better of him but mildly annoyed that it had happened again. That first woman had done something similar all those years ago, thinking she was smarter. Well, she'd wasted her time because all she'd done was get herself an even more painful death than planned. That was the thing with women, you just couldn't trust them to lie down and take their punishment, sneaky bitches.

TWENTY-SIX

Ben marched into the station like a man on a mission. He was angry, no, he was raging, and he didn't know why he was so mad. It wasn't as if Morgan had had a positive sighting of Marks; she said herself she couldn't be sure, and it had only been a split-second glance. But he was hot, irritable and just wanted to stop this case before any more victims had to suffer and die horrendous deaths. He was mad because he didn't want Morgan at home on her own. He needed her here working alongside the rest of the team and doing what she did so well, finding bloody maniacs. He slammed the office door open so hard it bounced off the wall and a chunk of plaster fell to the floor.

Amy looked at him. 'Everything okay?'

He nodded, afraid to open his mouth just yet. He crossed to his office and went inside, closing the door behind him. He knew that she would see Morgan wasn't behind him and realise something was wrong. That was the thing with having such a small team. They knew each other far better than they ought to. He threw his suit jacket over the back of a chair, removed his tie and unfastened the top two buttons of his shirt. He couldn't breathe. He felt as if his lungs were on fire. Turning, he stared out of the window, which overlooked the fells. He couldn't see the tops of them for the dark, ominous thunder clouds which were lingering over them. Which pretty much matched his mood. He heard the low rumble of thunder in the distance and began to count, waiting for the lightning flash to follow, when there was a knock on his door.

'Come in.'

He turned back to see Amy, a bright pink mug with the words 'nobody puts baby in the corner' emblazoned across the front in white.

'Coffee?'

He nodded. 'Thanks.'

Placing it on the desk in front of him she lingered. 'How did it go?'

'Not what I hoped or expected.'

She nodded. 'Thought so, you're in a pretty shit mood.'

'You noticed?'

'Hard not to, the wall now has a hole in it big enough to pass the brews through from the kitchen.'

He smiled. 'It wasn't him, he's just a patsy, a decoy, and we fell for it.'

'How were you supposed to know? It's a good lead. You did what you had to. So he's not our guy so now we just need to figure out who is.'

'That's the problem though, isn't it? This man's cleverer than I gave him credit for. He's probably laughing at us running around the north-west on wild goose chases, while he's hiding out somewhere with Sara Fletcher doing God knows what to her, if he hasn't already killed the poor woman.'

Amy sat down opposite him. 'Where's Morgan? Did you leave her in Manchester?'

'She's at home.'

Her eyebrow arched. 'Are you going to tell me why or do I have to guess?'

'It turns out Daryl Harper shared a cell with someone who we know very well, or at least whose information we know very well.'

'You're shitting me, Sarge. You're not going to turn around and tell me that he shared a cell with Gary Marks and thinks he might be the killer?'

'Seems everyone has worked this one out except for me.'

'Why? He's kept a low profile since he escaped prison. Why would he do this now?'

'Why does Gary Marks do anything? I'm not a hundred per cent convinced that it's him, it's just a theory at the moment, but we don't have anything else right now. Unless you're going to tell me that you have something that will turn this all around?'

'Me, nah, I hate to disappoint you, but I have nothing remotely as interesting as that little bombshell. I still don't get why you sent Morgan home.'

'Shut the door.'

She stood up and stretched out her leg, pushing the door shut with her foot.

'Blimey, you're being a bit paranoid, aren't you? There's only Des in there and he's oblivious to anything that involves working for his pay cheque.'

'Morgan thinks she may have seen him, only a quick glance, she wasn't sure, but if it was then it puts him in the area.'

'Well, she's going to be a bit on guard, isn't she? That's totally to be expected. The guy is a cold-blooded killer who also happens to be her sperm donor. I'd be a bit freaked out by it all too; in fact, I'd probably think anyone with the same hair colour was him.'

For the first time in over an hour Ben felt his shoulders relax ever so slightly.

'Yes, of course, she is.'

'Then why is she grounded?'

'Think about it, if it was him and he's killed two women and she never said anything.'

'Rubbish, you can't go laying that on her shoulders, boss.' She emphasised the boss.

He shrugged. 'Yeah, but the man is a cold-blooded killer.'

'Yeah, and there was a good chance it wasn't him. Stop persecuting her. No one needs to know; it's between us three. Anyway, I don't think it's him; he's not that clever, and where has he got the money to buy a campervan from?'

A loud knock on the door made them both look up. The door opened, and Tom walked in.

'Not disturbing anything, am I?'

'No, just having a bit of a brainstorm.'

'Good, well what happened in Manchester then? I'm guessing nothing exciting, or you wouldn't be sitting here gossiping like you have nothing better to do, would you?'

'No, sir. It was a wasted journey; Daryl Harper is not our man. He has a confirmed alibi; he did give us some information that might lead to something though.'

'Like what?'

Amy stood up. 'I'll leave you to it.'

Ben gave her a thumbs up. He felt better and was glad he'd shared his concerns with Amy, who always spoke the truth and didn't pussyfoot around anyone. She gave him a thumbs up and walked out leaving him with Tom.

'So, what's the next step?'

'I was hoping you might have a plan?'

He shrugged. 'I'm going to be honest with you, Ben, I'm not doing so good with all of this. I'm thinking we need to call in the Murder Investigation Team. I've already had DCI Claire Williams on the phone; she's away on a course but will be here tomorrow to lend a hand.'

Ben nodded. 'Of course, that's great.' This was protocol. He was surprised she hadn't been called in straight away, but it still felt like a sucker punch to his gut, confirming that Tom wasn't taking any chances.

'Glad to be working with her again. I'll take all the help I can get. I just want this bastard behind bars before anyone else gets hurt.'

Tom walked out leaving him staring after him, wishing he could go to the pub and have a drink or two, to settle the churning inside his stomach and blot the disaster of a day today had been out of his mind, just for a few hours.

TWENTY-SEVEN

Morgan sat cross-legged on the floor. She'd changed into a pair of leggings and an oversized sweatshirt, boiled the kettle and made herself a mug of herbal tea, but had barely touched it. Spread out in front of her was everything out of the brown folder Brian had passed to her. She was thankful that Ben hadn't even noticed her retrieve it from the boot; she hadn't wanted to anger him even more than she already had. She had sorted the papers into piles of statements, photographs, reports, forensics, and a pile of newspaper clippings. Brian was thorough if nothing else: there was an awful lot of stuff in here. She wondered if it would be better for him to come here, and they could talk things through. In fact, the more she thought about it the better it seemed. She dialled his number; the phone rang once.

'*Hello.*'

'Brian, it's Morgan Brookes, am I disturbing you?'

He chuckled.

'*Let me see, I'm currently sitting inside my campervan watching the blackest thunder clouds brew over the tops of the trees in the forest and waiting for a storm to strike, while twiddling my thumbs. Can I help you?'*

'Would I be able to come and pick you up, then would you like to come to my apartment for some lunch, and you could go through all these reports with me in detail?'

'Well, I don't seem to have any other offers at the moment, Morgan, so I suppose that would be a yes.'

'Really, that's fantastic thank you. I'll be there soon.'

She hung up. She figured she could handle getting in any more trouble than she already was by discussing things with Brian, besides he was one of them. He'd served his time on a busy police force. Not utilising his experience and knowledge was plain stupid. The FBI used outside consultants who were experts in their fields, and she didn't see why the police couldn't.

The first heavy drops of rain began to fall as the thunder rumbled in the distance; Morgan loved a good thunderstorm but she wasn't quite sure how she felt driving in one along a forest road under a canopy of trees that went on for miles. Hopefully, the lightning would stay over the Keswick area where the clouds were hovering and not move in this direction rapidly, although this was the Lake District, and it was renowned for having its own weather pattern unlike anywhere else. She drove through the entrance to Forest Pines Campsite and was amazed to see that it looked deserted. There were a few tents pitched further down from the caravans and a couple of campers, but it wasn't busy like it had been the first day she came, and she wondered if the publicity about Sara had scared everyone off. John and his wife weren't going to be so happy if they'd ruined their business. She parked in the deserted car park and saw a shadowy figure lingering under the porch of the reception hut. Her heart missed a beat and then a voice shouted.

'Morgan.'

She breathed out the breath she was holding and waved. 'Brian.'

He jogged over to her car and ducked into it as the steady patter of rain began to hammer against the windscreen hard enough to make it difficult to hear each other speak.

'That was good timing,' he shouted at her, and she laughed, nodding her head. Reversing, she drove out of the car park and back to her apartment in Rydal Falls, the only sound the rain and the swishing of the windscreen wipers as they worked triple time to keep the screen clear. A crack of thunder erupted above their heads making Brian jump.

'Bloody hell, that was right above us. Do you think we should take shelter?'

She shook her head. 'I'm not parking under the trees for anyone, Brian. I'd rather try and get home. At least the roads are quiet.'

By the time they reached Rydal Falls, the rain had slowed to a steady drizzle. She had indeed left the storm behind, driving much faster than the speed limit to get here. Getting out of the car Brian laughed. 'Have you seen that film *Twister*?'

She nodded.

'If you get fed up with being a copper you can at least become a professional storm chaser, that was some drive.'

'Thanks, I'll take that as a compliment.' Winking at him she led him into the communal entrance that led to her apartment. He shrugged off his damp jacket and she took it from him, hanging it in the small hall cupboard where she kept hers.

'Make yourself at home. Can I get you a drink? I only have herbal tea or coffee.'

'I'm partial to a mug of strong coffee, that would be great.'

She led the way. Boiling the kettle she heaped a large spoon of coffee granules into her only other mug, and she carried it over to the oversized chair where Brian was sitting. She sat down on the floor cross-legged, and he smiled at her.

'I'd give you the chair and be a perfect gentleman, but my back's knackered, and my knees won't withstand sitting like that. All those years of playing rugby have played havoc with my poor body.'

'Don't be daft, I'm grateful that you're here. I wouldn't dream of making you sit on the floor. You're my guest and I rarely get any of those. Well to be fair, I had one once who tried to strangle me and hang me from the staircase banister in the hallway, but apart from that I don't.'

Brian was staring at her open-mouthed. 'You need to find better house guests, that's really quite rude.'

She laughed. 'Ha-ha, that's funny. You better not try to get any ideas and murder me, Brian, because I'm having a really bad day already.'

He held up his hands. 'I wouldn't dream of it, I'm not the murdering type. I promise you are perfectly safe with me. Are you okay though, what's happened?'

Morgan found herself wanting to tell him everything, he was so easy to talk to.

'I'm in a spot of bother at work. I won't bore you with the details, but after I left you yesterday, we ended up going to visit a prisoner in Manchester whose name was on the keeper details for a blue van that we managed to get pictures of leaving the scene of a brutal murder.' She replayed what she'd told him: she was okay, no names or addresses had been mentioned so she wasn't breaking any confidentiality rules.

'You traced him; you found The Travelling Man?' The excitement in his voice made her feel even worse, and the sigh that erupted from her mouth was huge.

'Not really, but we really hoped that we had. I think it was a wild goose chase that he had planned if the police got close to discovering who he was. This man's clever, much cleverer than we've given him credit for. I think he's put more thought into planning this than we could ever imagine.'

'Damn it, that would have been stupendous if you'd managed to catch hold of him.' He took a large sip of the coffee and nodded. 'Not bad.'

She smiled. 'I really hoped we'd caught him. I wanted to be able to save Sara Fletcher, but I feel as if the time is flying too fast.'

Brian nodded. 'Yes, it is. I'm afraid if she's still alive, she's living on borrowed time unless he's gone to ground and got scared. Tell me, how did you connect the murder from yesterday morning to The Travelling Man? I'm fascinated to know what brought you to the conclusion it could be the same person.'

'It was so violent and horrendous, and not the sort of murder that happens in Keswick.'

'How so? What made you think that it wasn't an average domestic gone wrong or a mugging?'

Morgan looked into his soft brown eyes, with lines around the edges, and wondered if she was going a step too far trusting him, but what else did they have? Brian knew his cases inside out; he'd lived and breathed them for years. He wanted this sick bastard caught and brought to justice as much as she and Ben did.

'This is confidential, right?'

He saluted. 'Scout's honour, I would never betray your trust, Morgan. I know all too well the heartache that kind of thing can bring to the door.'

'The victim was eighty-two. Two days ago she rang 101 about a blue van in a car park with strange noises coming from the back of it, said the man driving it was rude to her. Yesterday morning I think she spotted the van again and, bless her, went to take a closer look at it, then whoever he was saw her and...' She paused as an image of Florence's battered body snapped into her mind like a polaroid camera still. 'And he beat her to death and left her dying in a pool of her own blood on the pavement.'

'That's awful.'

'It really was, but I'm going to find him, and make him pay. Which is where you come in. I was hoping you could talk me through these.' She pointed at the stacks of papers. 'Anything really to help find him. Tell me as much as you know about him.'

'Well, the body, as you know, wasn't discovered until a few years after he'd taken her. She was skeletonised and we had no DNA on our system to compare hers to, no missing persons' reports that matched the time frame, and the forensic anthropologist found that her throat had been cut due to the markings on the vertebrae.'

'That's his MO, the cut throat. The remains we found had a similar injury.'

Brian nodded. 'That fits and makes sense, it's all in the copy of the post-mortem report. Six months later, a body was discovered in Scotland, around seventy-two hours after reports of a missing woman, again in a wooded area, partially hidden under branches and trees. I managed to speak to the DI working that case. Again the same MO, her throat had been cut and he told me that they had a missing person's report for their victim from her boyfriend. The victim had been missing for twenty-four hours when he reported her. At least her family got her back; my victim was buried in a grave in the cemetery with no marker and no one to visit and leave her flowers.'

'That's so sad. How can someone disappear, and no one gives a shit?'

'You'd be surprised how many people do, but I couldn't let it go. It niggled away at me day and night, wondering who she was and who had done this to her, and then it all stopped; no more murders, at least not here in the UK. I'd managed to find a case in France where a lone female camper disappeared from a campsite. I tried speaking to the French police investigating the case, but they weren't interested. I kept on searching but nothing came up that was of any interest. I had set up alerts on my laptop should any news be reported with the search parameters to fit the criteria.'

'Where do you think he went?'

'Prison, I think he got put away for a long stretch but for something unrelated to these killings. Armed robbery, fraud, serious assault.'

'Murder and rape?'

Brian arched an eyebrow at her, then shook his head. 'Rape he would possibly be out now, but surely not for murder, unless it was manslaughter. What are you thinking, Morgan?'

She went to the kitchen and picked up her cold mug of tea. Sipping it she grimaced then poured it away. She could do with something much stronger but Brian needed driving back to the campsite.

'It's a long story and probably an even longer theory, but…'

He nodded; she had his attention. She told him about her relationship to Gary Marks and how she suspected he could be the man they were looking for.

When she finished Brian held up his hand. 'So, Gary Marks is your biological father, he's escaped from prison and they haven't captured him yet. Is that the key information?'

'Yes. I think the timeline all fits. Those murders of the women from campsites happened before he was put in prison. He used to travel around, he was a tree surgeon and regularly worked in the forests around here. Then my mum had me and my brother, and he stopped travelling for work.'

Brian was sitting forwards, his eyes wide as he listened to what Morgan was saying.

'If he was working in forests, he would know the deserted places to leave a body. He travelled around the country, he was a sick bastard and, who knows, maybe he turned to raping women when he could no longer travel, then he killed my mum and got put in prison.'

'And you think that he might be The Travelling Man?'

She shrugged. 'He escaped prison, and I'm pretty sure he's back in this area, though up till now he's evaded capture. If the skeletal remains that were discovered two days ago are linked to him, it means he started close to home, then realised it was too risky and when he travelled for work, he carried on killing. Now he's back out, he's a wanted man anyway: what's he got to lose? Maybe he figured out he might as well have a little fun before we catch him.'

'Whoa, that's a lot to take in. It's also circumstantial and I can see where you're going with this, it's a possible lead. What does Ben think?'

'He's looking into it.'

'So, if you've come up with this why are you sitting at home like a grounded teenager?'

She didn't want to tell him; she was embarrassed enough about her situation but she wanted someone to take her seriously, and she thought he deserved to know the truth.

'I thought I saw Marks a few weeks ago scurrying down the high street. I followed him but lost him. I wasn't a hundred per cent sure it was him, it was literally a fleeting glance, but the way he disappeared from sight when he knew I was there really bothers me. I didn't call it in because I wasn't sure and now, if I'm right and it was, then Sara Fletcher's abduction and Florence's blood is on my hands. I could have stopped this from happening before he started. I was stupid and pig-headed.'

She bowed her head, not wanting to cry in front of Brian, and not wanting to drop all of this onto his conscience. Her sins weren't his to forgive. She felt a warm hand on her shoulder and looked up to see him standing over her a bit like Stan used to when he tried to console her. She'd always shrug Stan's hand away. She didn't shrug Brian's.

'Hey, that's an easy mistake. We've all been there. How many times do you think I've been off duty and seen a wanted person and thought, sod it I'm not doing anything about it? I can guarantee you that every single police officer in the world has done the same and, besides, you weren't sure it was him, so this is not your fault. This is not your guilt to shoulder and I'm pretty sure that Ben will realise this.'

She blinked back the tears that were pooling in the corner of her eyes and smiled at him.

'Thank you.'

'The only person with any guilt or blame in all of this is the sick bastard taking women and killing them. So, why don't we take a look at the post-mortem reports for my victim and see if we can come up with a definitive timeline? There's also a map of the country there with every campsite on it. I got it from a mate of mine who was a member of the camping and caravanning club. It's out of date but should hopefully have all the relevant campsites on it. Have you got anywhere we can stick it up and put pins in to point out our locations? A map of this area would be pretty useful too.'

Morgan pointed to the blank wall behind Brian. 'Help yourself, I'll get some Blu-Tack to stick it with. I've also got a map. Hang on, I'll go get it.'

Ten minutes later they had dragged the chair out of the way and had both maps on the wall, with small, smiley-faced pushed pins from Morgan's kitchen noticeboard. There were four pins for where each victim's body was located in Rydal Falls, Kent, Scotland, France and also a pin to show Sara Fletcher's abduction site. Morgan had an A4 notebook and was writing down the dates of discovery of the remains, determined to put right any mistakes she might have made, vowing to put all of this right and end it before anyone else was taken.

TWENTY-EIGHT

It was almost mid-afternoon by the time Morgan and Brian sat back and looked at the mass of Post-it notes stuck all over the wall next to the maps.

'I think that's it; I think that's right.' Brian yawned as he spoke.

Morgan glanced down at her watch and felt bad. She'd kept him here for hours with only a short break for pizza. 'I think you're right. Thank you so much for helping me get this in order.'

'It's the least I could do. We make a half-decent team. I would have loved working with you if I'd had the chance.'

'Thank you, me too. I mean I'd have liked to have been in your squad. I'll give you a lift back to the campsite.'

He laughed. 'That's very kind of you, as long as you don't mind.'

'Of course, I'll drive you back.'

'You don't mind?'

'Of course not. I'm so grateful you've been here and helped me to sort this out. I can't wait to tell Ben.'

She stood up, stretching. She was ready for some fresh air

too. Her sunburned skin was feeling as if it was too tight for her arms and the back of her neck. She needed to put some aftersun on and lie down just for a little while when she got back.

They walked out to her car. The rain had stopped, and the air smelled earthy and fresh.

They drove back to Forest Pines in comfortable silence until they were almost there.

'How well have you looked into the backgrounds of the workers at the campsite, and how about the forestry commission? They will have workers who know the area like the backs of their hands.'

'We've done the campsite checks. I'm not sure how far Amy has got with any others.'

'Just a thought.'

She drove into the car park near to the reception building, and Brian got out. 'Well thank you for a pleasurable day.'

She laughed. 'Heck, I'm not sure if it counts as pleasure but, thank you, Brian. You've been a massive help.'

He gave her a thumbs up and shut the car door. She watched him saunter back to his campervan, afraid to drive away in case he didn't make it. There was no reason why he shouldn't, but she had a feeling of foreboding that something was on the verge of happening and she wanted to make sure he was inside before she abandoned him.

Satisfied Brian was inside his van, she turned the car around, feeling absolutely exhausted. It was so desolate out here, even in the late afternoon. She found herself pushing the button for the automatic locks before she drove fast enough for them to engage. She noted that the gravel road down to the main road was lit up sporadically but not well enough for her liking. She shuddered. What had Sara Fletcher been thinking accepting that pitch so far from everyone else in the dark? Did she like being secluded? Did she really not want to be near other people? They knew so very little about her. She decided that she would go and visit Sofie tomorrow, to learn more about Sara. Had she been here before, camping alone?

* * *

As she drove back into Rydal Falls she was tempted to go and tell Ben what she and Brian had spent the day doing; surely he wouldn't be angry with her. She didn't take the turning for Singleton Park Road, and instead she went in the opposite direction, to where Ben lived in the huge Victorian semi that was far too big for him on his own, with only the ghost of his dead wife, Cindy, to keep him company. His street was far better lit than the campsite, thank God.

Morgan pulled up opposite his house which was all in darkness. Damn it, she'd wanted there to be a light on somewhere so she could knock on his door. Bright headlights turned into the street, and she had to squeeze her eyes against them as the car pulled in behind her. Its engine still running, someone got out as it drove off, and she realised it was a taxi. She indicated to pull out, needing to go home and tend to her poor skin. There was a loud knock on her window, and she screeched, jumping off the seat of the chair. Ben's face pressed against the glass. Her eyes wide with fright she pressed the button for the window to slide down.

'How long have you been sat out here like some weird stalker staring at my house?'

Her cheeks burned. 'I just got here before you.'

'Yeah, a likely story.'

About to tell him to sod off, he smiled at her. 'Sorry about earlier, I panicked. Do you want to come in for a drink? There must be some reason you're here. You're such a weirdo, Brookes, but I like that about you.'

He laughed, and she shook her head but put the window up and got out of the car. He didn't step back to give her much room, and she could smell the faintest trace of his aftershave, combined with what she thought may be whisky fumes.

'Have you been drinking?'

'What are you, my mother?'

'No, I can smell it.'

'Had to let off some steam, it's been a hell of a day and we still haven't found Sara Fletcher, the blue van guy, or Gary Marks come to think of it.'

He wobbled and stepped away from her, leading the way to his garden gate, which he threw open much harder than he needed to and stumbled up the three steps to his front door. The security light came on bathing them in harsh, white light, and Ben took several attempts to get his key into the lock. Morgan took it from him, pushing it in first time. He gave her a little clap.

'You know after the shit day we've had, and the even shitter way I treated you earlier, I thought you may have gone home and downed that bottle of ice-cold vodka you keep in your freezer.'

He fell into the hall, and she followed, closing the door behind her, following him to the kitchen, picking up his suit jacket that he'd dropped on the floor and his tie that had been loosened so much he'd pulled it over his head. He sat down on one of the kitchen chairs, and she went to the sink to run the tap. Opening the cupboard she took a tall glass out and filled it with water, passing it to him.

'Drink this.'

He took it and began gulping it down.

'Where have you been?'

'The Black Dog, just for a few. I needed to do something to ease the guilt.' He hiccupped, the noise echoing around the huge kitchen.

'Well, while you've been consoling yourself with whisky, I've been very busy.'

'Have you now?'

'Yes, I have.' She stopped talking because Ben's eyes were beginning to close, and his head was drooping forwards. There was no point: she may as well save it for the morning. She walked around to the chair he was dozing on and shook his shoulder.

'Come on, let's get you to bed.'

His eyes opened and he looked at her, confusion in them, but he pushed himself up from the table. She hooked her arm through his and felt him lean into her. He was much heavier than her and she had a job to keep him supported. She looked at the stairs weighing up her options: it was either struggle to get him up them or make him comfortable on the sofa. She opted for the sofa. Pushing the door to the lounge open with the toe of her Converse, she flicked on the light and led him to the dark brown, worn chesterfield and pushed him down onto it. Arranging the cushions at one end for his head, she guided him until he was lying down, tugged off his shoes and looked around for the throw that had fallen to the floor. She threw it over him; there was no way she was undressing him, that was beyond the call of duty even for her. As she tucked him in, he opened one eye and looked at her. His hand reached out from under the woollen throw, and he gently traced a finger along her jawline and murmured, 'I love you, Morgan.' Then his hand fell onto his chest and his eye closed as a gentle snore came out of his mouth.

Paralysed, she stared at him. Crouched over him she could feel the soft warmness where his finger had touched her face. She straightened up. He was drunk, nothing more, everyone talked crap when they were drunk, but her finger touched the place on her face where the skin was tingling from his touch, and she wished that he would say it when he was sober.

She sat down in the armchair opposite him and sighed. She was beyond tired and not to mention a little bit on edge. There was so much happening, so much evil outside of this door, she wondered if she should curl up and spend the night here. She realised that she didn't want to be on her own and even a drunken, unconscious Ben was better company than being on her own, staring at photos of crime scenes, missing women and skeletonised remains that was now the new artwork on her wall back home.

She went to check the house was locked up, front and back, then grabbed a couple of cushions from the other lounge and another throw to wrap herself up in. She went back to where Ben was now in a deep sleep and turned a small lamp on. Pulling the blinds down she closed them and turned off the big light so she could curl up on the chair and get some sleep. As her eyelids began to flutter, she replayed those words in her mind, *I love you, Morgan.* She drifted off with a small smile on her lips.

TWENTY-NINE

Morgan opened her eyes; her neck was stiff, and for a moment she had no idea where she was. Then she realised and knew that she should have gone home instead of staying here. Ben was already up: the cushions were back in their place and the throw was neatly folded. She heard the sound of the shower running upstairs and wondered if she should leave, but he'd come home in a taxi, so he obviously had no car. She may as well wait for him to take him to work. She checked her watch and was amazed to see it was almost seven. The water stopped running upstairs, and she heard Ben walking around. His phone began ringing, and she looked around for it. Standing up she followed the sound into the hall, where she had hooked his suit jacket over the newel post of the staircase.

'Morning, do you want to get a shower and I'll make some breakfast?'

His voice startled her, and she looked up to see him standing at the top of the stairs with just a soft lemon-coloured towel wrapped around his hips. His hair was dripping water down his chest, and she felt her cheeks begin to burn. She nodded.

'Thanks, your phone was ringing.'

'I'll get dressed then see who it was. Help yourself to the bathroom. I think there's some aftersun in the medicine cabinet. You look like a fried tomato.'

She glared at him and thought, *well it was definitely the drink talking last night*. Running upstairs, she realised that she had no clean clothes to get changed in to, but at least she could run into her apartment and get changed fast.

Ben walked into the bedroom, closing the door behind him, and she walked into the bathroom, which was damp and steamy. Using the sleeve of her top she rubbed the condensation from the mirror and stared at her reflection. She did resemble a fried tomato and it wasn't a pretty sight. Shaking her head, she went to lock the bathroom door and realised there wasn't one. Of course, Cindy had died in here and Ben had to break down the door to get in. He probably didn't want a lock on it after that. She stared at the claw-footed bathtub and shivered, glad the shower was a separate unit, feeling bad that she was about to get naked in the room where his wife had died. Morgan undressed, leaving her clothes in a pile by the door to slow it down should he try and come inside. Half of her would have loved him to come inside and do the kind of things you only watched in movie scenes, and the other half of her was horrified that she was even thinking like this.

She stepped under the steaming spray and had the world's quickest shower, the jets of water feeling like tiny hot pricks of pain against her skin. She patted herself dry as gently as she could, then opened the pine cabinet. There were lots of expensive face creams and toners inside. She spotted a bottle of Hawaiian Tropic After Sun and took it out, slathering herself in the stuff. When it had soaked in enough she dressed, then squirted toothpaste onto her finger and rubbed it around her mouth and gums. There were no hairbrushes in here, not even a comb. Gathering her wet hair into a very messy bun she tied it up and went back downstairs.

Ben was buttering toast, and she sat down on the same chair he'd been in last night. It was like a complete role reversal as he placed a plate with a mountain of hot, buttery toast on the table and smiled at her.

'Feel better?'

She smiled. 'I was about to ask you the same question. How's your hangover?'

He shrugged. 'What hangover?'

'Are you for real?'

Laughing he sat down opposite her. 'I have a slight headache but nothing that a couple of paracetamols won't cure, or at least I'm hoping they're going to kick in soon. I had to let off a bit of steam. Yesterday was awful, and I should have rung you to apologise instead of going to the pub.'

'It's me who should be apologising. I screwed up.' She picked up a slice of toast, taking a bite.

'We all make mistakes. Anyway, what were you doing outside my house last night? I wasn't that drunk I didn't remember you parked outside like some stalker.'

'I spent the afternoon with Brian.'

He looked at her. 'You did? What's it with you and older men?' He was smiling but she didn't think it was funny.

'Don't be a dick. He gave me copies of his notes, and I wanted him to talk me through them. We ate pizza and spent a couple of hours poring over post-mortem reports, crime-scene photos and newspaper clippings and, besides, the man drove over six hours to get here to help us and you brushed him off the day before yesterday. I felt bad for him.'

'Sorry, was it helpful?'

She nodded. 'Very, do you want me to tell you now or at work?'

His phone began ringing again, and he stood up. 'Bollocks, I forgot to check who was ringing.' He retrieved it from his jacket pocket. 'Matthews.' He listened to the voice on the other end talking animatedly. Morgan knew it was female but had no idea what they were telling him.

'You're joking, where?' There was a pause. 'Well that's bloody fantastic. I'm on my way.' He hung up and turned to her.

'A couple of mountain bikers out on a ride have found Sara Fletcher in Grizedale Forest.'

Morgan jumped up. 'Is she alive?'

Ben was grinning. 'She is. She's been taken to Westmorland General.'

'That's incredible. But how, what was she doing there?'

'At this moment, I don't know, and I don't care. Come on, Brookes, let's go and speak to her.'

He was almost running out of the door, and she followed him. Outside he looked around and whispered, 'Shit, my car is at the pub.'

She shook her head. 'Good job I came here to stalk you then, isn't it?' She ran towards her car, and they got inside.

Ben reached out and touched her forearm. 'What a team we are.'

She smiled but it didn't reach her eyes and she didn't look directly at him. 'Yes, I'd say that we are.' She felt her heart tug the way it does when something exciting or painful happens and there's no controlling it.

THIRTY

The hospital took forever to reach, even with Morgan driving as fast as she could on the winding roads to get there. When they finally got to the car park she abandoned the car as near to the entrance without blocking the ambulance access, and they both ran into the accident and emergency department. An officer was already waiting for them to take them through to the cubicle Sara was being assessed in. Ben nodded at her.

'Sergeant Matthews, how is she?'

'Hello, I'm Shannon. She's shaken up, and has a head injury that needs attention, plus from what I could see a fair few bruises on her arms and legs. She's also suffering from shock. She's been hiding out for hours scared to death, bless her.'

'This is just brilliant. She's alive. Has she told you anything?'

The officer shook her head. 'No, bless her, she hasn't said much at all.'

Morgan was looking around for the scary doctor who had been here when Ben had been brought in a while back, but she couldn't see her. As they reached the cubicle a nurse came around the corner and held up one hand.

'Whoa, my friends, stop right there. What are you doing?'

'Ben Matthews and this is Morgan Brookes from Rydal Falls CID. We need to speak to Sara as a matter of urgency.'

'I know you do but give the woman half a chance, she's been through a terrible ordeal. Let me ask her if she's ready to see you at least before you go barging in there.'

She disappeared through the tiniest slither of a gap in the curtains. A few seconds later the curtain was held open for them to step inside. Morgan's heart was racing at the thought of seeing Sara face to face, relief that she was alive making adrenalin rush through her body.

The woman on the bed was huddled under a blanket, her face an explosion of bruises, and there was a deep wound on the side of her head where she'd been hit with a heavy object. Her dark blonde hair was matted with dried blood, twigs and leaves.

It was Ben who spoke first. 'Thank God you're okay, Sara. I'm Ben and this is Morgan from—'

'I heard you outside.'

Despite the trauma of the last few days, her voice was strong. She looked at Morgan.

'Sara, I can't tell you how glad we are to see you. I know this is a ridiculous question, but how do you feel?'

She met Morgan's eyes. 'Glad to be alive, shocked that some sick bastard dragged me out of my tent, tied me up and threw me into the floor of his converted campervan. He was going to kill me... and I almost let him.' Tears filled her eyes and she blinked them away.

Morgan crossed to the bed and sat on the blue plastic chair next to it, taking hold of Sara's bruised scratched hand as gently as she could.

'Do you want to talk about it or do you need to wait until the doctor has sorted your head out and maybe given you something for the pain?'

She looked at Morgan wide-eyed with terror. 'No, I need

you to know before he does it again. The next woman might not be so lucky.'

'What makes you think he'll do it again?'

She pushed her hand into the small pocket of her pyjama shorts and pulled out a single, silver half-moon earring and passed it to Morgan who felt in her pockets for something to put it in. She pulled out a glove and a small evidence bag that was crumpled but big enough for the earring and slipped it inside, sealing it then labelling it with her initials MB1.

'I found that when I was feeling around for a way out of that awful little hole. It's not mine. Why else would he have a woman's earring down there? He's done this before and he's going to do it again, because when I was hiding in the forest, he was shouting that if I didn't come out, he was going to look for someone to take my place and t-torture them to d-death.' She let out a sob. The tears began to flow and Morgan couldn't stop herself, she sat on the bed next to her. Wrapping her arms around Sara's trembling shoulders she pulled her close and held her.

When her sobs eased into small, hitching breaths Morgan pulled away from her. Ben was sitting on the chair, his head bowed, giving them a moment. The nurse who had been watching the whole thing placed a box of tissues on the bed next to Sara, who grabbed a handful and blew her nose. 'Thanks.'

Morgan felt awful, but they had to glean as much information from the distraught woman as they could. 'I'm sorry, Sara, I truly am but are you able to answer some questions?'

Sara looked at Morgan, her pale blue eyes locking with her green ones and nodded.

'I don't want to think about him but, yes, I can.'

She squeezed her hand. 'Thank you, you're very brave.'

Sara laughed. 'I'm not sure what I am, but at least dead isn't on the list.'

'No, it's definitely not. Could you talk me through everything, from arriving at the campsite to the time of the assault? I'm sorry but I have to ask you, did he sexually assault you in any way?'

She shook her head. 'No, thank God. I think he gets off on the violence and keeping someone against their will. He didn't touch me inappropriately that I'm aware of.' She took another tissue and blew her nose, then picked up the small plastic cup filled with water and sipped.

'I arrived at the campsite late afternoon around three. They told me there had been a mistake and they had let out the last pitch to a family, but there was one I could use if I didn't mind being a little far from everyone else.'

'Had you pre-booked your pitch?'

She nodded. 'Ages ago, but you know how the world has been so crazy. I kind of forgot and wasn't really expecting to come. I decided last minute it would be nice to get away and see Sofie. Oh God, does she know I'm okay? Was it her who reported me missing?'

'It was and yes, someone has gone to tell her that you're safe. They will bring her here to see you if you're up to it.'

She nodded.

Morgan glanced at Ben and could tell that he was raging inside. His fingers were clenched into tight fists at his sides. Whoever The Travelling Man was he had just made the angriest enemy he could wish for, and she was glad. That made two of them. She was going to hunt this sick bastard down and finish this today.

Morgan didn't feel as confident as she sounded.

'Until we catch him there will be a police guard outside your room. We're not taking any chances.'

'Thank you, I'm sorry for all the trouble.'

'You have nothing to be sorry for, Sara, this is not your fault.' She replayed Brian's words he'd told her last night. 'The only person who has anything to be sorry about is the sick fu–' She stopped herself. 'Sick man, who did this to you.'

'I was struggling to put my tent up, there was a guy cleaning up nearby, but I managed in the end. Then I went to the showers, came back, put my pyjamas on and lay on the grass reading a book and drinking some of those cocktails you get in a can. I was in heaven; the sun was warm on my face and I'd even turned my phone to silent so no one could disturb me. I ate a sandwich and a bag of crisps. Later on I demolished a couple of chocolate bars before climbing into my sleeping bag and falling asleep.'

'Did you see anyone hanging around while you were reading? Was anyone paying particular attention to you? Did you speak to anyone?'

'No one, apart from the guy at the main office who told me he'd screwed up my pitch and the worker who helped me. There was a family a bit further up who I waved at but they were busy with their three kids. To be fair I was relieved I wasn't right next to them. I wanted peace and quiet. I like kids but not when they're full-on screeching and arguing.'

Morgan smiled. 'Me too. When did you know something bad was happening?'

'I felt a strong breeze on my face. I was half asleep and I turned on my side wondering where it was coming from, because even though I'd had a few of those cocktails I'd definitely zipped up my tent, so there shouldn't have been any. I opened one eye and saw the side of the tent flapping and panicked, then I felt a shadow leaning over me. That sounds really stupid but it was so dark and I couldn't see an actual person. It was just a huge black shadow. I opened my mouth to scream, but something heavy hit the side of my head and it exploded with pain. It made bile rise up in my throat it was so hard. I felt sick, dizzy and it was hurting really bad. I couldn't even move. I was lying there wondering what was happening and then he must have hit me again because I blacked out.'

Morgan squeezed her hand, giving her a moment. 'You're doing really well. You must have been so scared.'

'Not at first, because I didn't understand what was wrong.'

'When did you?'

'I was being dragged through the forest, the leaves and pine needles were hurting my feet and I opened my eye to see what was happening. I was out of it; I was thinking I was having a nightmare but I realised that I could smell the trees and feel the scratches against my skin. He had his arms under my armpits and was grunting as he dragged me downhill. It can't have been uphill, or he'd have had a heart attack.'

Morgan smiled. 'What a shame he didn't.'

'I think I passed out again. My head was hurting so bad, and I could taste blood in my mouth. I thought I'd been in a car accident so I didn't struggle. I thought he was helping me, so I didn't fight. I let him take me.' She closed her eyes and let out a loud sob.

'You weren't to know. He smashed you in the head; you were disorientated and dizzy.'

'Why though, why me? I didn't do anything wrong.'

'You were in the wrong place at the wrong time. It has nothing to do you with you as a person. He found you and couldn't resist the opportunity. Then what happened?'

'I must have passed out again because I can't remember anything else until I opened my eyes. My body was moving from side to side so I knew I was lying down in a vehicle. I thought I was in an ambulance until I tried to open my mouth to speak and couldn't.'

'Why?'

'There was a piece of material tied around it. Then I tried to move my hands and feet and realised that I couldn't. It was so dark in there. I tried to move and my head hit something solid. I turned the other way and it did the same. I panicked then because I thought I was in a coffin, that's what it felt like. A confined space. But I could hear the engine. I didn't know what it was but figured it was a van or something. My head was hurting so much I kept passing out, but whenever I woke up and there was no movement, I did my best to bang against the sides of the van. At one point I was panicking so much I was even headbutting the wall with the other side of my head that wasn't bleeding.'

Morgan kept on squeezing her hand tight. She could feel the panic coming off her.

The nurse stepped in. 'I think that's enough now, don't you?'

Ben stood up. 'Just a couple more questions. Is that okay with you, Sara?'

Sara nodded and he continued.

'Did you ever get a good look at him? Can you describe him to me?'

'Yes, when he dragged me out of the van. I realised it was some kind of converted campervan. There were lots of trees, and it was almost dark. I could hear thunder rumbling but it wasn't raining yet. I lay there and didn't move; I was trying to think what I could do. The whole time I'd been kept in that small space I'd done nothing but try and loosen the ropes around my feet and ankles. I couldn't get them off, but they were loose enough and once I had a little more room I knew I could bend down and slip them off my legs. He was bending over me, screaming at me, calling me a bitch, and he kept kicking my thigh. He had heavy black work boots on, but they looked a bit different. A bit like off the cops shows on TV.'

Morgan looked at Ben, her eyes wide, alarm bells ringing inside her mind. *Please God, don't let it be one of us, not again.*

Ben opened the curtain and asked the police officer outside

to come in. 'Shannon, can you show Sara your boots, please? Were they like this, Sara?'

Shannon obliged, rolling up her trouser leg. Sara shook her head. 'They are a bit similar but it's hard to say.' She went back to the story. 'I didn't move. We were out in the open and he was wanting to get me into the trees. I knew if I did what he wanted I was dead.'

'What did you do?'

'I waited until he bent down really close to me and I did the only thing I could: I threw my head back and headbutted him as hard as I could in the nose.'

Both Morgan and Ben smiled at this amazing, courageous woman. Morgan leaned forwards and lifted the palm of her hand. Sara high-fived her back, and Ben began to clap, his head nodding.

'Amazing, you're a badass, Sara.'

She laughed. 'My poor head is never going to forgive me, but it was worth the pain to see his nose erupt and see him fall on his stinking arse onto the floor. I pushed the ropes off my feet and hands and stumbled into the trees. I had no shoes on, but I didn't care. I knew if he caught me there would be no second chance. I kept zigzagging. I could hear him shouting in the distance, but I kept on going until I found a fallen tree, and there was a small hole. I squeezed into it trying to pretend I was on *I'm a Celebrity* and not trying to save my life. I waited and waited; the thunder came, along with heavy rain, and I was getting soaked. At one point I heard him shouting and crashing through the trees, but he didn't come my way.' She shivered violently, and the nurse held up her hand.

'You said "his stinking arse", did he smell?'

'He smelled bad; his breath was awful, and he reeked of stale sweat. He was wearing camouflage trousers and jacket, and one of those fishing hats that was camouflage too.'

Ben looked at Morgan. 'Thank you, Sara, you are a legend

and you've been so helpful. We'll leave you alone now and let you get some rest.'

Loud voices somewhere in the unit filled the air and then a voice called, 'Sara.'

For the first time Sara's eyes flickered to life, and she yelled, 'In here, Sof.'

Morgan drew back the curtain and smiled to see Sofie pushing past the angry doctor and running towards them. She took one look at her friend and threw herself onto the bed, wrapping her arms around her, and even Ben had to blink hard to stop the tears from falling.

Morgan smiled at them both, relieved they had a happy ending. Although Sara would be scarred for life from her abduction, she was strong and Morgan didn't get the impression she was the kind of woman who would let it take over, or at least she hoped that she wouldn't let it with the right help. They left them to it.

THIRTY-ONE

Outside, Morgan inhaled deeply then exhaled and turned to look at Ben.

'That was intense. What an amazing woman, I'm so glad she escaped.'

'Yes, so now we're looking for an angry, unwashed man who favours camouflaged clothing and wears Magnums, driving around in a converted van. Who should be much easier to find now we have that little bit more information.'

They arrived back at the station full of hope and determination. As they walked through the ground floor, Mads came running out of the sergeant's office.

'What a turn up for the books. I wasn't expecting that.'

Ben nodded. 'I don't think any of us was but thank God she got away. Where are we? Has the area been flooded with patrols?'

'As soon as the call came in, the area where she was found was cordoned off, and the dog has been in. There have been no sightings of a blue van. If you ask me, it was long gone before we got there. I think he cut his losses and got out of there when he realised she was gone.'

'It's a huge area. Have the car parks been checked?'

'Give us a chance, Ben, we're on with it.'

He nodded, and Morgan knew he was beyond frustrated and itching for a fight, but Mads was right, everyone was doing what they could.

They went upstairs, where Amy and Des were already in the office; Tom and Mel were also there.

'How is she?' Mel asked before anyone else could.

Ben smiled. 'Surprisingly good, she's tough and gave us a full account except for the parts where she was rendered unconscious.'

'I hope she makes a full recovery; did she report any sexual assault?'

'No report of anything other than a violent physical attack, and she seems as stable as she can be given the circumstances.'

'Thank God for small mercies, the poor woman.'

Tom was pacing up and down. 'Plan of action? There's a violent criminal still out there. We need a briefing yesterday. Gather everyone that's not out searching in the blue room in ten minutes. I want this man caught today, not tomorrow. And definitely not after another woman has been taken.'

He walked out, and Mel stood up. 'Keep up the good work. This is harder than we ever anticipated.'

She smiled at them, and Amy shook her head. 'This is like the nightmare that won't end. I know he's right to be in a mood but it's not like we're not all going above and beyond.'

Morgan stood up. 'It's not Gary Marks.'

All three heads turned to look at her. Amy spoke. 'I wasn't aware we officially thought that it was.'

Ben's eyes met Morgan's. 'How can you be so sure? Yesterday you thought it could be.'

'Me and Brian worked late last night, I told you. We figured out the victims' timelines from the post-mortem reports. The skeletonised body found the day Sara was abducted is the first victim, Brian's victim in Kent the second, then the body in Scotland was the third, and the one in France with very little info the fourth.'

Amy was shaking her head. 'What does this mean, and where were you working with Brian?'

'At my apartment. I think that the first kill took place in a geographical kill zone that I think was central or near to where the killer lived back then.'

Ben asked. 'Well then why are you ruling Marks out? He lived in this area, and you said yourself he was a tree surgeon, so would have been familiar with the trails and logging roads in and out of the forests.'

'He's a good fit for the first three victims, there's no doubt about that. But here's the thing: he was arrested and sent to prison in 1999. We have so little information about the one in France, apart from the fact that we know she was taken and discovered in 2004, and by then Gary Marks had settled into life in prison. Then after 2004 there were no more until Sara Fletcher.'

'So we think the killer did a stretch inside from 2004 onwards until recently? Or they lived abroad for a good length of time maybe and we don't have access to those records? Amy, do a search on any recent prison releases. Can you find out how long the sentence was they served and when they were released, also where to?'

'I'll try; I should be able to.'

Ben's face was screwed up so tight there were deep furrows on his forehead. He looked at Morgan. 'Why would you get a stretch of ten to at least twenty years? There's a good chance he got more because if he served a good length of time he was probably released for good behaviour. What kind of sentence gets such a long term, and what links to the area does he have that have brought him back?'

Morgan was pacing up and down. 'I think we need to be

looking at someone who has links to the campsite or forest. It's a well-known fact that serial killers start out close to home where they feel comfortable. Who felt comfortable enough to take a woman from a campsite and kill them in the woods not too far from the site?'

Ben turned to the whiteboard and picked up a pen; uncapping it he began writing.

John Winder – previous for fighting

Eleanor Winder –

'Who are the other workers? Did we check them out?'

Amy nodded. 'Of course, I did, there's a Miles Gilbert and Luke Tarr. The only one with a bit of a record is Luke: he's been in a few times for theft from dwelling. Neither of them have served time.'

Morgan was shaking her head. 'Right well, what about the forestry commission? I wonder if there is anyone working there who has a prison record?'

Amy sighed. 'Well unless you go and get a list of names off them for me to check out, how are we supposed to know?'

Ben held up his hand. 'Amy, you and Des go to the main office in the forest after the briefing and ask them nicely if they have any workers who went to prison, or have they recently hired an ex-con? Maybe they do an offender rehabilitation programme or have workers come in through a charity. If you play nice it might cut down on the need for warrants and all the Data Protection crap. Morgan, we're going back to the campsite to ask them the same.' He looked at the clock on the wall. 'Crap, we better get to briefing; at least we have a plan when they ask what we're doing.'

All four of them piled out of the office to go down to the second floor and the blue room.

. . .

As they were filing in, DCI Claire Williams followed them in. Ben nodded to her, and she whispered, 'Sorry, I should have come earlier. It's been chaos at my end.'

She didn't elaborate, and he didn't ask her in front of a room full of people. Al was there along with Tom, Mel, and CSI were also there; Mads came rushing in, his coffee sloshing all over the side of his mug onto the table, followed by Trav, the duty inspector. He held up his hand. 'Sorry.'

Tom was standing up. 'Right, we have no time to lose. There's a press conference in twenty minutes. I've held off as long as I could but they're foaming at the mouth and it's far easier to give them what they want. What I want is a detailed plan of what we are doing to catch this monster before he strikes again. So, who wants to start?'

He was staring at Ben. Morgan felt sorry for him but that was the job: someone had to take responsibility and it looked as if Ben was the guy. If Claire Williams had joined in earlier, she'd be the gal to shoulder the blame. Lucky for her she was only just joining in.

Ben began relaying what he'd told them and the actions they were going to take. He didn't mention Gary Marks, but when he'd finished talking Tom clicked a button on the remote and a larger-than-life photo of him filled the screen.

'What are we doing about him? The infamous, slippery little toad called Gary Marks? Have you even considered him as a suspect, because to me he makes an excellent one. He's escaped prison from a lengthy sentence and no bugger has a clue where he is. I'm inclined to think that he's travelling around the county in a blue van, hiding from police and continuing his obsession with hurting women.'

Tom didn't even look Morgan's way, but she could feel the heat radiating from her cheeks just the same. Was she ever going to be rid of that piece of shit? He was always there no matter what she did, lingering in the background and making her life a complete misery.

Ben shook his head. 'With all due respect, sir, Sara Fletcher hasn't been raped or sexually assaulted. Marks is a convicted rapist and killer. I'm not sure that he'd be able to stop himself if he was the one who abducted her, it's just not his MO.'

Tom's eyes widened as he stared at Ben. 'Not his MO, are you having a laugh? Who else around here is that sick?'

'There's only one flaw with that theory.'

If Morgan thought her cheeks were red then they were nothing compared to the huge, deep red splotches on Tom's cheeks that were growing by the second.

'And what flaw would that be?'

'We have no confirmed sightings of him in Rydal Falls.' Ben never looked Morgan's way, and she wanted to crawl away. He was sticking his neck and career out on the line for her. She had never prayed so hard for Gary Marks not to be the one to blame for these brutal murders. If it turned out he was, both she and Ben would be signing on at the job centre before the end of the week.

'Right, well, we still can't rule him out. He may be hanging around here; after all, he has a good reason to.' Tom looked at Morgan, and she needed to refocus the room.

'Sir, I have looked at some detailed reports passed on to me from a retired DI from Kent. He had a similar situation: a missing camper whose skeletal remains were found years ago in a wooded area. There was also a missing female camper in Scotland, whose body was discovered in almost identical circumstances in the woods, six months after DI Walter's Kent victim. Five years later another camper went missing in France, again very similar circumstances, and Gary Marks was in prison while this one happened, and I don't believe he's responsible for them as much of a scumbag that he is. I have a plan to draw our suspect out.'

She felt everyone turn to stare at her, and she could feel Ben's eyes burning into the side of her head, but she was determined not to turn and look at him. She hadn't told him of her brilliant plan because it had literally only just occurred to her that it might be half decent.

Tom nodded. 'Well, put us out of our misery then, what is it, Brookes?'

Amy's head was moving in the smallest micro shake she had ever seen, and she knew she was telling her to keep her mouth shut whatever it was she was about to say, but she couldn't.

'I think that our suspect is going to very angry, frustrated and, well, he's probably raging that Sara got away from him. He likes to abduct lone, single females from a campsite, and we believe he keeps them alive for up to seventy-two hours before taking them back to the woods and killing them. I'm willing to be a decoy. I could camp where Sara did and see if it lures him in to try and abduct me.'

Ben slammed the palms of his hands on the table so hard it vibrated all around the room.

'Absolutely not, Morgan, have you gone nuts? It's a disaster waiting to happen. There is no way on this earth you are putting yourself at risk.'

He was staring into her eyes, and she stared back, her heart racing. She knew this was stupid but she wasn't backing down.

'What else have we got, Ben? This guy's going to be mighty pissed about losing Sara, and he'll want another victim so he can prove to himself he's still got it, that he's still the tough guy. It's worth a shot.'

Tom was nodding, and she realised that he liked her suggestion. Ben, on the other hand, looked as if his head was about to explode from his shoulders. He was glaring at Tom now.

'Sir, you're not actually considering this. You cannot think that this is a good way to catch him. It's too risky, especially with Morgan's past record.'

'What else have we got, Ben? Have you got any better ideas? This way we might just be able to flush him out. Obviously we would have the campsite surrounded with plain-clothes officers, armed officers would be on standby. There would be no way he could escape if he did take her.'

Ben shook his head. 'There is no way, shape or form that I will agree to any of this.' He walked out of the room, leaving everyone staring after him.

Claire Matthews, who had looked flustered when she arrived, now looked completely bewildered.

'Hang on, how did we go from checking out the campsite and forestry workers to putting Morgan out as bait for a sadistic killer to abduct? I'm sorry, Morgan, while it's a good theory it's not logical or safe. Gold command will never agree to it. It's so dangerous, and what if all the resources are tied up watching you that he takes another victim from somewhere else?'

Tom was looking at them both. 'I agree it's very risky, but sometimes you have to take the risks to get the results. If we have it all planned out to the finest details, it's got to be worth a go. Unless anyone else has a better idea?'

No one answered him.

'Well, there's your answer. I suggest you all go away and try and bring me this bloody man.'

Morgan whispered, 'The Travelling Man.'

'What?'

'The DI from Kent, Brian Walter, calls him The Travelling Man.'

'Well, whoever he is, I want to know that we've done our very best. Everyone dismissed, Morgan stays behind.'

Everyone stood up. Morgan glanced at Mads, who was looking at Al and twirling his finger around the side of his head, as if to say she's nuts. She didn't disagree with him. This plan was crazy, and she had no idea why the hell she had said it out loud. Claire didn't leave; she waited, sitting opposite Tom.

When it was just the three of them, Claire stood up. 'Tom, you can't even think this is a good idea?'

'Why not, Claire? We have a dangerous criminal at large who is on the prowl for another victim, if everything Morgan has said is true. What would be so bad about luring him out?'

'Exactly those reasons you've just said. I'm not saying that we shouldn't have plain-clothes officers keeping tabs on the campsites, because if this is how he likes to take his victims then the possibility of him striking again is very high.'

'I'm still going to see if I can get it authorised. We have to do something. Morgan, did you mean it, are you happy to be a sitting duck?'

She nodded, afraid to speak in case her voice broke and she cried, because listening to them discussing it like this had made her realise that it was probably the stupidest thing she had ever suggested in her whole life. If it was Gary Marks, then she would finally have her time with him face to face, to put an end to the misery he had wreaked on her entire life since she was a toddler. If it wasn't him, then she would be doing it for Florence and the four women who had died at his hands, because that was how he got his thrills.

'For now, let's get those enquiries ticked off that Ben has suggested. I'll get Al to arrange patrols to cover the campsite. I'll see if I can speak with someone who'll authorise it, Morgan. Thank you for offering to help.'

He left her and Claire alone. Claire waited until they could no longer hear his footsteps out in the corridor.

'Morgan you can't do this, please. If he does by some chance get someone to agree with him, although I can't see it, you just can't. The risk to yourself is far too high and, judging by Ben's reaction, I think you might give him a heart attack if you did.'

'I just want to catch him and stop this now before anyone else gets hurt.'

'And that's a very honourable thing to do, but what if you get hurt? What if he takes you and we can't stop him before it's too late? Christ, I'm late to all of this but even I can see the danger you'd be putting yourself in, even if you can't. If he tells you it's a go, then tell him you've changed your mind.'

She nodded and stood up. 'I better go and find Ben.' Although she had a feeling he wouldn't be anywhere for her to find.

THIRTY-TWO

Morgan walked back into the office and she was right, there was only Des in there.

'Where's the boss?'

'Gone to the campsite with Amy to get away from you. You know, after that suggestion, Morgan, I'm beginning to doubt your sanity.'

'Go screw yourself, Des.'

She sat down at her desk, a wave of misery coursing through her veins. He was standing looming over her, his arms folded. 'Come on, the boss said you were to accompany me to the forestry commission, and if you try to get out of it, I was to cuff you to his desk until he got back.'

'Like he thinks I'm safe with you?'

Des shrugged. 'Obviously, come on, Brookes, it's not all about you. For once in your life be a team player and get on with it.'

Morgan's fingers clenched into fists so tight she wanted to punch him, but she knew if she did that was her suspended. She stood up, grabbed her bag and followed him out to the car park, wishing that she'd kept her mouth shut in the briefing now. Ben must be really pissed with her, making her go out with Des.

* * *

They sat in silence all the way to Whinlatter Forest. She stared out of the window the whole time, willing a dark blue van to drive past them so they could pull it over. Although Des was such a wimp, he'd probably drive in the opposite direction so they didn't have to. She leaned forwards and jabbed her finger to turn the radio on. Tom's voice filtered through the car: she'd forgotten about the press conference. Quickly turning the station over, she leaned back to the sound of Smooth FM and thought about Declan. What would he say about her grand suggestion? No doubt the same as Ben, that it was stupid and far too dangerous.

Des turned into the road that led into the forest and drove slower. There were lots of mountain bikers and families walking and she wanted to scream at them to go home. Did they not care there was a dangerous criminal on the loose and that any of them could be his next victim?

When he drove into the busy car park, he glanced at her. 'Are you okay?'

'Yeah.'

'Good, let me do the talking.'

She closed her eyes; Des was giving her orders? Well, he could go take a running jump because he wasn't her superior, he was her equal.

They walked into the busy office, and he headed for the reception desk. Before he could open his mouth, Morgan spoke.

'Good afternoon, I'm Detective Constable Morgan Brookes

and this is my colleague, Des. Is there anyone we can talk to about staff? We have a serious incident that we're investigating.'

The man behind the counter nodded. 'Of course, is it to do with that missing camper? Come through to the back office.'

He opened a door for them to walk through. Morgan smiled at Des, who was staring at her with his mouth open, and led the way, letting him follow behind. He could go screw himself talking to her like that. She'd like to see him offer to put himself at risk to save lives. It took him all his time deciding what to have for lunch, which was like a daily ordeal for him.

'Please have a seat. I'm Justin, I run the office and do the admin, or at least I do while our usual office manager is on leave. To be honest I'm not very good at it; she's a whizz. How can I help?'

'Thank you, as you are aware we are investigating the abduction of Sara Fletcher, and I'm wondering if you can tell me if you have anyone working for the forestry commission who has recently been released from prison, or if you know of any workers who went to prison at least eighteen years ago?'

He let out a whistle. 'Wow, that's a big ask and I'm going to be honest with you, I don't know if I can help you much.'

Morgan had feared as much. 'Why's that, the Data Protection?'

He shook his head. 'No, as far as I'm concerned Data Protection can go screw itself when you're investigating something of this magnitude. I want to help you as much as I can, but I'm not too sure about the logistics of where that information would be stored.'

She smiled at him despite her frustration; Justin was a good guy. He stood up and began pulling open the filing cabinets behind him. 'I mean it's probably all on the computer, but I wouldn't have access to those files that are electronically stored. But hang on.' He pulled out a file and sat down, opening it.

'This is a list of past employees who have left; must be for references, you know, when they need to get another job.'

'It's not very big.'

'Ah, that's because we don't have a massive turnover of staff. That, I can tell you; most of us have been here years. It's a good job and there aren't a lot of us and, as far as I'm aware, we haven't taken on any new starts lately. To be fair I don't know exactly what you're looking for; you might do better yourself. How about I show you the new plans we have, Des, that are out in the main office for the expansion projects for the visitors' centre? Morgan, are you okay back here on your own while we go take a look?'

He stood up and opened the door. Des took his hint and followed Justin back out into the main reception area. Morgan did a quick check to make sure there was no CCTV camera watching her every move and, satisfied that there wasn't, she took hold of the file and began flicking through the papers for names and addresses. None of them stood out or drew her attention. Standing up, she took the file back to the cabinet and began working her way through them until she found one labelled 'volunteers'. Grabbing that one she began to look through it, not sure what she was looking for, but for a name that might have some significance. As her finger moved down the list she came to one that said, 'Edward Winder', and there was a thick, black line through it. Where did she know that name from and why was it the only one with a black mark? She could hear voices outside the room and, not wanting to get Justin into any trouble, she put the file back and shut the cabinet drawer. The door opened and Justin walked in with an older woman; Des was still outside.

'Josie, this is Detective Brookes. She was asking about past employees and any new starts.'

Josie stared at Morgan over her glasses. 'Well, you'd have to submit an application to head office for that, dear. We can't just give out information willy-nilly.'

Morgan stood up. 'Thanks, Justin; that's no problem, Josie. I'll do that. Sorry to have bothered you.'

'I'll show you out.'

Justin led Morgan outside. 'Sorry about the dragon. She's not supposed to be back until tomorrow.'

'That's fine, thank you for your help. I really appreciate it.'

'Anytime, Morgan, did you find anything useful?'

She shrugged. 'I don't think so.'

'Ah, that's a shame.'

Smiling at him she walked away, and he jogged after her. 'Hey, if you ever fancy going for a drink you know where to find me.'

'Thanks, if I ever get the time, I'll let you know.' She winked at him then got into the car, where Des already had the engine running.

'Well?'

'The only name I found that meant anything to me was Edward Winder. There was a black line through his name on the list of volunteers.'

'Who the hell is he when he's at home?'

She shrugged. 'The guy who owns the campsite is called John Winder, maybe they're related. Why would there be a black mark through his name?'

'Maybe he's dead.'

She didn't reply; instead she took her phone out of her pocket and pressed Ben's name. It rang and rang; usually he picked up straight away.

'He's really mad at you. Wait till I tell him the guy from the forestry commission was hitting on you. It will tip him over the edge.'

'You're such an arse. Why would you do that? because he wasn't, he was just being friendly.'

'Yeah, right.'

'You phone him; this might be important.'

Des rang Ben's number, and Morgan had to do her best from exploding when after a couple of rings, she heard Ben's deep voice answer. She was raging with them all; they could all go screw themselves.

'Morgan said to ask if the guy who owns the campsite knows an Edward Winder. Apparently his name was on the volunteers list but was crossed out.'

She couldn't hear Ben's reply and knew he was purposely speaking quietly, but she wasn't sure if he was, so she had no idea what he was saying or whether John Winder was in hearing distance. 'Ask him if he needs us at the campsite?'

Des asked and even she heard the loud, '*Absolutely not.*' He ended the call, and she looked at him.

'Well, what are we going to do now then?'

'Go get some lunch. There's not much we can do and if I'm babysitting you, I'm not doing it on an empty stomach.'

Morgan's burning rage was at boiling point. She opened her mouth then closed it. Let him take her back to the station while he went to get his lunch. She would do some digging and see what she could find out about Edward Winder.

THIRTY-THREE

Ben was sitting opposite John Winder in the small, cramped site office. There was some kind of silent stand-off going on between Eleanor, who was leaning against the wall with her arms crossed, glaring at Amy, who was staring right back.

'John, can you tell me if any of your employees have ever been inside? Or if anyone who worked here got sent away?'

Eleanor spoke. 'I heard it on the radio they found that missing woman. Nice of you to let us know.'

'You should have been told first. An officer was asked to come here and break the news. I'm sorry if that message didn't get passed. I'll look into it.'

John was glaring at his wife. 'They did, someone phoned earlier. Sorry, Ellie, I didn't get a chance to come and tell you.'

If Ben had been angry with Morgan for her stupid suggestion, it was nothing compared to the way Eleanor was staring at her husband, but she didn't say a word to him.

'At least she's okay though, you must be glad about that, saves you having to keep looking for her.'

'Yes, she's alive, but I'm not sure she would agree with you that she's okay after her ordeal.'

Amy turned from Eleanor to stare at John. 'So, as my boss was just asking, have you any employees that have been to prison or recently released?'

John shook his head. 'None. I couldn't employ anyone with a criminal record. This is a family campsite. They all have to have a DBS background check to make sure they're clean.'

'Which I'm sure you're aware of, Ben.' Eleanor's voice was shrill, and if Ben didn't know any better, he would say that she was more than a little bit anxious, highly strung maybe, but why would she be?

'Yes, of course, but we have to ask as a matter of course. Do you have any connection or know anyone called Edward Winder?'

Both Eleanor and John replied with a short, sharp, 'No.'

'It's not some relation or distant cousin?'

'No. Why are you asking?'

'We're just following different lines of enquiries, John, you know how it is. How are things now, are they getting back to normal?'

Eleanor laughed. 'You lot have no idea. You practically bankrupted us. Have you seen how dead it is out there? We're not even at half capacity thanks to you all tramping all over the place.'

Amy stood up directly in front of Eleanor. 'What's your problem, lady? A woman was taken from your campsite and could have died. The only people at fault here are yourselves for putting her in a situation that allowed it to happen, so wind your neck in.'

Amy walked out of the office. Ben stood up and followed her, turning to look directly at John.

'If you do think of a connection to anyone of that name, or anyone who has been in prison, then let me know as soon as you can.'

* * *

Amy was already in the car, the engine running, when he opened the passenger door and got inside. He didn't say anything to her in case John or Eleanor were watching, but as soon as she was on the long, winding driveway out of there he turned to her. 'What the hell was that about?'

'That woman is a complete bitch. Where does she get off talking to us like that? And as for her wimpy husband, what a joke.'

Ben shook his head, wondering how his day was turning into the world's crappiest day and none of it was even his fault for a change. 'Look, she is, there's no doubt about that, but you can't talk to people like that.'

'Why? As if she was accusing us of being the reason they're losing business. They needed to be told the truth. Why do we pussyfoot around these kinds of people all the time? Because we're all afraid they'll put a complaint in to the professional standards department for speaking the truth. This job is screwed, Ben, it's not like it was and those two are both culpable in Sara Fletcher's ordeal. I hope to God she sues the arse off them.'

'What did you think about their reaction to Edward Winder? I get the feeling they were hiding something.'

'Or they're just wankers, either way.'

Ben laughed. 'Say it as it is, won't you? Did you see his cheek twitch when I asked him about knowing anyone who had been inside?'

'I think you should bring them both in for questioning, or at least to help with enquiries, and put the fear of God into their smug arses for good measure.'

He nodded; they were definitely hiding something. His gut was telling him that they were on the right track. Morgan had suggested right at the very beginning that the pair of them could be involved. What if she was right? Just thinking about Morgan and her stupid idea sent shooting pains through his heart. He wanted to keep her safe more than anything, but she had this self-destruct button that she kept pressing, and he didn't even know if she realised she was doing it.

'Let's get back to the station and do some checks on Edward Winder.'

'Yeah, and you better face Morgan because she's going to be as mad as a hatter for sending her off with Des.'

'After her little stunt she's lucky I don't make her work with him permanently.'

'You better not, I mean you're okay, Ben, and no offence, but I like being able to boss him around a little. Plus, he's terrified of Morgan, you know that, don't you?'

'What, he's more scared of her than you and your big mouth?'

'I'll ignore that tasteless remark. Yes, he thinks she's like some cursed harbinger of doom and death. She puts the fear of God into him, so if you make him work with her much longer, he'll be going off sick with the stress and you'll never get him back to work.'

'Christ, what a bunch of arseholes you lot are.'

Amy began to laugh so hard that tears leaked from her eyes.

Ben glanced at her and grinned.

When she finally composed herself, she replied. 'Yes, we are but at least we're your arseholes.'

This set her off laughing again, and Ben joined in.

THIRTY-FOUR

Des left Morgan and strolled off in the direction of town. He turned around and shouted, 'Do you want anything to eat?'

She did, but she was too stubborn to ask him to get her anything. She'd rather starve or as Ben would say, *shit in her hands and clap*. She went inside the station, wishing she could speak to Brian and ask him what he thought of her idea. She took out her phone feeling guilty. She hadn't even had the courtesy to ring him and tell him that Sara was safe. Which was unforgivable seeing as how he'd driven this far to try and help them all. She rang him and was surprised when he didn't answer, although given the campsite she shouldn't be so shocked. It wasn't a fabulous reception area for phone signals. The forest was too dense of an area.

'Hey, Brian, it's Morgan. Good news, we have Sara and she's alive. Ring me when you can.'

She went inside the police station and made her way up to an empty office on the third floor. She didn't want to see Des for at least an hour, or Ben and Amy. As she was walking upstairs, she heard a voice call, 'Morgan, a word.'

She turned to see Tom behind her, beckoning her towards

him, and she wondered what she'd done now. This place was a nightmare; you were either the star of the week or the disaster of the month.

'Yes, sir?'

He opened his office door, and she followed him inside. 'Please, sit down.'

'Am I in trouble?'

A look of genuine surprise crossed his face. 'No, why do you ask that? Should you be? Are you wanting to confess to something? because if you are I suggest you get yourself to St Mary's for confessional. I haven't got time for any of that kind of thing. We still have a violent man to apprehend.'

She smiled, thinking if she told a priest what she got up to it may just finish them off.

'How did you get on with the forest rangers?'

'All we got was a name from the list of volunteers, of a man who is no longer allowed to volunteer. That's it.'

'Who was it that got themselves struck off a volunteer job? I mean that's some effort to not be allowed to work your backside off for free.'

'Edward Winder.'

Tom closed his eyes. 'Why does that name ring a bell?'

Morgan leaned forwards. 'It does?'

He nodded. 'Let me think.'

He screwed his face into a tight ball, and Morgan wondered at the number of lines. She made a note never to do this in case she ended up needing Botox years before she should. He slammed his fist down on the desk, making her jump.

'Got it, goes by the name of Ed. It was a hit and run; he killed an eleven-year-old on his way to the shop for some milk one rainy night in March. The bastard didn't even stop to see if he was okay or call an ambulance. He left him there like a broken rag doll at the side of the road. A bus driver saw him and phoned it in, it was terrible.'

'When was this?'

'In 1999, the hit and run. It took us a while to find the sneaky little bastard. He was hiding out at his cousin's campsite, where he worked.'

Morgan felt the tiny hairs on the back of her neck prickle, and goosebumps appeared on her arms.

'Forest Pines Campsite?'

'Yes, bloody hell, why didn't I think of this sooner?'

'With all due respect, sir, until we got that name there wasn't an awful lot to go on, and it's only by complete chance that we actually got his name.'

Tom was shaking his head; he was annoyed at himself, she knew that, but this wasn't his blame to shoulder.

'He must have taken the earlier victims and then got caught for the hit and run, which would explain why there were no more until now. I'll ask Des to do some checks on him when he gets back. How are we going to play this? We don't want to scare him away; he knows the area well and is possibly hiding out. Do you think that John and Eleanor Winder know he's here or in the area?'

'I hope to Christ they don't because if they do, it incriminates them, doesn't it? I think we may be able to flush him out, but I do need a volunteer, one that Ben isn't going to have a mental breakdown over. It needs to be a lone female, like you suggested earlier. I think if we were to put one there as bait, he wouldn't be able to help himself.'

Morgan was nodding. 'Let me do it. If he's still around, he's going to be furious that Sara got away from him and want to prove to himself that he's still got it.'

Tom smiled. 'Morgan, I would love to use you, I really would, but I think Ben might just kill me, and I've given it a lot of thought and I need you to be working it from our side.'

'You're the boss. What's the problem if I'm a willing volunteer? I've been in difficult situations before and survived. What did HQ say?'

'They're not as on board as I would have liked.'

'But, we have to do something. We can't let him drive around looking for another victim. What if we didn't tell them and did a covert operation?'

He looked at her but shook his head. 'I'm getting too old for this; I'm thinking of retiring after we've put this to bed. I haven't told anyone except Christine, but she's over the moon; she thinks I've served my time for Queen and country. I'd like to take it easy. I have a stomach ulcer, you know, and I'm not blaming you, Morgan, but since you joined the team things have been a lot more, what's the word I'm looking for?'

She shrugged, feeling bad for Tom. He looked tired. 'Intense?'

'Yes, intense and downright traumatic. I don't know how you're holding up. I suppose because you're young you can cope with it, but trust me, when you get older and begin to slow down these things can come back to haunt you. Make sure you get the counselling now to help you work through all these difficult situations you've been in. I'm not sure throwing you to the wolves one more time is such a cracking idea. It sounds perfect but on paper it probably is a terrible one.'

'I'm fine, I can cope. I want to do this, Tom. I want to catch this guy for Florence and Sara's sakes, before anyone else has to suffer like they have. Please, let me do it?'

He nodded. 'I'll see what I can do.'

THIRTY-FIVE

When Morgan went back to the office it was a full house. Des was crunching his way through a packet of pickled onion Monster Munch. Ben and Amy were also there. She nodded at them and sat at her desk. Her stomach was churning so much she thought she might throw up and she didn't know why. She wanted to do this more than anything, but it was Ben she was worried about. He hadn't been the same with her since she'd first mentioned Gary Marks, and when Tom had suggested this earlier he'd almost blown a fuse. Amy was typing away on her computer and didn't even look in her direction.

She coughed, standing at the front of the room waiting until she had everyone's attention. They all looked at her, and she cursed her cheeks for turning into burning red splotches of embarrassment.

'The boss said he remembers Ed Winder; he is a distant relation to John Winder and was working at the campsite when the first victim would have gone missing. He got sent to prison for a hit and run on an eleven-year-old boy who died at the scene, and he was hiding away at the campsite.'

Ben shook his head. 'I knew it, the lying little bastards.'

Amy whooped from behind her monitor. 'Found him, here he is.'

They all crowed around her desk to look at the mugshot of Edward Wayne Winder. Morgan was surprised to see that the guy who was dressed in a camouflage T-shirt with a dark stubble on his chin resembled an older version of Tom Hardy. He was good-looking which kind of threw her because she knew he was a monster and had expected him to look like one. The one thing which sent a cold shiver down her spine was how black his eyes looked. They were staring at the camera with an intensity that she found both terrifying and mesmerising.

'Obviously he's twenty years older now; he could be grey for all we know, but damn he's easy on the eyes, isn't he?'

Morgan was nodding. Ben and Des looked at them both, the distaste evident on their faces.

'He's a kiddie killer and probably a serial killer not to mention a killer of old women – how do you find that attractive?' Des was shaking his head.

Amy answered. 'I'm not saying he's the marrying kind, Des, but he's, you know, better looking than your average creep.'

Ben held up his hand. 'Enough.'

Tom threw the door open so hard it knocked another chunk of plaster from the wall. He walked over to Amy's desk.

'Yes, that's Ed Winder. Better looking than your average weirdo, or at least that's what the papers said when he was brought in for the hit and run. Right then, what's your plan to apprehend him? because if you don't have one then Morgan and I do.'

Ben tore his eyes away from the picture on the screen to stare at first Tom and then Morgan.

'And what is this grand plan? Tell me you've changed your mind and it doesn't involve putting Morgan at risk?'

Tom looked a bit sheepish for the first time since Morgan

had become a part of his team, and she wondered if they were taking this too far.

'Well, it's agreed we will set up a perimeter and try to lure him out. If we all ascend en masse to the campsite then we'll never see him again. He'll disappear for good; he has the transport and clearly has false plates, so I should imagine he'll slip through the net pretty easily.'

'Not if we put traffic officers on all the routes out of the area, he won't. What if he's already left? He could be long gone.'

It was Morgan who answered Ben's question. 'I don't think so, I think he's lying low and furious about Sara Fletcher getting the better of him. He's just biding his time to take another victim, to prove to himself and to us that he hasn't lost it.'

'No. On my life I'm not authorising this madness.'

'Come on, Ben, we'll have plain-clothes armed officers surrounding the area, pitched in tents and in the woods. As soon as he gets near to Morgan's tent, we'll swoop in and arrest him. Wouldn't be too bad if someone accidentally shot the bastard either.'

'You're insane, the pair of you.'

Tom shrugged, and Morgan looked back at the picture on the screen. Gary Marks was a similar type of man to Ed Winder: both of them handsome in a terrible way and as evil as the devil himself. She turned back to look at Ben and realised he looked distressed. She felt awful.

'We have to bring John and Eleanor Winder in first. How do we know that they aren't involved? They certainly weren't forthcoming with any information about him. If they're on site they will warn him. We need to arrest them at the same time and bring them in before they get the chance to get a message to him. If we arrest them, at least we can hold them for twenty-four hours while we give this a go.'

'I'll go get the warrants authorised.' Tom left them to it.

Ben was pacing up and down. 'There has to be a better way.

What if he's been hanging around and seen you there, Morgan? It won't work. It needs to be someone he won't have seen if we're going to do this.'

Amy nodded. 'I'll do it.'

Morgan shook her head. 'You've been at the campsite almost as much as I have, if not more. You can't do it either.'

There was a knock on the door, and Brenda from the front desk opened it, popping her head through the gap. 'Blimey, you lot look as if you're plotting something dreadful. There's a Sofie Ravetta at the front desk wants to speak to you, Morgan.'

Morgan smiled at her. 'Thanks, Brenda, tell her I'll be down in a few minutes.'

Brenda shut the door, and she turned to Ben. 'Sofie would be perfect.'

He rolled his eyes and shook his head at the same time. 'We can't ask her, that's just morally wrong.'

Morgan shrugged. 'I bet she would do it in a heartbeat. What's the harm in asking?'

Ben slumped onto the nearest chair, one hand resting against his chest. 'I think you're physically killing me. I have chest pains. Do any of you know where the nearest defibrillator is?'

Amy shook her head. 'That's indigestion, you idiot, off that meat and potato pie you rammed down your throat before.'

'At least let me ask her. If she won't, then I'll do it and we'll have to take the chance he doesn't recognise me.'

'She looks like you, Morgan. What's the difference?' Ben whispered.

'She did until the last time I spoke to her. Her hair is no longer red: she dyed it pink and purple. She'd be perfect.'

Before he could tell her not to, she was out of the door and heading down to the front office waiting area.

* * *

Sofie was the only person in there. She opened the door and grinned at her, waving her in. Leading her into one of the small interview rooms, she let her take a seat then shut the door, sitting opposite her.

'How's Sara?'

'Amazing, considering. I just wanted to come and say thank you.'

'I'm glad she's okay. Thank God she didn't let him get the better of her, and why do you want to say thank you? She did this all by herself. We weren't quick enough to find her.'

Sofie was shaking her head. 'Well, she's always been a bit stubborn, so I'm grateful she didn't just roll over and die. Yes, I do know how hard you've all been working to bring her back. I was a bit unfair the other day when I shouted at you all. So, thank you.'

Morgan grinned at her. 'I love your hair, and that's very kind of you.'

'Do you have any news on the sick fuck who took her? Have you caught him yet?'

'There's a lot going on at the moment, but we have some very good leads; in fact, Sofie, how would you feel about helping us catch him?'

Sofie stared into Morgan's eyes. 'Hell, yeah I'm in.'

Morgan nodded. 'This could be dangerous and it's a lot to ask of you. If you don't want to then you can say no and it's absolutely no problem at all.'

'What is it you want me to do?'

'I can't give you any details just yet because we would need to finalise them, and you can't discuss this with anyone, not even Sara. We need someone to camp where Sara did. We want to try and drag him out of the hole he's hiding in, but we need someone to act as bait. You won't be alone, the whole area will be flooded with armed officers; they'll be in the closest tents, and in the woods, watching you. He won't get near to you, but hopefully he will get close enough for us to arrest him.'

Sofie leaned over and high-fived Morgan. 'I'm in, babe, will there be lots of hot coppers with guns? And have you seen these nails? I'll claw his eyes out if he gets too near.' She waved her fingers in the air with the longest set of acrylic nails Morgan had ever set eyes on.

Morgan nodded. 'Good, make sure you do, but he won't get close. We won't let him.'

'What are we waiting for? Let's go.'

'We have to set it all up. We will pick you up later on and someone will drive you to the campsite once everything is in place. Thank you, Sofie, you have no idea how much this means.'

She stood up. 'No, thank you. It's like an episode of *Vera* only fifty times more exciting, and I'm not doing it for you, this is for Sara and the other women he thought he had the right to kill.'

'I'll phone you once we're ready to go. Is that okay?'

'I'll be ready. I don't like camping though, will someone make sure there's no spiders in the tent before I go inside?'

Morgan laughed. 'Serial killers are fair game, spiders aren't, that's fine. I'll make sure it's thoroughly checked.'

She saw Sofie out and went back to tell the rest of the team the good news; at least Ben should be happy that she wasn't putting herself in any risk of danger. She just prayed that Sofie wasn't either, because how would they live with themselves if the worst happened?

THIRTY-SIX

Gary Marks had shaved his hair after his escape from HMP Manchester. He'd also taken to wearing a camouflage baseball cap to keep his head warm. Getting older he felt the cold more than he had when he was younger. He left the cramped bedsit that he shared with three other men and wandered down the high street. It was surprising how often he saw Morgan as she went about her daily business, but Rydal Falls had never been a huge town. It was busy during tourist season and far easier to blend in, especially with the camera around his neck that he'd stolen from a chair outside a café while the Japanese owner had gone inside to order. He'd just walked past and scooped it up from the chair they'd left it on. He didn't use it; he didn't even look at the pictures on it because he wasn't remotely interested in them. He liked that it made him look extra touristy and not like an escaped convict, most of the time. He knew where Morgan lived. He'd seen the pictures in the newspapers when her brother, his son, had been arrested and recognised the old Georgian house on Singleton Park Road, although it had been a derelict home when he'd lived around here. While he'd been locked up it had been renovated into modern apartments. It was a fair old walk to reach it, but he'd done it on several occasions to try and catch a glimpse of Morgan at home. It was hard for him to comprehend how one of his kids had been a killer and the other a hunter of killers, and both of them supreme at their own choice of sport.

Did she lie awake at night pondering similar questions? he wondered. Did she ask herself how she had a family of murderous relations, yet she was the polar opposite? He shrugged, who knew? He had a sneaking suspicion that she did.

As he wandered around, he looked at the headlines on the local paper, the words ALIVE in big, bold print and a photograph of the missing camper underneath it filled the front page. That was a turn up; he'd fully expected her to be dead. He had his suspicions about who had taken her, and he doubted he was going to be very pleased with her escape. This was a very interesting turn of events; in prison he'd shared a cell for some time with a man who had lived around here. He used to brag that he'd done some terrible things, far worse than Gary, which had kind of pissed him off a little, but for all he knew the guy was a fantasist. People were so full of crap in prison. They liked to tell tales that you just knew were bullshit, but he'd taken an interest in Ed. Mainly because he'd come from the same area as him, but also because he'd wanted to know if he was as bad as he made out to be.

Ed hadn't been arrested for killing the women, he claimed; he'd hit a kid and killed them crossing the road. Ed had told Gary that the reason he couldn't stop was because he had a woman tied up in the back of his van at the time. He'd had to go and kill her and then get his van cleaned up before the cops came looking for him. Gary had assumed he was telling him porkies to make himself look badder than he was, but now he wasn't so sure. Had Ed Winder been telling the truth all along? Maybe he was sicker and more twisted than Gary had ever dreamed. But if so, it was time for him to up his game. There couldn't be two of them in Rydal Falls, although it was a nice distraction from him. While the cops were chasing their tails looking for Ed, it gave him free rein to do as he pleased.

He figured it was about time he paid his one and only daughter a visit. He'd neglected her for far too long. It was time to make things up to her, if she'd let him, and if that didn't work then it was time to finish this for good.

THIRTY-SEVEN

Ben was still pacing up and down when she returned to the office. His complexion was an unusual shade of white she'd never seen before and he looked ill. She glanced at Amy, pointing to his back and mouthed, 'Is he okay?' Amy shrugged. Ben looked at Morgan with an expression of quiet fury tinged with sadness, and she felt a yearning to throw her arms around him and hold him tight. They'd had so many missed chances. All she wanted was just one to show him how much she cared, but there was so much else to think about right now.

'Sofie is in.'

Ben shook his head. 'She's as nuts as the rest of you then, is she? Am I the only one who thinks this is a terrible idea?'

'What else can we do, Ben? You saw what he did to Florence, what he would have done to Sara given the opportunity. How else can we bring him in?'

'By doing the legwork, proper police work, surveillance on the campsite, on the last known addresses, patrols on the roads.'

'We haven't got the time. He's not going to let this one go, and all of the above takes a lot of time, effort and resources that we just don't have.'

'And what makes you so sure that he's going to strike again, Morgan? What, are you some kind of psychic now? Surely if he does, he's not going to go back to Forest Pines. You're telling me he's clever, and if he is then he's going to know that we're watching the place.'

Both Des and Amy were staring at them. Morgan could feel Amy's eyes burning into the back of her neck, but she wasn't backing down.

'I'm sorry, Ben, but I think he will. I think he's that cocky and full of himself that he'll go back there and try and take someone from under our nose, just to prove that he can. He worked there before he went to prison. He's going to know the area like the back of his hand. It's his hunting ground, we'll be in his territory, and he will be feeling so full of himself he won't expect such a huge ambush.'

'And what if it all goes wrong, he manages to abduct Sofie and she dies because we fucked it all up, what then?'

Tom, who was sitting in Morgan's chair, stood up. 'Then I'll take the blame. This was my idea, and I shall take the fall should anything awful happen. But I agree with Morgan, he's too sure of himself to think that he'll get caught. It's up to us to prove him wrong. I fully think that we can snare him in the act, or I wouldn't be putting my career and reputation on the line.'

Ben looked from Tom to Morgan. He shook his head, pulled his small leather warrant card holder out of his trouser pocket and threw it on the table.

'I can't be a part of this, I won't be a part of it.' Then he turned and walked out of the room, leaving them all staring at him open-mouthed. Morgan wanted to chase after him and beg him to come back. She didn't want to do this job if he wasn't here to boss her around. She felt all the bravado and confidence that had been brimming from her seconds ago dissipate and her shoulders drooped.

'I should go after him; we can't let him leave.'

Tom reached out and took hold of her arm. 'Let him sulk for a while, he'll be back. We don't have the time to go chasing after him just to make him feel better. This isn't about him, it's about Ed Winder. I've spoken to Al; he's gathering his team together. We're going to try and get both John and Eleanor Winder to come here. We can't go storming into the campsite and arrest them. Ed will know about it if he's hanging around and be gone before we know what's happened.'

Morgan had never felt so torn in her life. She wanted to run after Ben, she was on his team, but she also wanted to catch the killer. She stared at the door Ben had stormed through seconds ago then closed her eyes and prayed she was doing the right thing.

'If I can't go then neither can Amy or Des. We've all been there numerous times, hanging around asking questions. It has to be officers who haven't been the focus of everyone's attention.'

She crossed to the window and stared down onto the car park; Ben's car was idling away, fumes from his exhaust blowing in the wind, and she wondered if he thought she'd betrayed him, because she felt as if she had. Tearing her gaze away she turned to Tom.

'Yes, of course. That's true if he's been hanging around, then no one involved in the official investigation can attend the campsite.'

'What about Al, he was there?'

'He was in uniform though; he'll look different in plain clothes. I think he'll be okay. Right then, let's go and see what the plan is.'

Tom didn't wait for anyone to follow; instead he strode out of the room, a man on a mission, and Morgan felt as if her whole world had just been turned upside down. Amy, who had been surprisingly quiet, stood up.

'Well, what a complete balls-up this is going to be.'

Des was nodding, a smug grin on his face, and Morgan wanted to throw something at him. He'd done nothing but be condescending and a pain in the arse all day.

'What are we going to do?'

Amy turned to Des. 'For a start, Des, if you don't stop grinning like that, I'm going to punch you. It's not funny.'

'I never said it was.' He tutted under his breath, and Morgan saw Amy's fingers clench into tight fists. She stepped in between them.

'We need to bring Ben back. We can't do it without him.'

'He's pretty stubborn when he wants to be. I'm not sure we can.'

Tom burst through the door. 'The Winders have left the campsite. I want you two ready to arrest them and bring them in. There's a patrol car following at a safe distance. As soon as they get far enough away from public view, they'll pull them over. You two can do the honours and get them booked in and interviewed.'

Amy nodded. 'Yes, boss.'

Morgan waited for him to tell her to go with Amy, but he looked at Des. 'Chop, chop, Des, move your backside. There's no time to lose.'

Tom left again, followed by Amy and Des. Morgan looked around the room, a feeling of uneasiness settling on her shoulders. She wasn't sure if it was because Ben had walked out or if it was because of something else. Brian. They needed to get him out of the campsite or at least away from it for a couple of hours. He was bound to have been noticed by Ed if he was hanging around like they thought he was, and Ed would have seen her talking to him. Taking out her phone she rang his number and smiled to hear his soft, pleasant voice.

'Morgan, what can I do for you? Well done by the way, I got your message about Sara, that's just wonderful. Has she been able to give you any leads on The Travelling Man?'

'It is great news. There's a lot going on at the moment, Brian. I can't share everything with you but can I ask you a huge favour?'

'Anything.'

'Would you be able to drive to my house? You can either park up and stay the night on the drive or I'll meet you there and let you inside. Just until we have everything under control.'

'Ah, this sounds very promising. I like the sound of that. Can you tell me anything at all about the investigation?'

She paused, as much as she liked him and was grateful to him for all of his help and input, this wasn't something that she could comfortably divulge to him.

'I'm sorry, when it's all over I will, but for now I can't really say much.'

He laughed. 'Of course, I'm just being far too cheeky for my own good. Yes, I'd be more than happy to drive to yours, and I would love a hot shower if that's not too much trouble.'

She laughed. 'I'll meet you there. You help yourself to whatever you want.' She ended the call and felt a bit better that he was going to be out of the way and safe. She could nip home, let Brian in, then go and find Ben to check he was okay. There was still a dark, crawling sensation in the pit of her stomach just thinking about what the next couple of hours were going to bring. She wished she hadn't asked Sofie to do this now. She could have worn a wig or a hat to disguise herself.

THIRTY-EIGHT

Ben had driven away far too fast, but he was furious and sick to the teeth of all of this. He'd managed to get as far as the entrance to his street, but he hadn't turned into it. He was parked with the engine running, questioning his entire set of beliefs surrounding his role and ability to lead his team of detectives who were hell-bent on throwing themselves in harm's way on a regular basis. Actually, it wasn't his entire team, it was only one of them – Morgan. just thinking her name made his heart race, and he wasn't sure it was in a good way. Pulling down the flap of the sun visor he stared at himself in the small, illuminated mirror. His hair was greying faster than he had ever imagined it could, which was part of the reason he'd told the barber to shave it all off. He had subtle lines around his eyes, which were classed as laughter lines, he supposed, but there were deep grooves on his forehead which were definitely not from laughing. He felt old and way out of his depth, even though he was only in his late forties. Pushing the visor back up he leaned his head back, closing his eyes to try and ease the tension headache that was pounding inside of his temple and whispering to himself *what are you going to do, Matthews, ask her to stop putting herself in ridiculous situations? Maybe you could convince her to take a desk job in the call centre?*

Opening his eyes, he stared out onto the park opposite. He knew he couldn't do any of the above because Morgan Brookes wasn't his; she wasn't anyone's. She was her own woman who despite the worry and heartache, not to mention heartburn she caused him, would continue to do her own thing regardless of what he or anyone else asked her to do. He shook his head; he'd lost his wife because he'd been a lousy husband. He couldn't afford to lose Morgan because he was an even lousier boss who had thrown in the towel because the going was tough. A sharp pain ripped through his chest at the memory of losing Cindy. He had never thought he would recover from that. He'd been on autopilot until the day Morgan was abruptly thrown into his life. He had let his wife down badly; there was no way he could do that to Morgan now. As crazy as her ideas and work ethics were, he realised now more than ever that he wanted her in his life, and not just as a friend.

His phone began to ring, and he hoped it was her. Answering it he heard Tom's voice bark:

'Have you got over yourself yet? Are you ready to get back to work or do you need some time off, Ben? And I'm not asking this as your boss, I'm asking because I'm genuinely concerned about you. I know things have been tough and you never really took the time out to stop and grieve for Cindy.'

Ben rolled his eyes. 'Spare me the rest of that, Tom. I appreciate you taking the time to check up on me but I'm fine. I just needed to clear my head; it was getting a bit too intense not to mention downright dangerous. But I'm clear-headed now. So, what's happening and where do you need me?'

Laughter filled his ear.

'You're a smart-arse at times, Matthews, but I like you a lot and always have. You're a good copper, don't let your pining for Brookes cloud your judgement. When this is over maybe it's time

you did something about this schoolboy crush of yours. I mean it's great to see you getting on with your life, but when your feelings are affecting your professional judgement, well it's time to make up your mind about what you want and decide on a course of action. If she turns you down because you're just too old and ugly, not to mention depressive, then at least you know eh, and the rest of us can breathe a sigh of relief.'

It was Ben's turn to laugh. 'I see you've been taking lessons from the Amy Smith speak your mind school of thought.'

'It needed to be said and someone had to say it. I figured it might as well be me. I'm just sad I won't be around to see it.'

'Why, where are you going?'

'After this is over I'm handing in my resignation. If you think you're having a hard time getting to grips with all of this, then spare a thought for me. I was supposed to be winding down to retirement not leading a band of outlaws into gunfights at the OK Corral on a monthly basis. I'm hanging up my boots and going to drive Christine mad, but at least we'll have time together, which is more than we do now.'

'I'll miss you.'

'Thanks, like a hole in the head, eh? So, are you ready for an update of what's happening up to now?'

'Ready as I'll ever be.'

'Great, well the good news is John and Eleanor Winder left the campsite not long after you left the station on their way to pick up a Chinese takeaway from Keswick. Luckily for us a patrol car spotted them and tailed them until they were well clear of Forest Pines. They are now both in custody getting booked in, much to their distress and upset, especially about the wasted takeaway but, you know, shit happens. I've asked Amy and Des to interview them both, as Morgan so rightly pointed out that none of them should be anywhere near the campsite, because if Ed Winder has been lurking around there is a very good chance he'll have noticed them, and it will spook him.'

This news made Ben's heart begin to beat a little slower for the first time in over an hour.

'Who is watching Sofie? Is she there yet?'

He was hoping that Tom was going to tell him they'd scrapped that idea.

'She is being whisked there as we speak. One of Al's team is there and has already put a tent up for her. The pitches nearest to hers are now full of sweaty, plain-clothes officers, and there are armed officers in the forest, dotted along the way to the tent.'

'Surely if he enters the site that way he's going to spot them from a mile away?'

'They're not directly on the path he used, and if he does spot them they'll have to bring him in. I mean why would anyone be wandering through that forest in the dark, anyway? It's not ideal but it's a good enough motive to arrest him.'

'Where is Morgan?'

'That's a good question. She muttered something about picking something up from home then she was going to come back to the station to help with the interviewing of the Winders.'

Ben would have kissed Tom if he could, the relief was so strong that for once she was nowhere near a dangerous situation. 'Good, where do you want me then?'

'I think if you could go back to the station to be ready for when they bring our man in that would be best. You could even help Amy interview the Winders while we're waiting. It could be a very long night.'

'That's fine by me, I'll see you soon.'

'No, I'm at the campsite parked in the armed response vehicle with Al behind the main office. I'll see you when I get back.'

Tom cut him off as the line went dead, and Ben momentarily closed his eyes and whispered *thank you, God, I owe you big time*. Then he set off driving back to the station. Maybe this was all going to be just fine.

THIRTY-NINE

Morgan rushed into her apartment, turning on all the lights. She wanted to double check the information Brian had given to her in the folder, to see if they had missed anything that mentioned an Edward Winder as a suspect in any of the cases. She left the front door ajar for Brian who should be here soon. Picking up the brown paper folder full of printouts, she sat on the edge of the chair and began scanning the documents. There was a knock at the door and she heard a faint, 'Hello.'

'In here, Brian, come in.'

She was reading the police report about the murder Brian had been the DI for, to see if they had any suspects listed, and realised that Brian couldn't have heard her. Placing it on the chair next to her, she stood up and walked across to the long entrance hall to her apartment. There was a man standing there dressed head to toe in camouflage gear, and she felt her blood turn to ice as a fear raw and primitive ran down her spine, making her shiver. His head was lowered so she couldn't see his face, but she ran through Sara Fletcher's description of her abductor in her mind: male dressed in camouflage trousers and T-shirt, around five eleven with sandy-coloured hair.

He coughed then spoke in a voice so low she had to strain to hear him. 'Hello, Morgan, what's the matter, are you not pleased to see me? You left the door open. I assumed you were expecting me.'

Her eyes opened wide as she wondered how this man knew her, a crawling sensation at the base of her spine as she said his name, 'Brian?'

The man laughed, shrugging his shoulders. 'Maybe, I can be whoever you want me to be, darling.'

He kept his head bowed but he kind of looked familiar. Was it Brian? And then it struck her. 'Gary?'

'Close.'

She couldn't tell who it was. He had the same build as both Brian and Gary Marks. She didn't want to believe it could be Brian, that she could have been so wrong about him. He'd been inside here, they'd shared pizza. Her mouth dry, she gulped, realising that whoever he was she had to do something to protect herself. She had nothing; her cuffs and CS gas were in the glove compartment of her car along with her police radio. She took a step forwards towards him, then swung around and dived back into her lounge, her legs pumping to reach the kitchen and grab the biggest knife out of the drawer she could find. She would put him out of action first and then discover who he was. The drawer was in sight – she could almost reach it, but she knew he was there, right behind her. A whooshing sound as something heavy cut through the air behind her made her lunge to her right side. She glanced as a large hammer smashed into the side of her marble worktop, shattering the corner. Mute with shock, she realised that could have been her skull. While her would-be assailant picked up the hammer and tried to grip it after the shockwaves it must have sent up his arm, she turned and ran back towards the front door. If she could only get outside, she could hide from him. She hated running but she had never pumped her legs so hard, and she heard him clatter around behind her. She didn't turn to see how close he was, there was no time. Instead she threw herself out of the front door, then out of the open communal door, turning to slam it into his face.

As she began to run down the steps, she felt her foot connect with something large and heavy. There was a bloody huge Amazon box dumped on the top step. She couldn't stop herself as she began to fall forwards, taking the box with her. She landed on the gravel with a loud thud, the skin on her knees grazing as handfuls of tiny stones that stung like mad buried themselves inside the soft flesh. Loud footsteps behind her made her begin to crawl, even though her knees were on fire, the pressure of her weight on them embedding the stones further into the skin. Opening her mouth to scream she never got more than a 'He—' before she felt her head crack with the impact of the hammer blow, and she fell forwards, the world in front of her turning red and blurry. She lifted her elbow to protect her head, and a shooting pain as the hammer smashed into her filled her with a burning, white-hot pain so intense coupled with the head injury. She fell like a sack of coal and lay bleeding onto the white stones, which were quickly turning a deep shade of red.

FORTY

Ben was almost at the station when he realised that he couldn't sit around there waiting for something to happen at the campsite. If Morgan was supposed to be here he could relax a little and head to Forest Pines. Apart from the initial investigation, he hadn't been there much at all, and it was dark. He had a North Face jacket in the boot. If he swapped his suit jacket for that and the beanie hat he wore when it was cold he'd fit in just fine. It was better than being on pins pacing up and down waiting for news that they'd caught Ed Winder. Turning the car around he headed for the campsite and hoped that he wasn't too late, although there was complete silence on the radio. Tom had issued the order that only emergency calls be passed while this was ongoing, so it made a nice change not to have to listen to the constant chatter like usual.

When he drove through the entrance to Forest Pines, he had an urge to pull over and phone Morgan, but he ignored it and carried on driving. But it was there, a constant niggle in the back of his mind. He parked outside the reception building and took out his phone to ring her, just to satisfy himself that she was exactly where she was supposed to be and not here out in the woods, alone. Which if he was honest with himself was what he was expecting her to do. It rang until voicemail kicked in, and he hung up. She was probably annoyed with him for storming out before; he had been a little dramatic. Never mind, he'd make it up to her, and the rest of his team. He was entitled to let off a bit of steam now and again, especially working with those three.

As he got out of the car, he heard a low whistle coming from around the corner of the building, and he quickly slipped out of his suit jacket, throwing it into the back of the car, and grabbing the North Face one he hurried in the direction of whoever had whistled at him, tugging the beanie onto his head.

As he reached the corner of the building Al whispered, 'What the hell are you doing here? You could have been tasered. Everyone is on high alert. They watched you come along the road and two taser officers from Carlisle, who I had to borrow, were ready to red dot you the minute you opened the door.'

'Sorry, I couldn't sit in the nick twiddling my thumbs. How's it going?'

Al had hold of the sleeve of his jacket and was pulling him around the back out of sight.

'Not much happening. The girl is in the tent. I have officers all over the place and not one sighting of anyone looking suspicious. Well, that was until you turned up. I thought Tom told you to stay at the nick?'

Ben shrugged. 'Morgan isn't here, is she?'

Al shook his head. 'Nope, she is most definitely not. I wasn't having her messing everything up or getting herself in trouble. This is crazy enough as it is without throwing her into the mix. I can't believe Tom got the authority to go through with this.'

Ben looked at him, a slow realisation came over him. Come to think about it, Ben had been shocked, not to mention surprised, that they had been given the go ahead to carry this out at such short notice, and he felt a sinking sensation as he realised there might be a very good chance that he hadn't. He had been adamant this was what he wanted to do, but had he got permission? Because if he hadn't, and it all went wrong... Al's radio buzzed and a voice whispered, 'Movement in the trees, male, alone, walking along the path towards the campsite.'

Al answered, 'Is he heading towards the tent?'

There was what seemed like the longest two second pause of Ben's life, then the voice answered, 'No, he's not even heading in that direction. What should we do?'

Al looked at Ben. 'What do you think? Why is there someone out in the woods so late on their own?'

He shrugged. 'Tell them to take him down. If he's innocent and is a camper who's lost or been out for an evening stroll, we should soon be able to clear that up.'

Al nodded. 'Go, go, go.' Then he took off running in the direction of the tent where Sofie was curled up inside reading a book. Ben followed him, praying that this was Ed Winder who was sneaking around, and they were about to put a stop to the murderous bastard's fun and games and keep Sofie safe.

FORTY-ONE

Gary Marks arrived on foot across the fields that led from the high street to Morgan's apartment. As he was clambering out of the bushes, he saw a blue van come driving out of the drive gates far too fast. He turned to glare at the driver, wondering if it was some piece of shit copper or even Morgan, but it didn't look like anything the police drove. The one and only street light illuminated the driver's face and, for a split second, their eyes locked as they recognised each other, and then the van was driving down the quiet country road, and Gary had a sneaking suspicion that something terrible had just gone down. He jogged through the gates, and the security lights flooded the driveway, where he saw a dark stain on the pale white chippings and a crushed cardboard box. The front door was open. He knew Morgan lived in the ground-floor apartment; he'd been here before several times. Picking up his pace he ran up the steps and into the communal hallway, where her front door was wide open.

Inside, he called, 'Morgan.' He called again, louder second time, but he knew she wasn't here; he had come too late. A burning rage filled his chest: that sneaky little shit had been here, and it looked as if he'd taken her. A set of car keys lay on the small table in the hall, and he grabbed them and ran back outside, pressing the unlock button on the knackered VW Golf that he'd seen her driving around in. The car engine sounded like a tank as it came to life, and he put it into first gear and screamed out of the drive after the van, narrowly missing a campervan that was turning in. He could have phoned the police, but what good were they? By the time they arrived she would be long gone, and he realised with a burning fury that all the time he had spent pondering what to do about her had been a complete waste of time.

She was his daughter, his flesh and blood, and he owed it to her to stop whatever was happening. He had never felt particularly paternal towards either of his kids, even though Taylor obviously felt a deep connection to him. Yet he found his stomach churning at the thought of some weirdo hurting his child, which was a bit of a revelation for him because he'd fully expected to be the one to take her life. He wasn't sure where this deep-seated parental responsibility had come from, but he was going to make this right. He put his foot down on the accelerator and watched the needle as it went from thirty, to forty, fifty, sixty, seventy. He didn't dare drive any faster; the car was rattling, and it had been a long time since he'd driven these roads. A flash of red in the distance as a set of brake lights lit up the dark road ahead filled him with hope. He was catching up to him. They had labelled him a monster, well, if that little creep had hurt Morgan, he would show him exactly how much of a monster he was.

FORTY-TWO

Brian let out a high-pitched scream, almost deafening himself, as the VW Golf drove straight at him. He knew that was Morgan's car. He'd been inside it; but it hadn't been her driving, it was a man and, from the briefest of glimpses, he had a look of Gary Marks. Surely the man wasn't brazen enough to come here and steal his daughter's car? He parked the van and climbed out, his heart still beating way too fast at his near collision. The security lights came to life, illuminating the driveway as he walked towards the front door, which was wide open. Something wasn't right. He caught the deep, earthy, rusty metal scent that signified there was a large amount of blood nearby. Looking down he saw the large dark stain and bent low. Reaching out a finger he touched it then recoiled. It was blood. The years he'd spent as a detective had taught him well, and he kicked straight into investigator mode. Standing up he carefully made his way to the front door and wondered if Marks was injured. Was that why he was driving like a maniac?

'Morgan.' He called her name, managing not to sound too panicked. He was treading carefully, trying not to ruin any potential evidence. He had no idea what had happened, but he had an awful feeling it might be bad. As he reached the front door and went inside, her apartment door was wide open, and he just didn't think she would ever leave it like that. Especially not after everything she had been through. He stepped inside and yelled, 'Morgan.'

'Who are you and where is Morgan?'

He turned to see a woman dressed head to toe in Lycra, her brown hair in a high ponytail and a yoga mat tucked under her arm.

'I'm Brian, and I don't know, I'm trying to find her. Have you just come in or are you going out? Who are you?'

'Morgan's neighbour and friend.'

Emily didn't wait. She threw the yoga mat on the floor and pushed past him hovering in the entrance to her flat and ran straight in. 'Morgan.'

The silence told Brian everything he needed to know: either she was seriously injured, or she wasn't here. He followed her inside, where everything looked like it had the last time he'd been here.

'Look at the worktop.'

He came to stand next to Emily who was pointing at the shattered piece of marble. She already had her phone to her ear asking for the police and mouthed, 'Do you know Ben? Ring him now.'

He nodded, but he didn't have his phone with him, it was out in the van, so he rushed outside and saw that Emily had parked her car directly over the blood. Luckily, she hadn't walked right through it, and at least the car was shielding it from the elements. Grabbing his phone from the front passenger seat of the van, he scrolled until he found the number Morgan had given him for Ben and dialled.

'*Matthews.*'

'It's Brian Walter, I'm at Morgan's address and I think something awful has happened.'

There was a slight pause.

'*Where's Morgan?*'

'I don't know, but her neighbour, Emily, is ringing it in. There's a large pool of blood outside on the drive, a corner of the marble worktop is shattered in pieces and, as I arrived, I think, I'm not a hundred per cent sure that it was because it was such a fleeting glance, but I think I saw Gary Marks driving like a maniac in her car.'

The line went dead. He turned and went back inside to where Emily had just finished telling the control room operator a similar version of events. She turned to him, eyeing him up suspiciously.

'I've never seen you before. Do you work with Morgan?'

He noticed as she was talking she was walking backwards towards the cutlery drawer, which was open. She reached in, grabbing a large carving knife and brandished it in front of her.

'No offence, and I'll apologise when the cops arrive, but me and Morgan have been in some scary situations, I'm not taking any chances.'

He held his hands up and nodded. 'Good, that's good, just please don't get jumpy and use that thing. My wife is due home tomorrow evening from a week away with her sister, and she doesn't even know where I am. If she has to come and identify my body, she'll kill me.'

Emily laughed. 'I think you're okay, Brian, and as long as you stay away from me and don't try to attack me then we're good. Do you think we should go look and see if Morgan's injured somewhere?'

'If I was a working detective that would be my first priority but, seeing as we're in a rather awkward situation, and you have no idea who I am, it may be better to wait for the police to arrive and sort it out.'

'You stay here; I'm just going to check the bedroom and bathroom.'

He watched her walk backwards, not taking her eye off him while she navigated the apartment with the grace and ease of someone who lived here.

'Do you live here with Morgan?'

She had stopped in front of their wall of maps and Post-it notes and, fascinated, she began to study it.

'No, I live upstairs. Oh, damn, I shouldn't have told you that, should I?'

'I'm a retired DI, Emily, not some murderous freak.'

'Yeah, I bet that's what they all say.' But she smiled at him. 'What is this?' She was pointing at the maps Blu-Tacked to the wall.

'I was helping Morgan with an investigation, but it seems as if it's all gone horribly wrong.'

'She'll be okay, she always is. Has she told you about some of the stuff that's happened to her? A killer chased her into my apartment once and I had to knock him out.'

Brian smiled at her. He didn't mention the large pool of blood or the fact that he'd seen her wanted, fugitive father leaving the scene of the crime. Sirens filled the night sky, and he felt a wave of relief that he could hand this over to the professionals. He was getting far too old for all of this.

FORTY-THREE

Amy had flipped a coin with Des over who was leading the interview with John Winder. She had chosen heads, and heads it was. Eleanor was currently in cell four cooling off before her interview. She had kicked off big time when she'd been brought in to the custody suite to get booked in. Demanding to see a solicitor, demanding to know what this was all about, she'd even threatened to go to the newspapers, which had made Amy laugh. She'd replied that she was free to do as she pleased, but should their names be linked any further to Sara Fletcher's disappearance, she wouldn't be swanning around with her Louis Vuitton bags for much longer because they weren't allowed in prison. The silence had been blissful, and Eleanor hadn't uttered another word. John, on the other hand, had been nothing but stonily silent from the start, a little bit brooding and most of all polite, which hadn't been what she'd expected at all. He had been booked in and was currently waiting in interview room B for them to go in. Amy had a clipboard and had printed out the key questions she needed answering. Des was leaning over the huge desk, flirting with the custody sergeant who neither of them had ever seen before. She had to admit for some reason she was a little nervous.

'Are you ready, Desmondo?'

He turned and glared at her, and she smiled. He hated it when she called him that; but she also hated how he turned on the charm to every new woman he met, when he was a miserable bastard at heart.

He strode towards her and whispered, 'I hate it when you call me that.'

She shrugged. 'I know you do.' Then smiled at him, knocked on the door and walked inside to see an officer leaning against the wall, arms crossed, staring at the floor.

John was sitting on a chair behind the table. He looked up as they both entered but didn't walk in.

'Good evening, John, I'm Detective Constable Amy Smith and this is my colleague Detective Constable Des Black. Can I get you anything before we start? Are we waiting for a solicitor?'

John shook his head. 'No, I'm okay, and I don't need one.'

Amy sat down and pressed the record button on the tape. 'Can you state your name and date of birth for the record, please?'

He did.

'Do you know why you're here, John?'

He shook his head. 'No, well, obviously it has something to do with the missing girl, but I don't understand why I'm here.'

'Tell me about Edward Winder. How well do you know him?'

His shoulders, which had been stiff and straight, slouched down and he lowered his head. If Amy wasn't mistaken, he was breathing a sigh of relief. He stared down at his hands for a moment then looked her in the eyes.

'He's odd, very odd, but he's family.'

'When you say he's odd what do you mean by that? Can you explain to me how?'

'Ed is a cousin by marriage; he's a loner and he's been a bloody liability since he came out of prison. I told Ellie I didn't want him anywhere near the campsite, but she's always had a soft spot for him and a stupid family loyalty to her waste-of-space cousins.'

'Ellie's cousin, but I thought he was your cousin; he shares the same surname as you.'

He shook his head and tutted. 'My wife is very persistent when it comes to certain things. She didn't want to take my name which was Smith. No offence to you, Detective, she thought it was too plain and boring. When we married, I had to take her name.'

Des was jotting notes down furiously; obviously the John Winder whose record they had checked wasn't the same as the one sitting opposite him, and they needed do full checks on John Smith.

'You mentioned cousins, are there more working at the campsite?'

Her mind was spinning too many plates, trying to figure it all out.

'Yes, Miles. Miles is Ed's younger brother.'

'How old is Miles?'

She had him pegged as eighteen or nineteen; she didn't even know they were related. How had they missed this?

'Miles is thirty-two.'

Des leaned forwards. 'Do they have different surnames? I don't recall Miles giving us the name Winder.'

'He may have given you different names, but that would be Ellie's doing; she wouldn't have wanted you all sniffing around him. I don't know why she is so protective over those two, but she is.'

Des stood up. 'For the benefit of the tape, Detective Black is leaving the room.' He excused himself, leaving Amy staring at John.

She knew he was going to do intel checks on Miles, and also to let the team at the campsite know that Ed and Miles were brothers and might be in this together.

'It's a fucked-up mess, isn't it? I'm sorry, I should have come clean when it first happened, but Ellie is quite a force to be reckoned with. She would make a great gangland matriarch.'

'John, do you think that Ed took Sara Fletcher?'

He shrugged. 'Ed is certainly weird enough, but if you ask me it's Miles who you should be looking at. He's been missing in action since he spoke to Detective Brookes. He has a van that he lives out of, and it's usually parked up on site, but it was gone the day before that girl went missing and it hasn't been back since.'

'What colour is the van?'

Amy knew what he was going to say; she also knew that they were looking for the wrong guy.

'A dark, navy blue.'

She stood up. 'Interview stopped at 20.15.' She walked out of the door, turning to the officer. 'Please can you escort John back to his cell for the time being.'

Then she was out of there, running towards the heavy metal door. She hammered on it for the custody sergeant to press the automatic lock and let her out. It flew open, and she ran to the duty sergeant's office, bursting through the door, almost giving Mads a heart attack.

'I need your radio; they're looking for the wrong guy.'

'What, how do you know that? They're bringing a suspect in; apparently he was sneaking around in the woods, and Cain took him down. It's all gone to rat shit; Morgan is missing again. I'm just on my way to her house, and they think Gary Marks has taken her.'

Amy felt the blood drain from her face. 'Jesus, how long

have I been in interview for, a week? When I went in everything was tickety-boo and now...'

She keyed Ben's number into the keypad and pressed the button to make it ring. He answered straight away. 'Boss, it's not Ed Winder, and have you found Morgan?'

'*No, what do you mean not Ed Winder?*'

'He has a brother, Miles. Apparently Miles is much older than he looks, gave us false details, drives a blue van and has been missing in action since Morgan questioned him at the campsite.'

'Shit. Who has Morgan then? Where is she? Brian is sure he saw Gary Marks driving her car.'

'I'm on my way. Let me ask John if Miles has any favourite places he likes to go.'

She hung up, passed the radio back to Mads and rushed back to the custody suite. Hammering on the door to be let back in, the door clicked open, and she rushed towards the interview room, bursting through the door.

John was standing on the other side about to be led back to his cell. He jumped, along with the copper standing behind him, and she held up her hands.

'Sorry, where does Miles go, John, when he's not at work? Where does he live, does he have a favourite place to stay in this area?'

John smiled at her. 'I told you he's usually hanging around the campsite. He only came back to work here just before Ed was released. He moved to Kent, Scotland, and then France but when he realised Ed was coming home, he came back too. There's some caves he likes to go to, spends a lot of time alone in that area.'

'Rydal Caves?'

He shook his head. 'No, Millican Dalton's Caves in Borrowdale. They're situated under Castle Crag. I think there's a little car park that's very secluded that he likes to park up in. Just off the B5289.'

'Thanks.'

She was out of there and running back to the parade room. Out of breath, she ran straight into Mel, who was rushing in.

'What's happening, Amy? I got a jumbled message from Tom and came straight back.'

'We need to get to Millican Dalton's Caves. Come on, I'll tell you on the way.'

She ran into the locker room, where she retrieved her body armour, CS gas, cuffs and the radio she'd left in her locker earlier. High on fear and adrenalin, she led the way out of the station, grabbing the last set of van keys off the whiteboard, with Mel close behind.

FORTY-FOUR

Morgan lurched to one side, then the other, and she realised she was in a car. She lay on her back, the smell of diesel fumes filling her nose along with the underlying smell of defecation, and she wondered if she'd had an accident. Her head hurt so bad. Trying to lift it, she couldn't and a wave of nausea washed over her so strong that she had to try and take deep breaths to stop it, and that wasn't easy because wherever she was it smelled so bad that it was enough to make anyone puke. She reached out, feeling for the side, to see if she was on the floor of the back seat, hoping she'd find a door handle she could pull then throw herself out of. It didn't matter that she was in a moving vehicle, she'd rather take her chance on the road than with the man who had put her here. She had been right about one thing; he was pissed that Sara had escaped and was about to take his anger out on her. She couldn't let that happen; she wasn't going to be another decomposing body left to rot for years in a forest, lying on a carpet of pine needles. She closed her eyes. It would be so easy to sink back into oblivion, but she owed it to the next person who might come into contact with this crazy son of a bitch. She lay in the dark and moved her hands out as far as she could before they pressed against the wooden boards on each side. If she didn't know she was in a moving vehicle, she'd have thought she was in a coffin the space was so confined. No one knew where she was, or had Brian turned up and realised what had happened? She was praying that he had, and that he'd managed to get hold of Ben, who was on his way to rescue her just like in one of her favourite childhood fairy tales. She grimaced as the van turned a corner and she hit the side of her head, which was a bloody, throbbing mess, against the wood.

She could find nothing in this tiny space to defend herself with; she had no cuffs, literally all she had was her bare hands and harsh language. She moved her hands to reassure herself they weren't tied together, rendering her totally helpless. Why had he not tied her up? Surely he hadn't expected her to just lie here like a good girl and take her punishment. He hadn't the time to do anything else. He must have been worried that he was going to get caught. But why her? Why had he come for her? She hadn't done anything wrong as far as she knew. Except for maybe try her best to track him. She closed her eyes briefly; it was hard to stay focused, the thudding in her head making her eyelids feel as heavy as lead weights. Maybe she should have a little sleep, let Ben and the rest of the team come rescue her. It made total sense. This was where Sara had escaped from. If she could do it, then so could she. The van made a sharp turn, throwing her violently against the opposite side, and she hit her head and passed out once more.

The next time she opened one eye she let out a groan. She'd hoped this was all a bad dream, but she was still stuck in a confined space that smelled like shit and had the headache from hell. It took her a few moments to realise the van was no longer moving, and her heart, which had already been racing, felt as if it was going to jump out of her chest. The muffled sound of a door slamming made her want to cry out for her mum. The sound of doors being thrown open made her close her eyes. She wasn't going to make it easy for him. There wasn't room to move much in here, and he had put her in, so he was going to have to get her out. A small trapdoor above her opened, and she felt his shadow as it loomed over her in the dark, then a small bright torch was shone down into her box. She kept her eyes closed.

'Time to get up, sleepyhead, we have things to do.'

She didn't move or flinch. She could sense him leaning over her, staring. Watching her breathe to make sure she was still alive and, for a fleeting second, she wondered if death wouldn't be so bad after all.

'Get the fuck up, now.'

She stayed still, then a pair of hands grabbed her roughly. As they began to drag her upwards out of the hole she never flinched, lolling backwards as if still unconscious, letting him drag her dead weight out of the van. She hoped to God that he'd do his back in at the least. He was grunting and grumbling about how heavy she was, but he managed to somehow heave her out of the small space, then dragged her a few feet before dropping her out of the van onto the dark, damp, earthy floor of a wooded area.

FORTY-FIVE

Ben had arrived at Morgan's apartment in record time. He'd been speaking to Brian and Emily when he got the call from Amy, making him turn and run back to his car, leaving them both staring after him. He shouted at the officer on scene as he began reversing out of the drive and onto the road, 'Clear the scene and guard it.' He vaguely knew where he was heading, but he wasn't overly familiar with the area surrounding these caves, which he was ashamed about. He lived in one of the most beautiful areas of the country and he never made the time to go out and explore it. His stomach was a mass of nerves along with his racing heart. He didn't know whether Miles Winder or Gary Marks had Morgan, and right now it didn't really matter. Both of them were as deadly as each other. They had no proof who had taken her, but Brian had thought it was Marks driving her car. Why though? If he wanted her dead, surely he could have finished her off in the drive, where she was already injured. Why go to all the hassle of putting her into the car then stealing it? He'd have to act on the theory that it was Miles, and that they were heading to the caves.

He monitored the news coming through his radio. Cain had done well and taken out Ed Winder, who had been prowling around in the forest like some weirdo anyway. Thank God, he'd never made it to Sofie's tent. She was safe and bundled up, being whisked back to her home address to be reunited with her mum. Tom was lucky that had had such a happy ending. Now the question was: were Ed and Miles working together, or were Marks and Ed working together? He shuddered; the thought of two monsters working alongside each other to get their sick thrills was almost more than he could bear. The whole time he was driving, he was repeating the same words in his head, *please be okay, Morgan, please be okay, Morgan.*

Amy had a bit of a head start on him; the station was nearer to Buttermere than Morgan's house. He had demanded that every patrol not tied up at Forest Pines make themselves available; backup was travelling from Barrow and Penrith. Al and a team of armed officers were also heading in that direction, and it struck him that if, God forbid, Amy was wrong, then Morgan wouldn't stand a chance. This could all be some clever diversion to take them far away from the area. Morgan said the killer liked familiar places, woodland, forests, would he really bother to take her to a cave? Ben was seriously beginning to doubt that he would, unless they were surrounded by trees.

A sharp, shooting pain in his left arm temporarily made him forget everything except the eye-watering, breathless spasm. He squeezed his eyes closed for a second and felt the car begin to drift to the opposite side of the narrow road he was on. For a moment he wondered if he was about to have a massive heart attack and die in a car crash, in the middle of nowhere, while Morgan was fighting for her life. That would be tragic. But the pain subsided as quickly as it had come, and he opened his eyes, swerving and narrowly missing ploughing into a drystone wall. His heart racing, he directed the car onto the right side of the road, but not without ripping his wing mirror off in the process, and he heard it shatter against the wall then bounce to the ground. He kept on driving, slowing a little but not much.

* * *

Gary Marks hoped that the set of tail lights that kept braking now and again in the distance belonged to the van he was supposed to be following. There was a deep-seated fury inside him that was simmering away at this unfortunate turn of events. He knew this road well, had driven along it a lot when he'd been a different man, a family man, who hadn't begun to bring his sick, twisted fantasies to life yet. But this wasn't about him; this was about Ed Winder and his sick-in-the-head brother, who used to come and visit Ed in prison: his only visitor.

He lost sight of the van and realised that it must have pulled in somewhere. Swearing, he slammed his fist against the steering wheel. He'd been driving for far too long without seeing those red lights. He did the clumsiest six-point turn in the middle of the narrow road then slowed down and began driving along, looking for a turn off or car park that he must have missed. There was no way the van had managed to speed so far away from him on these roads that he wouldn't have spotted its lights in the distance.

He saw a small, hand-painted signpost that pointed towards a tiny, narrow road on the left that said, 'car park'. As he drove even slower, he put the window down and heard the sound of an engine stopping suddenly. He smiled and nodded to himself, *gotcha*.

Driving further on, he drove Morgan's car onto the side of the road into a thicket of bushes and abandoned it. He had no weapons on him. Opening the glove compartment he found a canister of pepper spray and a set of handcuffs. He shook his head but took them anyway, figuring anything was better than nothing. Shoving the heavy, metal cuffs into his jeans pocket, he uncapped the spray and clasped it tight in his hand. He would blind the bastard and then smack him with the handcuffs if there wasn't anything else more lethal to use.

FORTY-SIX

Morgan lay on the cold, rough floor afraid to open her eyes, until he stopped, leaning over her, and she could hear him banging around in the van. She was afraid to think about what he was looking for, but while he was busy, she knew this was her chance to at least try and get into the woods and out of sight, like Sara did. Unable to stand up, she turned onto all fours and began to crawl into the trees. Pine needles and stones were sticking in the palms of her hands, her head was too heavy to hold up and her knees that were already grazed and full of stones were agonising, but she kept on crawling. Looking for a branch or anything she could use as a weapon against him. It was pitch-black, there were no lights, but her hands crawled across a loose rock and she picked it up. It was big enough to do some damage if she had to, but not too heavy that she couldn't lift it. Then she heard his footsteps coming in her direction, and the bright beam of a torch wavered around the area.

'What is it with you women? For Christ's sake, why can't you just lay down and take what's coming to you, instead of always trying to get one over on me?' His voice called into the copse of trees she was heading into. His footsteps picked up the pace, and she tried to pull herself to her feet so she could run, but her legs were too wobbly. The beam of light fell onto her, and she dropped the rock gently on the ground.

'You tried, bless you. Sara had a bit more of a sporting chance, if I'm honest. She'd had a lot more time to recover from that first blow to her head. I bet that you're still disorientated and feeling as if your legs don't belong to you. Did you really think I was going to let you get away? She may have escaped, but you, Detective Brookes, were never that good.'

The harsh light was too bright, and she lifted a hand to shield her eyes and recognised her captor. 'You're good, Miles, you had me convinced you were a quiet lad when we first met, but you were never good enough to keep hold of Sara Fletcher; she was far better than you. So was Florence Brown.'

'Who?'

'The old lady you battered to death in Keswick.'

He laughed. 'Ah, she was a nosy old bird, feisty too. I did what had to be done. I'm not a granny basher though. I don't get off on that.'

'Really, I would have thought that you did. Beating an old, defenceless woman to death makes you a granny basher in anyone's eyes, you wanker.'

He lunged forwards, and she saw the axe in his right hand, swinging it at her feet. She rolled to one side and watched, amazed, as he was suddenly thrown off guard and taken down with a heavy thud as a dark figure came flying out of the trees and slammed into him. Miles let out a loud 'Ugh' as the wind was knocked from him. The torch flew out of his hand, and Morgan scrabbled towards it. She grabbed it, aiming it at the two men who were rolling around on the floor. She half expected to see Ben or maybe Cain: never in a million years did she expect to see Gary Marks throwing punches at Miles. She knew this was her chance to get away while the two men were beating the hell out of each other, but she couldn't move.

Gary lifted one hand and pressed the button on a can of pepper spray, aiming at Miles's eyes; he got a direct hit when a loud yell from Miles filled the air. Miles, who was rubbing at his right eye with the sleeve of one hand, ran at Gary, headbutting him in the chest and knocking him to the ground. Morgan let out a cry of horror as the beam from the torch glinted off the blade of the axe as it swung down towards Gary's head. He moved just in time as the blade buried itself into the ground, and Gary lunged for Miles's legs, this time taking him down to the ground.

She picked up the rock and stumbled to her feet, running towards them. Miles was on top of Gary, the axe still in his hand. She knew she had to make him drop it and did the only thing she could: she brought the rock down on the side of Miles's head as hard as she could at the same time that Gary slapped a handcuff onto his free hand. Miles grunted, but instead of falling to the floor in a heap like she'd hoped, he managed to bring the hand with the axe down and buried it into the side of Gary's neck with a loud thwack. The sound of the blade biting into flesh made her gag and she let out a scream. Lifting the rock, she hit Miles again and again, until he fell to the ground, and she kicked him as hard as she could in the kidneys. Then bending down she grabbed the hand that was now slick with Gary Marks's blood and cuffed it to his other. He lay there stunned and bleeding onto the forest floor. It was a complete role reversal, and this wasn't lost on Morgan. She kicked him as hard as she could in the nuts for good measure then turned and bent down to help Gary, who she could instantly see was bleeding to death.

She had never seen so much blood; his eyes were staring at her and, despite the horror at who he was and the crimes he'd committed, he had saved her life and she wasn't about to let him die alone without acknowledging that. She sat down next to him. Taking hold of his hand she squeezed it tight and whispered, 'Thank you.' He never took his eyes off her. Opening his mouth to speak a large, bloody bubble erupted all over his lips and chin. The axe was buried deep into the side of his neck. She couldn't pull it out to stem the bleeding; he was losing far too much blood. He tried again and this time managed a faint, single, wheezy word: 'Sorry.'

She clasped his hand as hard as she could and felt tears welling inside of her for the lost childhood she'd been denied because of the man who was close to death next to her. Despite everything, she pulled his head onto her lap as best as she could and held on to him. She had never felt such a mixture of raw emotions.

Sirens broke the silence in the distance. Miles, unable to move anywhere, let out a low groan as Gary Marks let out his last, gasping breath.

FORTY-SEVEN

Amy saw Morgan's car and the narrow entrance to the car park. Swinging the van in too fast, she almost took out a tree, scraping and dinting the side of the van, but she carried on until the van's lights illuminated the dark blue van in front of them, jumping out as Ben's car screeched into the car park behind them. Ben was out of his car and shouted, 'There,' pointing into the trees, where there was a single beam from a torch shining on the ground. Amy and Mel followed him as he ran towards it and the sight that was waiting for them just inside the trees.

Ben had the torch from his phone on, Mel had grabbed the large Maglite from the footwell of the van, and the pair of them shone it on the three bodies on the ground. Ben saw Morgan holding a man who was clearly dead, with an axe sticking out of his neck. Morgan squinted against the bright light, and he aimed it away from her eyes, relief that she was alive almost making his knees buckle. He rushed towards her. Bending down he saw the gaping, sticky injury on the side of her head and the blood, there was so much blood. Shining the torch on the dead man she was holding, he realised that it was Gary Marks.

Amy and Mel were standing over the other man.

Amy looked down at him and tutted in disgust. 'Miles Winder, you are under arrest.'

Ben heard her reading Miles his rights, but he had turned his attention back to Morgan.

'How, I mean what?'

There were tears in her eyes, and she looked more distressed than he'd ever seen her since the day they'd met. Inhaling, she whispered, 'I don't know, but he saved my life, Ben. He came out of nowhere and fought for me. I couldn't let him die without acknowledging that.'

He reached out and stroked her cheek, wiping the single tear that was rolling down it. He nodded. 'No, you couldn't. Are you injured anywhere else apart from your head?'

'Just the head, but I'm okay.'

Mel walked over to her. 'Morgan, love, you are far from okay but you're alive so we're not doing too bad. But what is this total disaster? I mean how did you end up having Britain's most wanted man come to your rescue?'

Ben smiled. 'It's a long story, but welcome to Rydal Falls, ma'am.'

Morgan looked down at Gary's lifeless body for the last time; they were done. He'd ruined her life then come back to save it, which was stranger than any fiction book she'd ever read.

Ben and Mel both grabbed an arm each and lifted him enough so that she could move away. She tried to stand up but lost her balance, and Ben reached out, catching her in his arms and for once she didn't fight him. More sirens as the backup began to arrive: better late than never, she supposed. This was going to be a nightmare of a crime scene to process, and she was covered in everyone's blood including her own.

Amy shone her camera torch at her and grimaced. 'You stink, Morgan, and you're never going to get that blood out of those jeans. But I'm glad you're okay, kid. Do you think that it's time you maybe considered a job in admin, out of the public eye for a while? because my heart cannot take any more of these kinds of disasters.'

She smiled at Amy but didn't reply. She had the headache from hell and felt as if she was going to be sick. She pushed Ben away and stumbled towards the side of the van, where she began to heave and then she passed out once more, and this time she didn't try to fight it.

FORTY-EIGHT

When she opened her eyes she was in a hospital room. She looked down to see a blue and white hospital gown and was relieved not to be in those heavily bloodstained clothes. There was a monitor beeping to the side of her. She lifted her fingers to the side of her head, which was covered in a crepe bandage, and she let out a sigh of relief.

'You're awake, welcome back.'

She looked over to see Ben in the armchair next to the bed. He looked exhausted; his shirt was creased and his trousers crumpled.

'How long have you been there?'

'A few hours. I came as soon as I could once the scene was under control. How are you feeling?'

'Like a bus ran over my head and like I've just woken from the scariest nightmare of my life.'

He smiled at her. Moving closer he sat on the side of the bed and took hold of her hand.

'I think you've lived the scariest nightmare of your life to be fair.'

'Is he really dead, did that happen?'

Ben nodded. 'Yes, Gary Marks is dead, and Miles Winder has been remanded in custody. There is no way on this earth he will ever see the light of day again.'

'I don't know how he knew.'

'I'll tell you what we know so far: Brian turned up at your place and saw Gary Marks driving off in your car. I think Gary was coming to pay you a visit, and talk about divine timing, but he turned up just as Winder had thrown you into his van and driven off. That van is a complete treasure trove of evidence, by the way; he may have been clever enough to avoid being captured but he was stupid enough to leave lots of evidence in the van.'

'Like what?'

'Like Florence's teeth for a start, or at least I would bet my left kidney they are Florence's. Not to mention the underfloor compartment he put you inside. It is a wealth of a variety of forensic samples; he didn't believe in cleanliness for one thing: it stank like a toilet in there. Miles has insinuated that Ed started the killings back in '97. Miles was nine years old and followed him into the woods, where he watched what he did to the first girl. It obviously made a lasting impression on him because when he was old enough, he decided it was time to follow in Ed's footsteps and carry on where he left off. Ed is denying all of that and blaming Miles, but as evil as the pair of them are, I don't believe a nine-year-old was able to carry out the early murders. It looks like the pair of them will never see freedom again.'

'That's horrendous, thank God, they won't. Can I go home?'

'Not at the moment, it's a crime scene.'

She nodded her head slowly.

'But you're welcome to come home with me, Morgan. I'm not telling you what to do but that apartment isn't a good place for you.'

This time she did laugh. 'You don't mind if I stay at yours?'

He shook his head, stroking her hand. 'I would very much like it if you came to live with me. We can sort out the logistics later. Let me take care of you for a little while, at least until you're better.' Taking her hand, he lifted it to his lips and kissed it softly.

She nodded. 'I'm tired, Ben. I want to get out of here.'

'Leave it with me, I'll see what I can do.'

He disappeared to go and find the ward sister, and she lay her head back on the pillow. Lifting up the hand he'd kissed, she stared at it, wondering at how good it had felt.

The door opened, and Amy walked in followed by Declan.

'You know I'm sure you're just an attention-seeker, Brookes. I think you're one of those people who crave it and enjoy being in hospital. Doesn't she, Declan?'

Declan smiled. 'What can I say? I'm just glad you don't like it enough that you end up on my slab, Morgan. I believe this was a close call. Isn't it time you took a desk job?'

She grinned at them both. 'Not you as well. No, I'm okay, thank you. I'll take a desk job when people stop killing each other.'

Declan began to clap. 'By God, you're good. What about taking up acting? I think you'd be great on a BBC drama series. I have some great news concerning our Jane Smith: the DNA samples we managed to retrieve from the skeletal remains brought up a close match on the database to a Lukas Bonas, who was arrested while over here looking for his missing sister, Anna Bonas. I've spoken to him and he told me that Anna came to the UK in 1997, to work as an au pair in Manchester; she left the family after a few weeks. They didn't report her missing as she'd taken her belongings with her. Lukas came over here to look for her after they didn't hear from her for a couple of weeks, which was most unlike her. He traced the family she was staying with and got into a fight with the husband, who had him arrested. Lukas filed a missing person's report then went home. He said that Anna always wore a silver crucifix that was given to her by their grandmother.'

Morgan's eyes filled with tears. 'That's so sad, Miles was wearing a silver crucifix when he dragged me out of the van. I bet it's the same one, we need to get it back to Lukas to see if he can identify it.'

Declan nodded. 'I know, but at least she can go home now and her family can lay her to rest.'

Ben walked in followed by the ward sister. 'I have it on good authority that you are not going home alone and are going to stay with your friend until you feel better. Is this true?'

Amy and Declan were grinning at each other, and Morgan's pale face flushed a deep shade of crimson. 'Yes, I am.'

'Right then, if the doctor says you can go, I'll get the paper-work sorted.'

Declan was still grinning. 'Well, isn't this just lovely? Party round at Ben's when you're up to it, Morgan.' He bent down and kissed her cheek.

Amy winked at her. 'We only came for a short visit, we'll leave you to it.'

Tom knocked on the door and squeezed into the tight space that was left. He pulled something out of his pocket and handed it to Ben. 'Here, I think you'll be needing this.'

Ben took his warrant card from Tom. 'Yes, thank you.'

'You're in charge. I've handed my resignation in and as of' – he looked at the clock above Morgan's bed – 'as of now, I'm on annual leave until my notice is up. I'm glad you're okay, Morgan, well done.'

Before anyone could speak, he turned to leave. 'Drinks on me at The Black Dog once you're fighting fit, just us lot mind you. I can't be bothered with the whole of section turning up.'

And then he was gone, Amy and Declan following behind.

Ben sat back down on the bed and took hold of her hand once more.

'Now what do we do?'

'We take it one day at a time and figure it out as we go along. Nothing will change. Except for us maybe, but that's your decision.'

He leaned forwards and pulled her close. She let him, sinking into his arms and enjoying every moment. She wasn't sure what she wanted or needed right now, except Ben in her life, and for now it looked as if that was a real possibility.

A LETTER FROM HELEN

Dear reader,

I want to say a huge thank you for choosing to read *Find the Girl*. If you did enjoy it, and want to keep up-to-date with all my latest releases, just sign up at the following link. Your email address will never be shared and you can unsubscribe at any time.

www.bookouture.com/helen-phifer

This book was one of those rare books that was a dream to write and I hope you loved *Find the Girl as much as I did writing it* and if you did I would be very grateful if you could write a review. I'd love to hear what you think, and it makes such a difference helping new readers to discover one of my books for the first time.

I love hearing from my readers – you can get in touch on my Facebook page, through Twitter, Goodreads or my website.

I also have a Podcast for any aspiring writers out there who need some inspiration and maybe some advice, hints or tips. You can find it on any of the usual podcast platforms or www.unleashyourcreativemagic.com

Thanks,

Helen

KEEP IN TOUCH WITH HELEN

www.helenphifer.com

facebook.com/Helenphifer1

twitter.com/helenphifer1

ACKNOWLEDGEMENTS

It takes a whole team to make a book, so I would like to say a huge thank you to my amazing, wonderful, brilliant editor Emily Gowers for all her patience, hard work and input to help make these stories really come to life. Thank you, Emily, I love working with you.

A big thank you goes to the rest of team Bookouture for everything you do, to make these books stand out and look amazing. The cover designers, editors, marketing, audio, there is so much work involved and I appreciate each and every one of you.

A massive thank you to the gorgeous Noelle Holten for her support and love on pre-release and release days; you make the whole daunting process such a dream.

I'm very grateful that I get to work alongside you all, not to mention drink lots of Prosecco with you all at the summer parties.

A big thank you to my husband, Steve, for holding the fort at home while I go lose myself in my stories and all the other stuff that being a writer brings with it.

As always I have to thank my gorgeous kids Jess, Josh, Jerusha, Jeorgia and Jaimea for the daily distractions and lack of sleep. I've named a wrinkle after each and every one of you. A big thank you goes to Tom and Danielle for being an amazing part of my family. It goes without saying that my beautiful grandkids are always there to provide the hugs and smiles when my brain needs a rest so Gracie, Donovan, Laurence, Matilda, Bonnie and Sonny, I love you all lots.

I'm so lucky to have great friends especially Sam and Tina who keep my sanity in check and are my coffee besties; thank you ladies for always being there.

A huge thank you to the one and only Mr Paul O'Neill for always being my superfast final reader, you are amazing, Paul.

Another massive thank you to the team at Audio Factory for bringing these stories to life, and a special thank you to the wonderful, hugely talented Alison Campbell who narrates Morgan's stories so perfectly.

Thank you to my gorgeous book club members for our monthly catch-up and natter about everything including books. A special mention to the Costa gals and guys who keep me going on a daily basis.

I'd also like to say a special thank you to my writing tribe, The Write Romantics, for all your support, especially Jo Bartlett who very kindly let me use her late dad's name and is the utterly wonderful, retired DCI Brian Walter in this story also Sharon Booth and Jessica Redland.

Whilst we're on the subject of names I have to say a special thank you to retired Inspector Paul Madden aka Mads who was my boss for the first half of my career as a PCSO. His sense of humour is legendary and when he wasn't making us walk the streets of Barrow for hours at a time in the pouring rain, he was making us laugh in the office – most of the time.

I'd also like to thank Al McNulty for answering questions about the role of a POLSA lead, I hope you don't mind that I named him after you Al, it seemed only right.

The wonderful Sofie Ravetta is truly one of the nicest gals I've ever met and thanks to Mel Whitehouse for the added inspiration about lone camping.

Last but by no means least the biggest thank you goes to my amazing readers; you all make this possible. Your love of my stories is what keeps me writing and I'm so very lucky to have such a fabulous, supportive group of readers and bloggers who are just the best.

Much love

Helen xx

Printed in Great Britain
by Amazon